ABOUT THE AUTHOR

Elizabeth O'Roark spent many years as a medical writer before publishing her first novel in 2013. She holds two bachelor's degrees from the University of Texas, and a master's degree from Notre Dame. She lives in Washington, D.C. with her three children. *The Devil Gets His Due* is her twelfth book. Join her book group, Elizabeth O'Roark Books, on Facebook for updates, book talk and lots of complaints about her children.

ALSO BY ELIZABETH O'ROARK

THE DEVIL GETS HIS DUE

ELIZABETH O'ROARK

PIATKUS

PIATKUS

First published in Great Britain in 2023 by Piatkus

1 3 5 7 9 10 8 6 4 2

A CIP catalogue record for this book
is available from the British Library.

ISBN: 978-0-349-44073-6

Printed and bound in Great Britain by Clays Ltd, Elcograf S.p.A.

Papers used by Piatkus are from well-managed forests
and other responsible sources.

Piatkus
An imprint of
Little, Brown Book Group
Carmelite House
50 Victoria Embankment
London EC4Y 0DZ

An Hachette UK Company
www.hachette.co.uk

www.littlebrown.co.uk

To Deanna Heaven—who combines Graham's fiscal responsibility with Keeley's willingness to say exactly what she's thinking. I'm so grateful to the extroverts who led us to become friends.

1

Sept 9, 2022

I don't know how to begin, so I'm just going to say it: I fucked up.

I can't fix anything at this point. I'm putting it all on paper simply because I hate that I hurt you. It's the worst thing I've ever done, which is really saying something.

I was thoughtless and I was irresponsible, but that's nothing you don't already know. So just let me tell you the rest.

2

KEELEY
JANUARY

"I have two goals," I announce, handing Gemma a margarita and sloshing it all over my hand in the process. This is either because the margarita is too full or because it's not my first of the day. I have a feeling the Langham Hotel is going to regret letting me host an event here.

Gemma smiles. "Only two? Let me guess, neither of them involves a savings account."

I pinch her. "Two goals for your *party*, asshole."

Gemma, to my vast irritation, ran off and married her boyfriend in an entirely elegant and dignified manner, a situation I hope to rectify this weekend. That was the plan, anyway, until her new brother-in-law, Graham, got involved.

"Okay." Gemma blots the stem of her glass with a napkin and places it on the table. "Let's hear these 'goals.'" She does air quotes around the word *goals*, which feels a little unfair to me when she hasn't even heard them, but is entirely fair based on our six-year friendship—she knows how I roll.

"One, to throw you the wedding party of a lifetime. Two, to bang the hell out of Six Bailey. Not necessarily in that order."

Six Bailey, one of her husband's many famous friends, is a hot, tattooed man-child, the kind of guy who will fuck like a machine and take off before I can tire of him. Will he reciprocate my interest? Probably. I'm blond and blue-eyed and look just like my mother, who once had two semi-famous rock stars get into a fist-fight over her *on stage*. The interest part seems to take care of itself.

Therefore, Six Bailey is already a sure thing, and possibly the one part of this weekend Gemma's awful brother-in-law won't manage to ruin.

"I'm just relieved you and Graham managed to agree on something," Gemma says. "I was beginning to think this party wouldn't even happen."

"I'd hardly say we agreed," I mutter. Because what's left of my proposed week-long party in Santorini? Happy hour in a hotel bar today followed by an afternoon party tomorrow. Yes, an *afternoon* party. Like we're celebrating a fucking baptism.

"I *told* Ben the two of you would make a terrible couple. Oh, before I forget, they've got a new color of the Sydney stiletto in stock at Stuart Weitzman and—"

"Wait, *what*?" I cut in. "Ben thought we *wouldn't* be a terrible couple?" What sentient human possibly could have believed that Graham Tate and I wouldn't shred each other to pieces, and not in a sexy way, if given the option?

As I've discovered thanks to *way* too many phone calls, Graham is the kind of guy who does what he's supposed to at every juncture. *Other* women would call him a "keeper": he saves money, tracks his macros, and has the next ten years planned out. He will take you out on a series of polite, respectful dates while assessing your ability to bring up his children and say the right thing at work events.

Personally, I have no desire to procreate, say the right thing or meet someone's standards. I mostly don't ever want to be "kept" and, therefore, I avoid keepers like the plague.

"It was ages ago," she says with a wave of her hand. "Graham had—oh, wait, they're here!"

Her fingers dig into my arm as she drags me across the room toward her tall and extremely handsome new husband... and the even hotter man beside him, who is supposed to be Graham but absolutely can't be.

I've developed an image of Graham in my head after spending six straight weeks bickering with him by phone, so I know he must be bald and tiny and look two decades older than Ben somehow—though he's actually two years younger. He carries an abacus or encyclopedia with him everywhere he goes and uses them to discuss things no one but him cares about. Like taxes or healthcare or politics.

Therefore, the broad-shouldered guy with the bone structure of a young superhero and wearing the hell out of a very nice suit can't possibly be Graham.

Can I picture this guy with an abacus? No. Can I see this guy with an encyclopedia? Yes, but only in a kinky way. Like maybe he's about to fuck you in the back of the library and doesn't bother to sweep the books off the table before he pins you there.

He *is not* Graham. Except he does look a lot like Ben—the same dark hair, the same perfect bone structure, the same quarterback build—and Gemma is currently saying "two nemesises come face to face" in a British accent as if she's narrating a nature documentary.

"I think the plural is *nemeses*," the guy who can't be Graham says with the ghost of a smirk on his face. He has the bluest eyes I've ever seen. "I looked it up in anticipation of this meeting."

I recognize his low, gravelly voice—even sexier now that I'm seeing the face that goes with it. I also recognize the corresponding desire to punch him.

Ugh. It *is* Graham. I suppose that means any moment now

he'll be asking me how much these margaritas were and deducting them from his share of the costs.

What a waste. You could sharpen a knife on that jawline. Alas.

His eyes meet mine, though I don't miss the way they went to my cleavage first. *Good.* I bought this dress hoping to make the most of my assets, and if even boring *Graham* is looking, Six Bailey is in the bag.

"Well, well, well," I say. "Look who put down the actuarial tables long enough to show up at the party."

"I don't use actuarial tables in my work. I—"

"I'm already bored, so clearly you're Graham." I extend a hand.

"And you're rude and drunk at noon, so you must be Keeley," he replies with a smirk. His hand swallows mine in a firm handshake, and I briefly imagine him consuming me, that massive body of his pushing me deep into a mattress. I'm not sure why the idea isn't as dry-heave-inducing as it should be. Maybe I should slow down with the margaritas.

I glance over at Gemma, hoping she finally sees how terrible he is, which I've been discussing at length for weeks, but she's paying no attention whatsoever. Her arms are draped around Ben's neck, and the two of them are all *whisper whisper whisper* while they smile at each other, lips a hair's breadth apart.

"Jesus Christ," Graham groans, just as I whisper, "gross."

He raises a brow. "I imagine that's the first and last thing we'll ever agree on."

I turn toward the bar and he follows. "Ideally we won't need to agree or disagree because I very much want you to stay away from me this weekend."

"Have I somehow given you the impression I want you to stay close? If so, I apologize. Nothing could be further from the truth."

I give the bartender my most beguiling smile. "I'm going to need several more of these," I say in a stage whisper, lifting my drink. "It's the only way I'll survive today."

"If you *not* surviving today is somehow an option—" Graham points at the bottle of whiskey in the bartender's hand. "—it would probably save me some money."

～

GO BIG OR GO HOME, is what I say. And by *"go home"* I mean *die*, which is what I'm likely to do relatively soon anyway.

The O'Keefe women die young. That my mother, Melinda O'Keefe Connolly, made it to thirty-six before dying of colon cancer was nothing short of a miracle. Her sister, Mary O'Keefe, had never smoked even once in her life but still died of lung cancer at thirty-four. My grandmother died at twenty-eight of melanoma, and my great-grandmother died in childbirth, but I bet cancer would have gotten her if childbirth hadn't.

Therefore, I simply strive to make the most of the time I have on Earth, and this weekend feels like the kick-off. My dermatology residency is officially behind me, which means—once I get through a three-month observership—total freedom and a doctor's salary are about to be mine. I am going to wrest every ounce of fun from this weekend if it kills me, and if it does kill me—O'Keefe curse and all—I suspect Six Bailey is a good way to go: he is inappropriately dressed, drops the word *fuck* like it's the only adjective or noun he knows, and is currently ogling his sister-in-law's breasts. Openly.

"Holy shit, Drew, your rack got fucking *huge*," he tells her before he turns to me. "It's okay for me to comment because I dated her first."

He is in no way a keeper, and he might be my soulmate.

My two-night soulmate.

"It's not okay," growls Josh, Drew's husband. "I'm not sure how many times we will need to have this conversation, but I'm happy to end it the way the last one did."

"Cut it out, Six," says Drew. "This is my first night away from the baby in *months,* and I want my husband in a good mood."

Six takes a long sip of his drink. "With a rack like that, I don't think you'll have to worry about his fucking mood."

"I'm going to kick your ass"—Josh places his beer on the table—"if you say one more goddamn word."

Heavy drinking? Threats of violence? A serious lack of boundaries? I've clearly found my people.

"No fights," says Drew, looking between them. "I'm serious." She grabs Josh's hand, and when she looks at him, he just *settles* as if he has everything he needs in the entire world.

Nothing about marriage appeals to me, aside from being able to blow through someone else's income, but watching them now makes me feel like I'm missing out.

Gemma and Ben affect me similarly. She's so happy all the time now I barely know who she is—I wish there was a subtle way to take a blood sample so I could make sure Ben's not drugging her.

Six's eyes travel over me, head to foot. "Jesus fucking Christ, you're hot. I'm sure you already know that. So how charming do I need to be, on a ten-point scale, to get you to—"

Before he can finish this especially intriguing question, a dark shadow looms over us.

"Can I borrow you?" asks Graham with a hand on my elbow. It's like being dragged out of a kegger by my dad, if my dad was really hot and young and involved enough in my life to drag me anywhere.

I smile at Six as I step away. "This will be fast."

Which is something I bet a lot of women say before walking off with Graham.

"What is it?" I hiss once we're around the corner. "I have

very specific plans for Six Bailey, and you're currently interrupting all of them."

"Glad to hear you actually have some life goals," he drawls. "Our previous conversations had not conveyed that impression. The happy hour component of this thing is over. I paid the tab."

I groan. Trust Graham to do something nice that also makes me feel guilty. "You didn't have to do that. I told you I'd cover half of everything."

"And I told you that wasn't necessary."

"Based on how cheap you are, I have to assume you can't afford any of this." Six is looking our way, so I hold up a finger, asking him to wait before returning to the dreary conversation with Graham. "Tell me what it was and I'll Venmo you."

"Just because I exercise restraint doesn't mean I'm *cheap*. If I left it up to you, we'd be on a flying yacht, throwing hundred-dollar bills off the back like confetti."

I stop. For the first time ever, I'm interested in something Graham has to say. "Flying yachts? Is that a *thing*?"

His mouth twitches, his eyes dragging over me and resting on my lips before he scrubs a hand over his face. "No, Keeley, it's not a thing. But it's not that far off from the week in Santorini you kept talking about, as if either Ben or Gemma was ever going to take that much time off work."

He's right, but I refuse to let him think holding the party on an LA *golf course* was a good idea. "We could have held it on Catalina. I could have reserved—"

"My ninety-year-old great aunt came in from Boston for this. She shouldn't have to get on a boat after a cross-country flight."

Six grins, watching me, and licks his lower lip. I really need to wrap this conversation up.

"Ah, so you were constraining this party around what would make the attending *ninety-year-olds* comfortable. I thought you just wanted to minimize the fun at all costs."

"If this is you not having fun," he says, his eyes falling to my empty glass, "I'd be scared to see what happens when you are."

HAPPY HOUR MOVES TO DINNER, which then moves to a club in the hotel. All the boring married people are gone, but for some reason the boring curmudgeon, Graham Tate, is still going strong...and steadily drinking, which seems unlike him given his hatred of spending and love of misery.

If he's simply waiting to see how drunk I get, the joke's on him...I'm already *extremely* drunk. Fortunately, my superpower is impersonating a sober person when necessary, though I guess it's only a superpower if you're a functional alcoholic or a teenager trying to escape her father's condemnation when she walks in at one in the morning.

Six wraps a hand around my waist and then pulls the neckline of my dress away from my chest. He's getting handsier by the minute, which I find oddly...irritating. As someone who is only hanging out with him for one reason, I'm not sure why I care—it'll just make it that much easier to ghost him in a week or two.

Six checks his watch, and I know he's about to suggest we leave, but I'm just not ready. I pull away, telling him I'm going to dance. I have no idea why I'm stalling. And where's Graham, anyway? I expected him to be looking on, figuring out how he could ruin this.

I slip onto the crowded dance floor and begin to move. There is something about the combination of alcohol and dancing that makes it seem like anything is possible. It's a soaring, gleeful feeling, the one you get when you contemplate making a reckless decision: *Blow all my savings on a trip to Croatia? Quit my job and spend a few months sleeping in and surfing? Spend five grand on a Birkin bag?* You know these are bad decisions and yet...just contemplating them makes you feel like there might be a whole other life out there for you, a better one.

I want more of this feeling and I'm wondering where to find it when a hand wraps around my hip and an exhale grazes my ear.

"Tell me you're not actually planning to sleep with that guy," says a voice I *know* I hate, though oddly I don't feel any of that hatred at the moment.

I turn to find Graham standing close, so close I have to crane my neck to meet his gaze.

He's looking at me in that way of his, as if he knows me better than I know myself, and resentment flares. He thinks he can loom over me, with his perfect nose and his lovely mouth, and make me feel guilty. He's wrong.

"Why shouldn't I sleep with him?" I ask and his hand rises to slide over my jaw.

"You really want to know, Keeley?"

I nod because, being this close to him, my mind has suddenly gone blank. He's near enough that I can smell the bourbon on his breath, which shouldn't be nearly as appealing as it is. He shouldn't be appealing at all, and yet—*God*—I'd challenge any woman to stand this close to him and not be drawn in.

"Because he isn't who you want," he says, his fingers tangling tight in my hair, "and you fucking know it."

And before I can tell him how staggeringly wrong he is, he pulls my mouth to his.

I am kissing Graham Tate.

No. *He* is kissing me, and there's nothing tentative about it. He kisses like a man who's thought of nothing else for the past decade. As if he's angry he ever had to wait. As if he resents me for pushing him this far.

While my disdain for Graham is still a living, breathing animal inside me...*Oh my God* he can kiss.

His scruff abrades my skin, his hand tight on my hip, pulling me against him. The kiss is skilled. And *filthy*. It is, in conclusion, nothing I'd have expected from Graham. And yet... maybe I did. As shocking as it is, I'm not actually shocked at all. It sort of feels like I was waiting for this very thing.

He pulls me farther into the darkness and I'm definitely going to stop this in a minute. Maybe two minutes at most.

"Six is a guitarist," I say as my back hits the wall. "He's known for his manual dexterity."

His mouth moves, just a hint of a smile as he pulls me against him again, his sizable erection pressing into my stomach. "Just wait until you see what I can do with my tongue."

3

KEELEY

The sun is blinding, streaming in through the balcony doors like long steel knives.

Except my room didn't have a balcony. *I definitely would have noticed a balcony, right?*

I roll over to see a pair of broad shoulders, the back of a head shaved to near military perfection. Not a single tattoo, therefore...

Not Six Bailey.

What the fuck happened last night?

More pressingly, what's up with this guy? Because he is *extremely* still.

"God," I groan, reaching over to feel his carotid artery, "not again."

"Did you just check my pulse?" asks a gravelly voice. And that's when I feel my first spike of terror.

No. No, no, no, no.

He rolls over, sleepy eyed, swollen-lipped, and in need of a shave. Someone else might think he looks pretty fucking good in the morning, but that would need to be someone who's never held a conversation with Graham Tate.

He runs a hand over his face while I try to piece the night together. Margaritas, more margaritas. Arguing with Graham, the arrival of guests. And Six. I remember talking to him. I remember him smiling at me in the way of someone who very much wanted to fuck me. And then I remember Graham.

His lips on mine in a dark corner.

Him looming over me, pushing my dress above my hips. Mostly I remember how badly I wanted him to do it. Telling him to hurry, the pleased half smile that tugged at his lips in response.

God, how embarrassing.

"This didn't happen," I proclaim, jumping to my feet, ignoring that my whole body feels bruised, especially the area between my legs. My vagina took a beating last night. It *deserves* a beating for choosing to avail itself to the enemy when I was in a vulnerable state.

I step over a condom wrapper to reach my dress, which is on the floor along with my bra, and yet another condom wrapper. No sign of my panties, so I guess I'm writing them off. "We speak of it to no one and put it out of our heads."

He watches me from the bed, arms folded across his broad chest, sheets bunched low at his waist. "Because you're still on your mission to fuck the rock star."

I drag my eyes away from him because the sheet is riding low enough for me to see his happy trail, and I'm tempted to keep looking. "If mankind let every simple mistake get in the way of its goals, we'd still be communicating via cave drawings," I reply, stepping over another condom wrapper. *Jesus Christ, how many times, exactly, did we do it?*

He reaches for his phone while one hand goes behind his head, his bicep flexing impressively with the movement. "Fair enough, slugger. Knock 'em dead tonight. Though not literally, which is apparently something that happens to you."

"I'm sure it happens to everyone at some point," I mutter, and he laughs.

It's a nice laugh, and there's a part of me that wishes I could hear it again. I take one last look at him, with that unshaved jaw, those biceps, and that mouth before I head for the door.

As terrible as Graham Tate is, he comes in deceptively nice packaging.

I SHOWER and collapse in my own bed for two hours, hoping I'll forget what occurred. Unfortunately, I wake feeling deliciously *overused*, which means I either ran a marathon last night or had repeated sex with someone twice my size.

If my life was a movie, this would be the wake-up call, the moment when I realize I need to pull my shit together: stop drinking, quit medicine, and do something meaningful with my life—like open a restaurant and join *The Real Housewives of Beverly Hills*.

Except I can't afford to have a wake-up call right now, because the only way I can play hostess next to the loathsome, oversized Graham is through a little more drinking.

I order eggs, bacon, and a mimosa, and am informed that they are no longer serving breakfast, which leaves me feeling judged. I settle for the mimosa and put on my bikini, picking right back up where I left off last night: with no food in my stomach and a strange unhappiness I'm eager to dull.

I walk outside. We got lucky with the weather—January in LA is not reliably warm enough to be considered pool weather, but it's in the seventies today and sunny. Apparently, I wasn't the only one with this idea, either. Gemma is lounging under the shade of a cabana, surrounded by her new friends, and it's hard not to think about how different things are, how different she is. I'm so happy for her, but I can't deny there's this little pinch in my chest.

We used to be a mess together. I was bad with all things adult, and she was so emotionally detached I sometimes wondered if she might be a sociopath. But it turned out she was simply damaged, and now she's fixed—madly in love and always doing grown-up shit with her well-adjusted husband and friends. She's tried to include me, and I always make an excuse to get out of it. Being around all of them makes me feel like the only flower in the garden that's failed to bloom.

I have to force myself to walk over. Gemma makes room for me to squeeze in, and once I'm seated, Tali, the very-pregnant wife of Ben's best friend, taps my foot.

"So...mission accomplished last night?"

"Mission?" I repeat, looking from her to Gemma.

"We had a whole conversation about your plan to sleep with Josh's brother. You don't remember?"

Her daughter walks over, dripping wet, and Tali wraps a towel around her before tugging her to her side for a cuddle. My mom was like that with me, even when I was nearly grown. If I was anywhere nearby, I was getting a hug.

I swallow and look away. "It didn't go as planned."

Gemma laughs quietly. "That's ironic. Your plans failed while Graham apparently had a *very* busy night."

My gaze darts to hers. "Oh?"

"Ben said his room looked like he'd held a rave there last night. I think—" her voice drops to a whisper, "he might have been with Elise. I don't know if you've met her yet."

Obviously, this whole Graham situation would be far less awkward if that were the case. I wonder if Elise is the reason he stayed out so late, and if so, how he wound up with me instead.

Tali's husband, Hayes, appears at the foot of the chair, smiling at his wife and kid with so much affection in his gaze that I have to look away. All these fucking couples with their shared looks and their quiet complete-ness are pushing my mood lower by the second, and it was already on the edge anyway.

I was ready to finish up my residency, but I'm sad about it too. I'm going to miss my friends at the hospital. I'm going to miss the chaos, though I've spent four years saying I couldn't wait to put it behind me. And I've got three months of training at NIH with no job lined up afterward, so what was supposed to be a celebration feels a bit less so, and I really don't need all this endless proof that everyone else is moving forward right now, getting jobs or getting married, or exchanging long affectionate glances over their children's heads. My bitterness makes no sense, given I don't even *want* most of those things, but I feel it anyway.

Hayes lifts his daughter into his arms and her head rests against his chest as she pops her thumb in her mouth. She's an adorable little thing. I'd have liked a daughter like that if things had gone differently.

"I need a drink," I say, jumping to my feet.

I need a lot of drinks.

I walk to the bar. This is my last weekend at home before I leave for DC and I'm finally free of Dr. Patel, the world's worst attending. I'll be damned if all these happy fucking people are going to ruin it for me.

I smile at one of the guys behind the bar, and he hustles right over. "I'll have—"

A hand lands on my ass.

"Two gin and tonics," says Six to the bartender before he looks down and grins at me like the sure thing I am. "What happened last night? You went to the dance floor and never came back."

I press a finger to one temple. *Goddammit*. My plan was one hundred percent on track and then Graham Tate somehow came in and ruined everything.

"I really don't remember. I must have gone to bed."

With someone else. By accident. So classy.

"We've still got today," Six says. He signs the tab and slides me one of the gin and tonics. "Slam it. I just challenged people to a chicken fight, which should be right up your alley, little wild thing."

He makes it sound like a compliment, while Graham could undoubtedly produce a long list of why being a *little wild thing* is not a desirable quality.

"According to my predictions," he'd say, *"you, Keeley, are ninety percent more likely than an average woman your age to be in a car accident, forget to pay a bill, or get reprimanded for dancing suggestively on a cafeteria table."*

Six leads me down the pool stairs, into water as warm as a child's bath. He sinks as low as he can. "Climb on."

"Who are we fighting?" I ask as I sling one thigh over his shoulder.

"Me," says the deep voice behind me, and goose bumps rise on my arms. I turn as Graham wades in, looking a thousand times better than anyone as boring as him should. He does not have a single tattoo, but when you're that sculpted, you don't need any—his body is a work of art all on its own. If only he didn't have to ruin it by running his mouth.

"Keeley, this is Elise," he says, indicating the girl beside him, who I'd somehow failed to notice. She's my exact opposite, by which I mean she appears too elegant and refined to be participating in a chicken fight in the first place. I'm going to *destroy* her. "She's at Ben and Gemma's firm."

Ugh. A lawyer. How perfect for him. They can bore each other for hours on end.

My bruised pubic bone presses to the back of Six's head—the universe reminding me Graham is, perhaps, not *always* boring.

Six and I wade farther into the pool while Elise climbs on

Graham's shoulders. "She's tiny," I tell Six. "This will be over fast."

"You're tiny too, wild thing."

Tiny, yes, but fucking fierce. I'm pretty sure that's Shakespeare, but I'm not sure Shakespeare used the word *fuck* all that often, so I keep it to myself. If I'm botching it, Graham will be sure to overhear and point it out.

"Ready?" Graham asks, and we turn.

He's holding Elise effortlessly atop his broad shoulders with a smug grin on his face, and in response, I shiver. It's probably horror, but it doesn't entirely *feel* like horror. I have a few very distinct, sharp memories from last night. None of them involve horror. The opposite, really, but they give me the burst of energy I need to knock Elise off Graham's shoulders in five seconds flat.

Six whoops. "That's my fucking *girl*!"

"It was supposed to be fun, Keeley," says Graham, helping Elise—her wet hair plastered to her face, mascara running—out of the water. "Not a death match."

I give him a small smile. "Looks like you were out of your league."

His eyes drift over me slowly, possessively, from my lips to my breasts and down to my hips before he steps close. I shiver as his hand brushes against my waist, as his breath grazes my ear. "Keeley," he says, so only I can hear, "we both know that's not true."

When he walks away, my nipples are pinched so tight that I have to fold my arms over my chest as I walk out of the pool. And I'm pretty sure it's not the air temperature that got them that way.

~

THE PARTY IS to be held on the hotel's long, sloping back lawn. It's a black and white theme, over Graham's strenuous objections. He was probably worried someone would enjoy it too much.

Thanks to my spray tan and lash extensions, I didn't need a lot of makeup tonight, so it's mostly a soft red lip and some highlighter. I pile my hair high on my head with a few loose strands escaping around my face—the sort of look men will laud for being *low-maintenance* and *natural* because they have no fucking clue how long it took. Those are the same guys who will tell you you're lucky to be "*naturally pretty*" because you "*don't need all that shit other girls use,*" never realizing you spent forty-five minutes on contour alone.

My white dress is sleeveless and fitted, with a v-cut down to my ribs. I lean closer to my reflection to ensure no tell-tale marks from last night are showing, like the hickeys I discovered on my breast and inner thigh this morning. And then I admire the nice hint of side boob revealed by the dress. Oddly, it's Graham's reaction I think of first before I shake my head and force myself to focus on Six instead.

I take the elevator downstairs with a small pit of dread in my stomach. When I leave with Six at the party's end, it will undoubtedly be under Graham's watchful eye and make me feel as if I'm doing something wrong. Honestly, how could I have chosen him last night? Do I have multiple personalities, one of whom is a deeply boring girl who'd rather talk about inflation than hook up with a rock star?

I walk out the back doors, and the first thing I see on the lawn is Graham, of course, dressed in head-to-toe black and discussing something with the caterer. For a moment—before disgust rushes in—I just look. He wears clothes like a dream and *God* that mouth is wasted on him. He should be on a movie screen with a mouth like that. Okay, maybe I don't have multiple personalities. Just one that's particularly shallow.

He turns then, as if sensing my gaze, and takes me in, eyes drifting from my face and then down—to my breasts, the curve of my waist, and back up. His nostrils flare as if he's an animal who's just picked up my scent.

"All set to seduce your rock star, then?" he asks.

For a second, I'd forgotten about Six entirely.

"Well, it would have been easier if you hadn't nixed the tequila luge I wanted."

His eyes fall closed. "I don't think you'd need to get anyone drunk, Keeley," he mutters. He reaches into a folder and puts a piece of paper in front of me. "We need to go over the seating plan." He points at one table that is full of little .5 marks. "What's this?"

I roll my eyes. "That's the table for people with kids. You know, your concern about this is coming a little late in the day."

"And they're far from me?" he asks.

"Far from us both," I reply. "Thank God."

He raises a brow. "You don't like kids?"

I feel a small sigh release somewhere inside me. I *do* like kids, actually, but since I don't plan to have any, their presence always produces this tiny voice in the back of my head asking if I've chosen the right path. I'd rather not spend the rest of the evening trying to drown it out.

"It's my understanding they get in the way of attending Coachella and taking spontaneous trips to Cabo."

"That," he replies, "is the first sensible thing I've heard you say in six weeks."

～

THE PARTY IS A REFINED, elegant affair that goes without a hitch. I'll never admit this to Graham, but I suppose it's a much more *Ben and Gemma* event than I'd have come up with if left to my own devices.

I also don't *need* to admit this to Graham because he already knows and is gloating about it. "It appears a party held in LA isn't the 'opposite of fun'," he says, stepping beside me.

I look up, up, up. It's really hard to appear condescending or disdainful when you have to practically tip over backward to meet the guy's eye. "Like you know what's fun."

"I didn't hear any complaints last night."

My head jerks up toward him again. "First of all, I thought we agreed that last night never happened." I glance around me. "Secondly, I'm surprised you *remember* last night." Surely, taking me back to his room wasn't a decision he'd have made sober.

His gaze falls to my mouth. "I remember enough," he says, and there's something there, in his voice. Something gravelly and interested, and a memory flickers to life: his palm, flat on my stomach as he went down on me, holding me in place. His gaze on me while he did it: hungry, a hundred percent in.

"Huh," I say aloud, though I didn't mean to. Because I suddenly know, beyond a shadow of a doubt, that there's another side of him, and I liked it. A lot.

Six is waiting nearby and I should be running away from this little chat as fast as I possibly can, but...but... "So, what exactly do you remember?"

His gaze drifts over my face, assessing me. His mouth opens to reply and then Six's arm is around my shoulders and a tray is shoved in front of me. "Shots," says Six. He grins at Graham. "You too. Even though you're hitting on my girl."

"I didn't realize she was *your* girl," Graham bites out.

"No worries, bud," Six replies, oblivious to Graham's tone. "I don't hold grudges, and your brother got me out of jail on two different occasions, so I consider you family."

"You've been to jail twice?" Graham smirks as he lifts a shot from the tray and toasts me. No one has ever made being a smug prick sexier. "Sounds like you two are perfect for each other."

Graham's sarcasm goes right over Six's head.

"Damn straight!" he says, slamming his drink before nodding at Graham. "We're all heading to this bar downtown since this is wrapping up. You in?"

I brace myself, silently willing Graham to bow out, to excuse himself so he can go chart the comparative GDP of small countries no one's ever heard of or whatever he considers a fun Saturday night. But instead, his gaze lands on me.

"Yeah," he says. "Why not."

To play designated cockblocker once more, I'm sure. No surprises there—ensuring no female leaves pleased is probably his personal motto.

Those hickeys, that ache between my legs...they don't prove anything.

4

KEELEY

Boom, boom, boom.

The sound is like a basketball hitting a microphone, or cannon fire.

It takes me a second to realize it's my *head* making this godawful racket.

My eyes open slowly, blearily, as I struggle to make sense of what I'm seeing. Where am I? Every single room at the Langham faces the golf course, a boring and endless sea of green. Except I'm looking out over...a city.

A city that isn't LA.

I'd like to claim I've never woken up in an unfamiliar room —obviously a lie, since I just did it yesterday—but I can at least say I've never woken up in the wrong *city*, until today.

Please be Six, please be Six, I think as I roll over.

Graham Tate's pretty face is mashed against the pillow.

Goddammit, Keeley.

Suddenly, music starts, and water arcs high in the air outside the window from a fountain—one I'd know anywhere because I always stay at the Bellagio when I'm in Vegas.

I'm in fucking *Vegas*.

How? How is this even possible? Vegas is a five-hour drive from LA. *None* of us were sober enough to make this trip, and as grossly irresponsible as I am, I would never get in the car with someone who'd been drinking.

I close my eyes, willing my stomach to stop rolling and my head to stop throbbing as snippets of the night before materialize: Graham beside me on a dance floor, looking very certain and very serious, which means I probably did something bad. And then, standing outside a nightclub in downtown LA with Drew, Six's sister-in-law—one of those drunken, emotional conversations, though I have no idea what we discussed, and honestly...it's unlike me, drunken superpower and all.

I extend a hand blindly, hoping to discover my phone and put this whole mystery to rest, when it *clinks* against the nightstand.

Even before my eyes open, the horror is spilling inside me like a stain. Because it's the sound of a ring, which is something I don't wear.

My stomach sinks as I look at the simple platinum band. I roll over, my head throbbing in protest. Graham's hand is currently splayed on my pillow. And he's wearing one too.

No. No, no, no. I squeeze my eyes shut. *Keeley, please don't have done this.*

My eyes open and *yep*, I did this.

Sometime over the course of the night, Graham and I went to Vegas and got married.

It couldn't have been premeditated. But somehow, we got to Vegas and one of us was drunk enough to say, *"hey, we're walking by this little chapel, and wouldn't it be funny if we got married by Elvis?"* and the other was drunk enough to say, *"let's do it."*

And while I do have some vague memory of walking down an aisle, I decide here and now that this didn't happen. We *talked* about it, bought rings, arrived too late and fell asleep.

Though judging by the condom wrappers on the nightstand, we didn't fall *directly* asleep.

God, why do I remember so little? There are only flashes of last night in my head: a champagne bottle opening and Graham's dark gaze on me as I tugged at his belt in the back of a limo, his teeth grazing sensitive skin, the urgency of it all. His voice against my ear, saying, *"Fuck, I'm gonna come so hard."*

How very *Keeley* of me to only remember the sex, and not the part where we traveled for five hours from another state and committed to each other for life.

And when Graham wakes, he'll be even more horrified by this situation than I am, which is when the blame will begin, as I'm pretty sure the wildest thing Graham Tate has ever done is declare a home office deduction on his taxes.

Therefore, only one possible solution exists: to slide out of this bed, find a way back to California, and pretend it didn't happen.

But, holy Lord, I've got to stop drinking.

5

GRAHAM

I wake in a hotel room in Vegas, deeply hungover.

When my mother begged me to relax and have a little fun this weekend, I doubt this was what she had in mind.

The room is a disaster—somehow, we managed to knock over a barstool at the kitchen counter, tear down a curtain rod, and crack a framed picture on the wall. I couldn't care less. And in spite of the night we just had, I'm already hard as a rock.

I roll over to greet my new wife and discover the bed is empty. I look toward the bathroom, but slowly realize there's no trace of her: the trail of clothes she'd left around the room last night is gone.

The only surprise here is that I'm surprised. That I ever thought it could have worked out any other way.

6

KEELEY
APRIL

Every movie in which a woman is transformed involves a rock-bottom moment: her heel snaps and she blows the big pitch to a client through no fault of her own. She's fired immediately and the skies open as she walks outside, drenching her as the cabs blow past, refusing to stop.

My rock-bottom moment, waking up married to the odious Graham Tate four months ago was a little seedier and a lot less blameless. I've tried to come up with a way that it isn't entirely my fault, but I haven't, just yet.

When a movie is eventually made about my life (*Keeley Connolly: The Doctor in Dior*), we'll have to finesse this whole situation so I come across a little more sympathetic. And why not? The movie will bear little resemblance to reality anyway. I will be played by a sixteen-year-old, for instance, which is twenty-nine for women in Hollywood years, and Graham will be played by an actor in his late fifties, which is a Hollywood thirty-four for men. The National Institutes of Health—where I just completed my three-month observership—will be ivy-covered and idyllic rather than a soulless concrete jungle in the middle of DC's blandest suburb.

I'm sure they can find a way to make my rock-bottom moment sympathetic to the masses in much the same manner.

I still can't believe it happened, but the one silver lining to this mess is that it provided me the kick in the ass I clearly needed; I haven't had a single drink since that night. Initially, this was because I was horrified I'd married Graham. Then it was because I was exhausted— something about the long hours and DC's endless gray winter have sapped my will to live. Thank God I'm finally back in LA.

I drag my bags to the curb at LAX where Gemma now stands, waving.

Her smile fades as I approach. "My God, Keeley, you're skin and bones."

Yet my jeans wouldn't button this morning. I don't want to think about that now.

I sling my suitcase into her trunk. "DC sucked. The weather was miserable, the food made me sick, even the smell of the *air* made me sick."

She raises a brow. "I grew up in DC and I've never once noticed a difference in the food or the smell of the air."

She's wrong. The smell is revolting. And the smell of the damp paper towels in the hospital bathroom will haunt me the rest of my days. I nearly passed out every time I peed, trying to hold my breath.

"I was busy," I tell her. "Too busy to eat. And now I need tacos. The Tex-Mex there left much to be desired."

We go to my favorite restaurant, where I want one of everything on the menu but don't have the stomach for more than a few bites.

I push the plate away. "I guess DC is still in my blood." I yawn. All I want in the whole damn world is to sleep.

"Keeley, you look green right now. Has this been going on a while?"

It's the precise conversation my mother had with her best

friend, at our kitchen table. I was fourteen at the time, and I can still recall the way my stomach began to sink, how I went from thinking everything was okay to realizing I could lose my mom, too, just like my cousins lost theirs the winter before.

"I'm just tired. It's been a long few months."

Gemma stares at me. "You're not pregnant, right?"

I roll my eyes...she should know me better than *that*. "My IUD is ninety-nine percent effective, and condoms are ninety-eight percent effective...which leaves me a hundred and ninety-seven percent unable to get pregnant. I'm pretty sure that means it could reverse an *existing* pregnancy."

Gemma's laugh is muted. "I don't think that's what it means. If you're not pregnant...I mean, given your family history, don't you think you should get checked out?"

I wince. I've tried very hard not to put it all together—the unexplained fatigue, the nausea—but when my pants wouldn't button this morning, my first thought was of my mom. She'd barely gotten her diagnosis before the build-up of fluid in her stomach began, a sign her cancer was far more advanced than we knew.

"I'm too busy to worry about this now," I insist, willfully ignoring that I once heard my mom say the exact same thing. "My job starts Monday, and once I get settled here, I'll be fine."

But even if I can lie to her, I can't lie to myself; I'm really dying, or I'm pregnant—and I don't want to be either of those things.

KNOWING your time on this planet will be brief is kind of like taking a trip: you're not going to house hunt or attempt to make anything *meaningful*, but you'll splurge on good restaurants and have a lot more pina coladas at noon.

Honestly, dying young is not all bad. People will still talk about how pretty I was at the funeral, for instance, and I will never have to worry about outliving my retirement savings, not that I'd ever have put money away in the first place.

Okay, I guess the silver linings are limited, but I can deal with that as long as I'm not leaving someone behind. I don't want to subject anyone to what I went through when my mom died, what my cousins went through when *their* mom died.

And that's why I finally take a pregnancy test—many hours after Gemma dropped me off—and burst into tears at the sight of two identical pink lines; because I'm okay with dying, but I can never be okay with saddling a kid with the grief that follows.

"You appear to be about sixteen weeks along," says Julie, my ob/gyn, the next day.

Sixteen weeks. It's somehow worse than I was expecting to hear, though I know it's dated back to the last period, not conception. I'm just a lot further into the stupidest mistake of my life than I imagined.

She continues sliding the transducer over my stomach. I make a point of looking at her, not the screen, because I don't want to get attached to the sight of something I might not choose to keep. "Due October eighth. I assume you haven't had a period for a while."

I shake my head, stunned. I thought it was stress. I just...I don't understand. "IUDs are foolproof."

"Only if they haven't fallen out."

I blink at her. "Without me even *noticing*?"

She hitches a shoulder. "Well, it's out, and you didn't notice, right? It's rare, but it happens."

Only me. This could only happen to me.

She hands me a paper towel. "You didn't have any nausea? Fatigue?"

I assumed it was cancer so I ignored it. Yes, I just spent three months studying metastatic melanoma, while perhaps ignoring something just as bad inside myself. Sometimes even I am shocked by the insanity of my thought processes.

I wipe off my stomach while she puts the transducer back. "I was busy. I just thought it was stress."

"Is the father in the picture?"

"I don't know," I reply, which comes across better than *"not if I have anything to say about it." God, why of all people did it have to be Graham?*

She meets my gaze and her shoulders sag. I know exactly what she's about to ask.

"Do you know what you want to do?" She says it as if she already knows the answer and she probably does. Our residencies overlapped and I've never exactly hidden my priorities. Only professionalism is keeping her from saying, *"you can't bring a baby to Burning Man, FYI. You can't bring a baby on a surfboard."*

"I don't know," I whisper. "The timing of this...could not be worse."

I'm starting a new job Monday, and I have no savings, nor any family who'll help out. I also decided long ago that a child wasn't in the picture.

When I leave the appointment, I wander listlessly around Brentwood. A child doesn't fit in with my life plans. Hell, it doesn't even fit in with my plans for the next year, which include surfing in Costa Rica this December, Carnival next February, and trying a jetpack once I find a place that will allow me to do so.

I'm all for people not being pregnant if they don't want to be pregnant. The problem is...I'm not sure I'm one of those people.

Yes, I wrote it off, but right now I'm remembering who I once was: the little girl who used to pretend her Barbies were pregnant, who'd already chosen her future children's names and occupations. Of course, I also thought I'd be married to JC from NSYNC when it happened, but even so...it was mostly about having kids.

For a full decade, I spent every lonely Christmas—half the day alone with my mom, half the day with my dad—dreaming of the big family I'd have as an adult. I'm not sure how I managed to forget all this until now.

Except I guess I didn't forget. I just put it all out of my head because I knew, even as a fifteen-year-old, that it would be a selfish thing to do. I'm about to turn thirty, only a few years younger than my mom when she died, and *she* was doing everything right. I don't have any siblings, my father is old, and Graham is awful. So what happens if I have this kid and the O'Keefe curse strikes again?

I go into Malia Mills and think about how many bikinis I could buy for the cost of a crib. I go into Goop and try to convince myself I'd rather have a Mara Hoffman dress than a stroller.

And then I walk outside and some little kid with a British accent is saying, *"very clever, Mummy"* as he swings his mother's hand, and my eyes fill with tears. Maybe it's simply because I didn't get knocked up by a Brit and my kid will never have a cool accent. But it's mostly because I *want* that. I want a kid placing his little hand in mine, his trust absolute. I want to care for someone other than myself, and I want it so much more than any purse or shoes or trip I've ever lusted after.

I want this baby, and even as I tell myself how selfish that is, I've got that soaring feeling in my chest—the one I always get before making the worst possible decision.

In the end, all I end up buying are prenatal vitamins.

I'm going to be a mom.

7

KEELEY

"**Y**ou're perfect for us," Kathleen Fox said when she hired me, and I was under no illusions about what she actually meant. It was above all about my ability to work long hours without complaint, but it was also *me*. She approved of my looks, my Hermes belt, my Balenciaga purse. Everything about Beverly Hills Skin is aspirational, and the staff is no exception; employees are unblemished and lovely. Though mostly it's just good genes, they *look* like women who have a secret or two, things their patients hope they'll share.

But now I legitimately *do* have a secret: everything they hired me for is about to change. I'm about to have commitments, and any day now I will no longer be a designer size two or fit into a Hervé Léger bandage dress.

And how am I supposed to tell them that? It's not like they'll believe I, a grown woman and doctor, didn't know this when I interviewed a month ago. I guess it'll be clear soon enough, but I definitely don't plan to make it clear today.

I'm shown the facilities by Trinny, who works at the front desk and could easily pass for Zendaya, but with better skin. They're in a hurry to get me up to speed because I'm replacing

Dr. Lee, who left three weeks before, and Dr. Fryer, who left in February.

The modern glam décor is just as it was when I interviewed: white fur throws in the patient rooms, black lacquered floors, a glass-front fridge stocked with Voss in the waiting room. After the chaos of working at the hospital, all I wanted was a quiet, air-conditioned office where inoffensive music would play through speakers and the air would smell like potpourri. That and a big fat paycheck I could blow on Louboutins at the month's end, all without Arjun Patel pulling me forward to diagnose a rare skin disease associated with malaria in front of everyone.

And I got it, but I have no idea now if it will last.

"We've been putting everyone off until you arrived," Trinny says, wincing. "So, it'll be a lot."

"I just came out of four years of residency," I reply. "As long as I get to drink free Voss and am not doing overnights, I'm sure it will be fine."

She smiles but she does not look convinced, and an hour later, I see why. Already, my patients are double-booked and every one of them is irritated; they can't believe they had to wait this long, and they can't believe they're being forced to see someone new. They wanted Dr. Fox or Dr. Joliet and got me instead.

"First, Dr. Brown and Dr. Fryer leave and then it's Dr. Lee, and now they're telling me *you're* my doctor?" demands a testy woman with rosacea. "How long will it last before they're pushing me off onto someone else?"

My smile flickers with uncertainty. *Is* it weird that so many doctors have left? I figured it was simply junior associates getting their feet wet and going off to greener pastures, but I guess it's a little strange that *no one* has stayed.

Not everyone has a kid arriving in mere months, however. So no matter what I'm in for here, I won't be going anywhere.

"I'm staying," I assure her.

She snorts. "Yeah, we'll see."

GEMMA and I meet at Louboutin in West Hollywood at the end of my first week for "celebratory shopping", in theory over my new job. I do my best to appear cheerful, though if the past few days were any indication, there isn't much to celebrate.

"These are you," Gemma says, wielding a sky-high purple suede stiletto at me.

I feel that old, familiar hunger I get when I want something. I reach...and then stop myself. They're probably eight hundred dollars at *least*, and now I have to buy...Jesus, I don't even know what I need: a crib, a changing table, a car seat? Given how much people bitch about the cost of raising children, I doubt it ends there.

She glances inside the shoe. "Try it on. You're a seven, right?"

I mean to say *"okay."*

"I'm pregnant," is what I tell her instead.

She pales. "What?"

I drop into the plush chair behind me. "I'm pregnant. Due in October." I feel a little calmer as I say it aloud. That's two seasons away. *In two seasons you can figure out anything. I've got loads of time.*

She doesn't seem as reassured by that as I am. "Who...? What—" she mumbles, dropping into the seat beside me. It's the first time during our long friendship that I've ever seen Gemma speechless. "Do you know who the father is?"

I tense. This is where it gets tricky. I probably need to tell Graham now that it's official. What stops me, mostly, is that I don't *want* to tell Graham.

My parents split when I was two and I spent most of my

childhood as the epicenter of their bickering. Over who was responsible for taking me to the dentist, over how weeks would be divided and whether my clothing was returning to the parent who bought it. My father stepped in to ruin every plan my mother tried to make, and he even threw the socks she bought me in the garbage when I arrived at his house with them in hand. *"She isn't going to tell me what socks you can wear,"* he'd said.

I don't want to do that to a kid, and I don't want to do that to *me*, spending the next eighteen years fighting Graham through lawyers because he disagrees with me about school, or braces, or deodorant.

And if Gemma tells Ben and Ben tells Graham, I'll be forced to.

"I've got some idea," I reply. "I haven't decided if I want him involved."

"Keeley," she says with that warning note in her voice, the same one she gets when I suggest I might not pay my taxes, "you shouldn't have to do this alone. And you sure as hell shouldn't have to *pay* for a kid alone."

God, I don't even know what Graham does for a living. Given how cheap he is, it can't pay well. After all the millionaires I've dated, trust *me* to get knocked up by a thousandaire instead.

"I have my own money," I reply, at which she raises a brow, because I spend like it's my last day on Earth, every single day. "I *will* have money, once I start saving it," I amend.

"It also isn't fair to this guy, whose name you still haven't told me."

I exhale. "Gemma, your parents had an ugly custody battle. You know how this shit goes. I don't want that for my kid, and it would all be so much easier if I just...avoided it."

"Ben and I are not going to let anyone take the baby from you," she says. "You know that."

Except I don't know that, not once they learn who the father is. Because Ben will definitely take his brother's side, and Gemma will be divided, and the way I see it, that means seventy-five percent of the vote has already gone to Graham, no matter how little interest he has.

And he doesn't *want* kids. He said so himself. Therefore, it's kind of generous of me to keep it a secret, from one vantage point.

I press my fingers to my temples. "I just have to figure some stuff out, okay?"

Like whether there's even a chance I can get away with this.

Can I? He's Ben's brother, but he lives on the East Coast. I haven't heard his name once since the party, so isn't it entirely possible he'll never hear mine again either?

We both leave the store empty-handed. Gemma hugs me goodbye, and I stop on the way home for donuts and then an açai bowl full of gross healthy stuff to make up for them. Sometime over the past week, food stopped making me sick, and I have not wasted any time getting reacquainted with the things I love: pizza and cookies and tacos, eating like someone who's just emerged from a famine.

I eat one donut after another and only realize when I'm going to bed that I forgot to unpack the açai bowl, which makes sense since I never wanted it in the first place.

I'm going to be an outstanding mother.

8

GRAHAM

I've been waiting for Keeley's name to be thrown in my face every day for months. This is, after all, the woman who told complete strangers about her plan to seduce a rock star. It stood to reason that she'd be unable to keep our Vegas wedding to herself. And if it's going to come out, it'll probably happen here, during my first family dinner since the holidays.

God, the *irony*. Ben, Simon, and Colin...they all went through a wild period, but now Ben is happily married, Colin's about to be, and Simon—well, Simon is still single, but he's young and making the most of it. They'd have a field day if they discovered that the only careful, responsible member of the family married a stranger he'd known for twenty-four hours.

My mother's focus tonight, fortunately, seems to be entirely on Colin and the wedding he and his fiancée have yet to plan. But just when I think I might escape unscathed, she turns and asks me how things are with Anna.

If Keeley told Gemma, who'd undoubtedly tell Ben, this is the perfect chance for him to say, *"Haven't you heard? He's got a wife."* But no one says a word.

"It's still over, Mom," I reply. "Just like it was the last time you asked." Her eyes dip, but I ignore her sadness. I have to. She wants too many things for me, and I wish she'd just stop wanting them.

The conversation reverts to Colin's unplanned wedding. It's too good to be true, and weirdly disappointing at the same time. I guess there was still a part of me that hoped something might come from the whole thing with Keeley, though I can't imagine it would have been anything good.

"How's your friend Keeley, by the way?" my mom asks Gemma, as if she's read my mind. "I had such a nice time chatting with her at the party."

I thought I was ready for this, for the sound of her name, for the news that will follow. I'm not, though. Not even close.

Gemma glances at Ben. "She's good." There's a tiny uncertain note in her voice, and my heart begins to pound.

Ben shrugs. "It's not a secret anymore, right?"

Gemma frowns. "I guess not." She turns to my mom. "She's pregnant."

I freeze, the drink I was about to casually sip suspended in mid-air.

"Pregnant?" my mother asks. "I didn't realize she was seeing anyone."

Gemma's laugh is small, diplomatic. "I'm not sure that she is. It's a bit of a mystery."

"What does *that* mean?" I demand.

Ben's brow raises, irritated at the tone I've taken with his wife, as if *Gemma* is some fragile flower in need of his protection. "What do you think it means? She's pregnant and she isn't telling anyone who the father is."

It can't be mine. She'd have told me by now.

Which means she's having someone else's child. I know I should simply be relieved...instead it feels as if something is lost.

"I did not see *that* coming," says Gracie, my stepsister. "When's she due?"

"October," Gemma replies.

My mother's eyebrows raise. "She must have gotten pregnant right around the time of your party."

The cup I'm holding cracks in my hand.

9

KEELEY

I meet up with a group of friends for dinner, the burgeoning swell of my stomach cleverly hidden by a tiny, waistless dress that ends at the top of my thighs. I pair it with the highest, strappiest heels I own. Perhaps appearing to be all legs will distract from the fact that I am now, at nineteen weeks pregnant, built like a Barbie doll—the anatomically incorrect version whose weight is so off balance she defies gravity just by staying upright.

I still haven't told work that I'm pregnant. How can I when they're so backlogged from the previous departures? How can I not, when I'm bursting out of every bra and can barely button a single skirt? I won't be able to pass it off as bloating for much longer.

I also haven't told Graham, of course. It's not like the kid is here. It's not like I'm *depriving* him of something. And I already know how he'll react if I call, as if this is all some scheme I've sucked him into. And why should I have to put up with that?

I order a seltzer with lime and let everyone think it's a gin and tonic. I could tell them the truth—unlike my family, unlike Graham, they won't insist I'm too incompetent for motherhood

—but they'd find the whole thing hysterically funny, a lark, and I *don't* think it's funny, or a lark, so I'm keeping it to myself until I do.

They regale me with what I missed while I was in DC, but their stories aren't nearly as hilarious as they think. There's the night Jason had a threesome and later found out one of the girls had just turned eighteen, which is a little disgusting. Then there's a story about them getting misspelled tattoos on purpose, which I'm glad I wasn't around for because I'd probably have done it.

These were my wildest friends, the ones who made me feel like *adulting* was a waste of time because there was too much fun to be had, but our fun was clearly alcohol-induced. Sober, I realize their jokes are stupid, their stories are barely engaging, and they're kind of shitty to the waitstaff.

"Keeley, what's wrong with you?" demands Erik. "You used to be the life of the party!"

I did. And if they bored me, I drank more or made everyone go dancing.

I force a smile. "I just need another," I say, shaking the ice around in my empty glass.

I go to the bar, and some guy in a suit tries to buy my drink for me.

"It's just seltzer but thanks anyway," I tell him. What I want to say is *"you're not my type"*, but who knows if that's even true? Because somehow, I chose a guy in a suit last January over much better options, *twice*, and I haven't wanted anyone else since.

When I return to the table, they're prank calling someone's ex, which seems like the kind of shit we should have outgrown around middle school.

"Keeley's too quiet!" shouts Candace. "Which means we need shots!"

I shake my head. "None for me. Work tomorrow."

"Why does DC make everyone lame?" Aaron complains. "Snap out of it."

I blink. "You know I'm a doctor, right? I don't have the kind of job where I can just fuck around all morning because I got no sleep."

"Never stopped you before," he says.

He's an asshole—they all are—but he's also not wrong, which leaves me wondering if maybe I was an asshole too.

I leave by midnight, painfully early by my standards, but pregnancy is honestly...exhausting. I used to think pregnant women were kind of sandbagging when they'd complain about the fatigue. *The baby plus all the extra crap is maybe twenty pounds at best, so how bad could it be?* I was wrong, though. Just the act of getting out to my Uber has me breathing like I just ran a 5k. Which is, coincidentally, something I'd never do by choice.

I yawn as I grab the mail downstairs and take the elevator to the sixth floor, shuffling the bills behind the catalogues so I can pretend they're not there.

Turning toward my apartment, the mail falls from my hands.

Graham Tate.

Stands at my door.

And he looks really pissed off.

I don't know if I should kneel to pick up my mail or simply make a run for it. I do neither. Instead, I just stare in shock as he walks toward me.

Did he grow? He looks even bigger than I remember, and I already remembered him being big. I'm not sure my body was built to carry offspring his size. My vagina definitely wasn't built to *deliver* it.

He squats to pick up my mail. His gaze catches on my legs as he rises, then rests on my face as he hands the mail to me. I feel a little...spellbound, looking up at him, noting the smug lilt of his upper lip, the curve of his cheek, and how blue his eyes are. How did I not notice just how lovely his face was the first time we met?

"Is it mine?" he asks, and the spell evaporates.

I fucked up by waiting. I know it now. But what am I going to *do*? How do I crawl out of this Keeley-sized hole I've created?

I could lie and tell him it's absolutely not his, but when this kid turns out to be an oversized geek whose favorite toy is a graphing calculator, he's going to demand a paternity test. He's probably going to demand one anyway. He seems like the type who'd be a stickler about that kind of thing.

"Keeley, answer me."

I fumble for my keys to avoid his gaze, and all the inevitable condemnation that will accompany it. "If I thought someone else might be the father, I'd be a lot more cheerful."

He slumps against the door. "Jesus Christ," he whispers. "Are you serious?"

Ugh. A brief, tiny wave of guilt sweeps over me, promptly chased away by resentment. "Right, Graham. *You're* the one who's inconvenienced here."

"I'm not *inconvenienced*, Keeley!" His voice echoes through the hall, undercut by a note of panic, and he blinks, surprised by his own outburst. "I'm fucking stunned. I mean, I'm having a kid and...were you even going to tell me?"

I elbow him out of the way and push my key into the lock. "I know for a fact I wasn't planning to tell everyone on my *floor*."

I enter and he follows. My apartment is delightful—full of bright cozy furniture and splashes of color everywhere you look, but it's seen better days. I haven't had time to unpack my bags, and my luggage is now open and strewn over the surrounding areas. I also haven't had time to tell my cleaning lady I'm back, nor recycle all the donut boxes I've brought home.

He's too upset to even notice as he paces, doing his best to avoid the clothes on the floor.

"So what was your plan?" he asks. "Have the kid and demand half my stuff?"

I love how he's assuming *he* has anything I'd want half of. "I'm a doctor and you're *you*. What would we be dividing— some off-brand men's shoes and a Turbo Tax coupon? Look, I only learned I was pregnant three weeks ago. This is all new to me too. I wasn't even sure I was keeping it until recently."

That muscle in his cheek twitches on overtime. *Oh, that did not sit well with him.*

He folds his arms across his chest—I'd forgotten how nice his arms are. And his shoulders, currently straining the seams of the fabric, like Superman about to burst from his clothes. "And you'd never even have included me in the decision?"

"Make up your mind," I say with a weary sigh. "Am I a gold-digging whore, or a heartless bitch trying to deprive you of fatherhood? Because it can't be both."

"Well, it was initially number one, but clearly we've moved on to number two."

I'm irritated, but he's also not wrong. I kick off my shoes and flop on the couch. I barely have the energy right now to argue on my behalf, and I'm not sure I even have much of an argument. Yes, I fucked up. And yes, I'm probably not a great person. But what's done is done.

"If I'd called you and said, 'hey, Graham, based on the hickeys and the condoms on the floor, I assume we slept together in Vegas and you knocked me up', you'd have doubted me, right? You'd have said *prove it*."

"I still intend to make you prove it. I mean, to be perfectly honest, maybe I wasn't even the only man you slept with that weekend."

My fists clench. It's mostly easy to ignore what Graham says —if the opinion of some uptight East Coast finance bro was going to mean anything to me, I'd start with one who's actually *successful*—but that weekend and its culmination in Vegas is something I might never live down, not even with myself. "Believe me, nothing could thrill me more. The last guy who asked me out was an NFL quarterback. Can you imagine the genetic potential? All your kid will do is recite actuarial tables."

"That isn't actually what I—"

I hold up a hand. "Please stop. I'm already bored by this conversation." It's bad enough that I'm having his kid. I shouldn't have to listen to him run through his job description too.

He glances around, looking for any clear surface to sit. I kick a bra off the chair across from me and he watches, appalled, before he finally sinks onto it and buries his head in his hands. "Jesus, Keeley." His voice is hoarse. "Were you even going to *tell* me?"

There's blame in that sentence, but what I hear most is how stunned he is by this entire thing. Which makes sense. Two hours ago, he was a single guy living his best life, and now he's got a major, lifelong albatross around his neck.

I release a breath on a long sigh. "Probably. To paraphrase Churchill, I do the right thing eventually, after I've tried everything else first." My aching body sinks deeper into the couch cushion, and I let my eyes close for a moment. *God, I'm tired*.

He sighs. "Fuck. At least we're married."

My eyes shoot open. I'd conveniently forgotten about that, for the most part. "*Were* we legally married?" I ask. "I sort of assumed it was just...a joke. I don't see how we could even have gotten all the way from LA to Vegas in time."

His tongue prods his cheek as he holds back what he wants to say. "Well, the signed marriage certificate I found the next day would indicate that we somehow managed."

It's sort of a relief that he doesn't remember either. As

appalling as much of what I've done over the past few years is, to have this monumental night be almost entirely a blank slate rankles. My father and stepmother constantly assume the worst and, in this, I'm forced to agree. "So I guess you were drunk too."

A hint of a flush graces his cheeks. "You can't possibly imagine I'd have chosen to do something like that sober?"

No, I guess not. While a fuck-up of this magnitude is just a day in the life for Keeley Connolly—I'm honestly shocked I hadn't gotten drunk-married in Vegas *already*—for Graham Tate, it was an appalling, life-shattering error. Temporary insanity he'll now be stained by for the rest of his days. It's hard not to feel a bit guilty for dragging him into my crazy.

"Look," I say, exhausted. "I have to work in the morning. Can we discuss this later?"

"My mom's armed their security system by now. I'll need to sleep here."

"*Here*? No. Get a hotel. Or go stay with Gemma and Ben."

"Keeley, for fuck's sake...Gemma and Ben are asleep, and I don't feel like finding a hotel at one in the morning. You must have a guest room."

"Sorry, Lord McRichPants. There is no *guest room* available. You can take the couch."

He pushes a hand through his hair. "That's a loveseat, and I'm six-four. We've shared a bed before, apparently. It won't kill us to do it again."

"My room isn't...fit for company."

He glances around him. "Believe me, my expectations were already low."

Ugh. I guess I deserved that. "Fine, whatever, but no judgement."

I walk to my bedroom, which looks even worse than I remember, and I remembered it looking pretty terrible. The bed is unmade, and atop it rests several days' worth of clothes, plus a wet towel, a half-eaten bag of popcorn, a makeup mirror I haven't hung up, and my beloved Birkin bag.

He arches one perfect brow, that tiny flare of his nostrils accompanying it. "You're sure you're actually a doctor?" he asks, looking around. "Because you live like a teenage girl who just profited from a sex tape with Kanye."

"I'm going to take that as a compliment."

"I assure you it wasn't one. I mean, are you letting circus folk use your bedroom as a staging area? I don't even understand how one tiny person could make a mess of this size."

How the hell did I sleep with this man? How the hell did I convince myself to *marry* him? God knows *he* couldn't have been the one who did the convincing...He can barely stand to look at me.

I carefully pick up the Birkin before sweeping everything else onto the floor. "Climb in, remain *dressed*, and go to sleep."

"Where's your bathroom?"

There is absolutely no way he's seeing my bathroom if he's this judgmental already. "Guest bath," I say, pointing toward the door. "Off the closet."

"Your closet has its own bathroom?"

I ignore the question, entering my bathroom and slamming the door behind me. And then my jaw locks and I swallow against the tightness in my throat, because coming face to face with myself, and only seeing my mother reflected back at me, is not ideal at the moment. She wanted so much for me and so much for herself.

I brace my hands on the vanity and try not to cry. "Keeley, you've really fucked up. You've fucked up so badly."

Because *look at this place*. There's half a donut on the sink. Last night's pajamas are still on the bathroom floor, where I shed them this morning. I haven't taken out the trash in two weeks and it's beyond overflowing.

I can't *parent*. I can't even take care of myself, and it's only now, when I finally have a witness to it all, that I see it clearly. No wonder he's horrified. I wouldn't want me raising my kid either. But I absolutely can't fall apart right now, not with Graham Tate stomping around my apartment, looking for signs of weakness.

I wash my face and pull on last night's pajamas, then emerge from the bathroom to find Graham sitting up in my bed, leaning against the headboard with a t-shirt on, arms folded. He looks like someone's cranky dad.

A really hot cranky dad, I'll admit.

Which is what he already *is*. The man I'm looking at right now with those drool-inducing arms is the father of my child. My *husband*.

I shake my head as I stand in the doorway, patting on my eye cream. "I feel like I've landed in some kind of bizarro alternate universe."

"Me too," he replies. "But that's mostly about the state of your apartment."

I ignore him, shutting off the bathroom light and crossing the room to my side of the bed.

"I can't believe you've turned an entire *bedroom* into clothing storage," he grouses. "Why do you even own that many clothes?"

I climb in, pulling the blankets up to my neck. "I need clothes. It's part of my brand. Eventually I'll save someone's life and be propelled into reality show fame, and when that happens, there are going to be a lot of premieres and cocktail parties, and I'll need clothes."

He glances at me, brow furrowed. "Your 401k must be a disaster."

"Joke's on you. I don't have a 401k." I make a show of fluffing my pillows, placing them all the way over to the halfway point of the bed. I swear to God if his body crosses the midline of this mattress, I'll stab him in his sleep. I keep a knife on my nightstand, so I wouldn't even have to exert myself.

"You have *no* retirement," he repeats. Now I know the one thing that can upset him more than impending fatherhood. "Jesus, are you serious? You should be contributing the maximum every year. I bet your company even matches it."

"Ugh. You sound just like Mark." I flip off the light and lie down beside this massive almost-stranger I'm stuck with for the night. Movies make this situation look sexy, but in truth it's just *weird*. His side of the bed is for outfits I chose not to wear and for the makeup mirror I haven't found time to hang, not for other humans.

"Who's *Mark*?" His voice is icy.

I'm startled out of my reverie. "A friend."

"What *kind* of friend?"

Dread slowly crawls into my stomach. This is what I'm in for. For the next eighteen years, it's going to be my childhood all over again: *Your mother left you with a sitter to go out? With whom? She isn't allowed to introduce you to someone without informing me first. Who the hell is Daniel? Does this quote-unquote neighbor sleep over?*

I'm not going down this road with him. I'm just not fucking doing it.

"Let me make something *crystal* clear," I hiss. "We might be having a kid together, but that doesn't mean you have some kind of dominion over me. I don't owe you explanations about *anything* unrelated to the pregnancy."

He tenses beside me—I assume because he wants to argue. "For our kid's sake," he finally says, "we should probably at least be civil to each other."

Yeah, that's what my dad used to say, too, when he wasn't getting his way.

～

My ALARM GOES off in the morning and I'm assaulted by the sight of skin.

So much male skin.

Graham took his t-shirt off sometime during the night, violating a rule he agreed to six hours earlier, which doesn't bode well for sharing a child.

And the man sleeps like the dead. I cough and shove him, but he doesn't budge.

With a sigh, I go into the bathroom, twisting my hair on top of my head before taking the world's fastest shower. When I walk out, wrapped only in a towel, he wakes, and the first thing he does is look me over, from head to toe—the way he might if we'd just slept together and he was thinking about doing it again.

For the briefest second, there's a pulse between my legs, a muscle clenching low in my abdomen.

I clutch the towel around me tighter. "You need to get out."

He raises a brow, pushing himself up and leaning against the headboard. I'd forgotten about his fantastic abs. "You're a ray of sunshine in the morning, aren't you?"

"I'm a ray of sunshine the whole goddamn day," I huff, "but I don't need a naked stranger lounging in my bed when I get up."

"Turning over a new leaf then, are we?" A smug smile lifts his mouth. "I was implying you do this a lot, in case that wasn't clear."

My eyes narrow. "It's a shame you hadn't done it *more*. Maybe you'd have known how to put on a condom."

A quiet light flickers in his eyes as if he's remembering something about that night. *Nights.* That traitorous muscle in my gut clenches once more.

"Leave," I demand as I march into my closet.

Inside, I manage to find a skirt that still fits, along with a cardigan just baggy enough to disguise the whole mess. And when I enter the kitchen, he's sitting at the counter. Apparently, he didn't understand what I meant by "leave."

I pop a bagel in the toaster and act like he isn't there.

"Is that your breakfast?" he asks.

"This is for Mark. I don't eat breakfast."

His eyes darken. "Mark, your *friend*? You make his breakfast?"

I could tell him, once again, that it's none of his fucking business. I only answer because the truth will bother him more. "He sleeps outside the building. I've told him he can come make it himself, but he never takes me up on it."

Graham grips the counter and breathes slowly, in and out of his nostrils. "So let me get this straight: the guy advising you about your finances is *homeless*, and you've offered him access to your apartment."

"You shouldn't judge people based on their occupation."

"I'm not judging him on his occupation, Keeley," he replies, mouth ajar. "He doesn't *have* one. Do you have any idea what parenting even requires? You need to have money. You need to have some food in your refrigerator. You need to not offer random homeless men the run of your apartment. And I really hope to God you're not still drinking."

Jesus, *of course* I'm not drinking. Did he miss the part where I said I was a doctor? Has it escaped his attention that if I'm living in this very nice—albeit messy— apartment I must be doing *something* right? I'm also taking vitamins and choking down green juice and salad every day, but I'm not going to waste time defending myself. And since he's going to think the worst of me no matter what, I might as well have some fun with it.

"We'll see about the drinking," I chirp. "All bets are off when I go to Coachella. I get *so* thirsty."

"You're not seriously going to Coachella...with all the pot

fumes and cigarette smoke you'll breathe in? What if you accidentally take an elbow to the stomach, or get trampled?"

I return the cream cheese to the fridge. "FYI, getting trampled would kind of be an issue, pregnant or not, medically speaking."

He ignores this, suddenly focused on the purse I've slung over the chair beside him. "If you're *actually* a doctor, why do you have a closet like a Kardashian? And how the hell did you buy an Hermes bag on a resident's salary?"

"It was a gift."

He stiffens. "Anything *that* expensive is an 'arrangement', not a 'gift.'"

I slam the knife down on the counter. "What, *precisely*, is that supposed to mean?"

He doesn't answer because we both know exactly what he was trying to imply.

I nod at the door. "Time for you to leave, Graham."

He hesitates before he rises from his chair. "I'll call you."

"Don't feel compelled," I reply, as the door shuts behind him.

10

GRAHAM

I thought the answers would quell the panic in my chest, but I have the answers and a full night of sleep, and I only feel worse.

I mean, of all the people with whom to be producing a child, something I never wanted in the first place: a woman who eats popcorn in bed, seeks financial advice from the homeless, is being "gifted" shit worth thousands of dollars, and who still doesn't seem entirely sure she even wants the kid.

There's a piece of me that thinks it would be better not to know, but better for whom? Not our child, who'd then be raised by Keeley alone, with no supervision. She probably thinks she can let him sleep in a pile of designer dresses in her closet and feed him Skinny Pop when he cries. Maybe she'd ask "Mark" to check in on the baby during the workday if she was feeling extra responsible.

And how the hell am I supposed to fix anything when I live three thousand miles away?

When I get back to Newport, my mother grins at me from her seat at the kitchen table. "*Someone* had a late night," she teases, undeniably pleased. She'd begun to worry I'd always be alone, something I'd assumed as well and was fine with. Trust Keeley Connolly to fuck up every one of my carefully laid plans.

I cross the kitchen to the coffee pot. If I admitted where I've been, she'd be thrilled. She'd dance across the kitchen, then hire a skywriter to shout it to the rest of Newport. But I'm not going to tell her she's got a grandkid on the way when I have no fucking clue what Keeley's going to do between now and the next time I see her.

"Anyone special?"

"No, Mom. It wasn't a big deal."

Her smile wavers and I get a sudden glimpse of the worst days of my childhood. And possibly a glimpse of my kid's childhood too.

I won't fucking stand for it.

I tell my mom I need to pack. I'm already calling my lawyer by the time I hit the stairs.

"I need you to write something up for me," I tell his voice mail.

Maybe Keeley isn't the same as my mom, but she might be even worse.

And I'm not fucking living through that again. Neither is my kid.

11

KEELEY

I arrive at the office, waving half-heartedly to Trinny at the front desk.

She winces, and I already know what she's going to say.

"Your schedule is packed. Dr. Fox had something come up."

Ugh. I'm nearly through the backlog, but my days are just as long because Dr. Fox and Dr. Joliet seem to have a lot of shit that just *comes up*, always to my detriment. And maybe if they knew I was pregnant they'd stop doing it, but it's still early in my tenure here and they already don't seem pleased. There have been comments about my attire—my cardigans would be more flattering if belted, apparently—and there are vague complaints about the way my new patients aren't thrilled with me. Why would my patients be thrilled? They thought they were getting a well-known doctor and got dumped on the one who's still wet behind the ears.

I can't say I'm thrilled either. I'm putting in as many hours as I did as a resident, and they somehow feel *longer*. At least at the hospital, my day was exciting. There were burns and lumps and deformities. There were blisters the size of my hand and the occasional cutaneous *larva migrans*. Now, my day is always some version of the same thing: *"I'm breaking out"* or *"I don't like these lines"*. Psoriasis is as exciting as it gets.

I glance at the schedule. There are now three patients shoved into time I blocked off for my nineteen-week exam.

"I've got a doctor's appointment today," I tell Trinny. "That's why I blocked it off."

She looks at me, eyes wide. "Do, uh, *you* want to tell her?"

My shoulders sag. I already know how that will go...Dr. Fox takes disappointment poorly, to say the least. "I'll change my appointment."

But this is going to have to stop. And I'm wondering how I'll ever gather the courage to tell Dr. Fox *why* it has to stop when I can't even ask for a lunch break.

JULIE IS able to fit me in at the end of the day. I hope her irritation over this is why she's coming down on me so hard about everything else. "Keeley," she says, "you've put on ten pounds in a week."

"It's all gone to my rack, though," I argue, glancing down. Out of nowhere, I'm suddenly spilling out of every bra I own.

"You'd dropped weight early on and you had some catching up to do," she says. "It's just something we'll need to keep an eye on."

"I thought we were here to discuss the *baby's* health," I mutter, feeling judged. "Not *mine*."

"This *is* about the baby. A serious spike in weight might be a sign of gestational diabetes. Didn't you do an obstetrics rotation?"

Various facts pop into my head. *Between six and nine percent of pregnancies, excessive thirst and urination might be the only signs.* It's easier to play dumb, though, so I simply shrug.

"Yeah, but I was hooking up with Lowell Chambers at the time. Remember him? Maybe you were gone by then. Anyway, I was in a lust-induced fog, and it all went in one ear and out the other."

She gives me one of her polite *Julie* smiles, the kind that say, "*I can't believe this woman and I got the same degree.*" I get that look from colleagues quite often, surprisingly.

"Is the father going to be involved?" she asks.

I glance away. "I'm not entirely sure."

It's been two days since Graham left and there's been absolute silence. I assume this means he's gone back to his soulless and tidy apartment in New York, run the numbers, and written it off.

I'm mostly relieved. Yes, there's the occasional thought about how fucking *easy* it is for men to bear none of the consequences, but then I remind myself: I didn't want him involved and I don't need his money.

I mostly don't need his money. Any day now, I'm going to turn into the kind of person who stops buying designer clothing and taking trips to Cabo.

"Well, let's take another look," she says, grabbing the jelly for the ultrasound.

My heart beats a little faster. I watch the screen as the transducer glides over my stomach. And then...a profile. A nose, a leg, a tiny, fast-beating heart, flickering in and out like a flashlight in a storm.

My throat tightens unexpectedly.

My child. Something I never thought I'd see.

"The baby is kind of facing away," Julie says. "I'm going to start doing the measurements and maybe he or she will turn for us here in a second so we can figure out the gender." A tiny foot comes into view and a flutter in my stomach matches the movement. I want to see more, so badly, and at the same time, I can feel panic bubbling in my chest. I'm not ready for this to be any more real than it already is.

"That's okay," I whisper, my throat clogged with tears. "I don't want to know."

It's already too real.

"Keeley," she says, her voice soft, "you're probably going to need some help, you know? It's a lot."

Which makes me cry the entire way home because she's right...it's a lot. And I'm going to be a disaster at it.

GRAHAM CALLS THAT EVENING. I'm tempted to let it go to voice mail until I think of that tiny flickering heart I saw this afternoon. This isn't about me or him, and I probably need to start trying a little harder.

"Can we meet this weekend?" he asks. "I'll come to you."

If he's willing to fly all the way to LA, he either wants something or plans to demand something, and I'm not interested. "That seems like a lot of trouble for what you could probably say right here in thirty seconds."

He exhales. A heavy, *weary* exhale. If he's tired of me now, just wait 'til he gets to know me.

"There's a lot to discuss, Keeley, and nuance is lost when you're discussing things by phone. We'll go to dinner, and that's it."

A dinner he'll spend badgering me, pushing and pushing for whatever it is he wants. For that little flickering heart, though, I guess I can agree.

THE RESTAURANT he's chosen is not, to my vast surprise, the all-you-can-eat, buy one-get-one-free buffet I'd expected. And if

Graham is shelling out for this place, he must be after something big. *"I've bought you this nice steak dinner,"* he'll say, *"and now I need you to sign a twenty-page contract agreeing to my demands."*

It's another tactic I remember from my childhood. *"Your father is cooperating,"* my mom would say with a sigh. *"He must want something."*

And she was always right. So I don't know what the hell Graham wants, but I wish he'd just texted his request from New York so I could have said, *"no,"* and also, *"fuck you,"* without this performative dinner.

I find him waiting in the bar, reading something on his phone. His jacket is off, his tie loosened, his five o'clock shadow looking more like ten o'clock—and the effect is devastating. While I have a thousand regrets about the way my life is currently unfolding, I've got to say that simply from a genetics standpoint, I didn't do so bad. If Graham was anyone else, someone I didn't know to be a cheap, judgmental asshole, I'd say that he was *appallingly* hot, the kind of hot that probably had women doing double takes all the way through the airport this afternoon.

He looks up suddenly, catching me staring, and awkwardness descends; I've never had a guy fly across the country to see me without sex being the entire purpose. I'm not sure how to proceed. *Hug? Parisian almost-kiss to the cheek?* In the end, we opt simply for a nod—two business colleagues who hate each other but have accepted the position they're in.

"No offense," I tell him, "but I was kind of hoping you'd no-show."

He frowns. "For Christ's sake, Keeley, this isn't a dispute in small claims court. It's a child. Of course I wasn't going to no-show."

I'm wondering, again, if I should have just lied through my teeth the night he came to my apartment. My mother's life would have been so much easier had she just quietly slunk off to raise me without ever involving my father. Instead, she spent the last fifteen years of her life being told, *"no"* to every single thing she wanted. *"No"* to a summer in Morocco, *"no"* to letting me audition for a Disney show, and *"no"* to letting us tour with her boyfriend's band.

Have I just signed up for the exact same future? One in which not a single decision is mine?

Graham walks over to the supermodels moonlighting as hostesses to tell them we're here. They're the kind of women who act bored regardless of circumstance, but even *they* brighten a bit as he approaches. Sure, they do—he's big and broad-shouldered and disgustingly handsome, and they haven't been forced to endure a ten-minute speech from him yet entitled: *Just Because I Can Afford to Pay For a Tequila Luge Doesn't Mean I Should.*

He motions me in front of him as we're led to the table, his hand briefly on the small of my back. When he holds my chair, the stupid fucking hostess has stars in her eyes.

"Your waiter is a little busy right now," she says only to Graham. "Can I get you something to drink?"

"Water, thanks," he says.

"I'll have the same," I reply, not that she seemed to be asking me. She walks away, and I roll my eyes. "You could have gotten a drink. I'm not so tempted by alcohol I won't be able to resist if I see yours."

"I stopped drinking. Our night in Vegas was a wake-up call."

Well, that's flattering. Marrying me was so horrifying that it made him stop drinking. Of course, it made me stop drinking, too, but *I'm* a treasure.

"Ditto."

His mouth tilts into a smug smile. "I assumed that weekend was par for the course for you."

"You're awfully judgy for a guy who got so drunk you don't

even remember *marrying* me. To be honest, it implies you might have some issues with alcohol."

His jaw falls open. "*You* don't remember either."

"And now you're deflecting blame, which is also a sign of alcoholism."

He laughs quietly. "Will murdering you be a third sign?"

I hold the menu in front of my face. "Well, it certainly wouldn't be an argument *against* it."

The waiter returns with our water. Graham and I both order the New York Strip, served in a red-wine reduction, except he asks for spinach in lieu of fries. It feels like a criticism, and I bet I'm in for more. I bet I'm in for a whole lifetime of him silently but obviously doing things better than I do and gloating about it.

"You seem tense," Graham says.

"I came here straight from work. It takes me a minute to unwind."

"It's seven-thirty." His brow furrows. "I hope your boss realizes you won't be able to work this late going forward."

Oh, here we go. The inevitable discussion where he points out all the ways I'm not cut out for this. Where he produces a graph showing me how badly I'm about to fail.

"*Don't,*" I warn. "This is all new to me and I'm figuring it out. But this is a kid, not something you can plug into an actuarial table and—"

He makes a noise—it's a laugh or a growl, I'm not sure which. "For the last time, I do not use actuarial tables. What is it, exactly, that you think I do?"

"Something with money? Taxes? I think I just tend to lump all the boring professions into one."

He takes a sip of his water. "I tell people what to do with their money."

A basket of bread is delivered to the table, and I tear into it, trying not to groan volubly. "That still sounds like taxes to me."

"You need a CPA to do taxes," he says.

"So, what I hear you saying is that you're not *smart enough* to do taxes."

He makes that noise again. I'm pretty sure it's a laugh, but this time it also sounds an awful lot like a prolonged, weary sigh. "Yes, Keeley, you've nailed it. Anyway, I've spent the week thinking about this situation and, well, you didn't want kids, and—"

"I didn't," I say, cutting him off. "But I want this one. And you didn't want kids either."

He looks at me for a long moment, and I get the oddest feeling that something just changed, and I have no idea what it was. "I didn't. But I want this one," he says softly. "So maybe I should move in, just until you give birth."

I swallow the bread in my mouth so rapidly I nearly choke. "Move in," I say blankly. "You mean...with *me*?"

"Yeah, I can work from LA for a while. At least until the baby comes. And it makes sense, doesn't it?"

"In what possible way does you moving into a stranger's one-bedroom apartment make sense?"

"Keeley, you have a second bedroom and none of the shit in that 'closet' is going to fit you in a month anyway."

Oh no he didn't.

I draw myself up straight, politely returning the rest of my bread to my plate. "I have no idea what you're talking about."

He scrubs a hand over his face. "You realize how pregnancy works, right? Your stomach is going to get bigger. *All of you* is going to get bigger. And I've seen how you dress. I'm guessing your closet doesn't abound with loose clothing."

Wow, just...*wow*. "Are you trying to say my clothes are *slutty*?"

His eyes graze over me before he looks away. "It wasn't a complaint." His voice is deeper than normal, gravelly. And I see a flash of something from our brief past—unapologetic hunger in his eyes, his hand sliding inside my dress, the sound of panties tearing.

That's why I couldn't find them the morning I left. He *tore* them. He tore them and he wasn't the least bit sorry. I feel a tiny spark in my core, one I immediately extinguish.

But...*huh*. I would not have guessed he was the type.

He swallows. "Weren't you going to have to clear that room out for the baby anyway?"

I suppose telling him I hadn't thought that far ahead won't especially help my case here.

"I was kind of hoping a Saudi prince would just buy me a house between now and the delivery, but I guess that window is closing."

"Pretty sure that window already closed," he says, with a glance at my stomach.

Unbelievable. In less than five minutes he's said my clothes won't fit and that no Saudi prince would be interested in buying me a house.

"Well, you're certainly doing a *stellar* job of persuading me thus far," I say dourly. "Why the fuck would I let you live with me?"

"Because I'll pay your rent the whole time I'm here. I'll buy everything you need for the baby and help you get it all set up. Think about all the shit you could buy with that much extra money."

"You don't even know what the rent is."

Amusement flickers somewhere behind his unmoving mouth, his unreadable eyes. "I'll manage."

If I trusted him, I'd be willing to hear him out, but there's *got* to be a catch, some mean little legal trick at play here —*eminent domain* or something that will mean I can't kick him out when the time comes.

"Why? Because nothing about this offer makes sense to me."

His tongue slides between his lips. "I guess saying I don't trust you to make responsible decisions for our child wouldn't be a compelling argument?"

My eyes narrow. "I hope you're not in sales because you're terrible at it."

"Based on the sheer number of purses you own, I'm assuming I don't *have* to sell it. You probably haven't got a penny saved. Look, I want to be a part of my child's life, even before he or she is born. I don't want to miss this. And I'm worried I'll always feel like I'm on the outside, given the situation, if I'm not invested from the start."

Ugh. It's the kind of appeal that's impossible to say *"no"* to.

I move my bread plate out of the way so the waiter can place my steak there, and the sight of fries makes me lose my train of thought.

I spear a piece of steak into my mouth along with a single fry and let the flavor explode on my tongue. "*Ohmygod,* it's so good," I groan.

For a millisecond, his face is feral, all sharp bones and glittering eyes before he swallows. "You shouldn't let yourself get that hungry."

Already the lectures begin. "Sometimes my job means I don't have time to get downstairs for lunch. The baby will survive. You think cavewomen had breakfast, lunch, and dinner?"

His mouth opens to argue before it closes again. And that's why it will never work. Because currently, he has to cooperate with me, but once this child is born, he'll have no reason to be polite.

He's not even all *that* polite right now.

"Your company is really just going to let you work from here all that time?" I ask. "It's *months.*"

One corner of his mouth lifts. "I think it'll be okay."

God. I'm going to have to put up with his smug face for four months. Four. And we will kill each other. How am I the only one seeing this?

"Doesn't it make more sense to, I don't know, save your leave up?" I argue. "You can come back after the baby is born. Nothing is even *happening* now."

His eyes darken. "*Everything* is happening now."

I sigh. "I don't know, and you're not going to push me into deciding anything *here*, so let me just enjoy my steak."

He smirks. "I didn't get the sense I was stopping you."

I look down. My steak is half-gone already. "Just stop talking," I tell him.

WHEN THE MEAL CONCLUDES, he pays the bill and walks me out to my car, eyeing my convertible MINI Cooper. Any second now he'll say, *"that's not a good car for a kid. Have you considered replacing it with a used minivan?"*

"I know you need some time to think," he says instead, "but I'm only here until Sunday. Can we meet tomorrow morning to discuss it some more?"

"Do you promise you won't trash any hopes I have about the Saudi prince?"

His mouth twitches. "Do you really think a Saudi prince is going to fall for a woman who's five months pregnant? It's not like he wouldn't have other options."

My arms fold across my chest. "You've got this weird habit of doing exactly what I just told you not to do."

He smiles to himself. "You've got a weird habit of entertaining wildly unrealistic hopes and dreams."

"Whatever. I'll meet you at the Starbucks by my apartment at eleven."

"Eleven? That's hardly morn—"

He stops himself at my raised eyebrow.

"Fine. Eleven."

He holds my door while I climb into the car. Holding some-one's door is honestly the most useless action. Were women once so weak they couldn't close a door on their own? But I guess...it's not all bad. Maybe it's a little sweet.

I can see exactly who he'll be as a father: bossy, demanding, full of unreasonable expectations. But he just flew across the country, tried to get me to eat vegetables, paid for my meal, and saw me safely to my car.

The truth is, he'll likely be a far better parent than I'll be.

12

GRAHAM

I stay in a hotel that night so I don't have to lie to my family about why I'm here, a lie that would be dissected by each of them *ad nauseam*.

She breezes into Starbucks ten minutes late, of course. Probably had to discuss some critical financial issue with her homeless friend Mark. Her pale blonde hair is falling out of a loose bun, the sparkle in her eyes could stop traffic, and she's smiling at everyone she passes. It's only when she sees me that she grows wary.

"You came," she says, making no effort to hide her disappointment.

"Did you think I'd fly across the country for this conversation and change my mind that quickly?"

She shrugs. "I would."

Yes, I know. I know because you fucking married me and ran off without a word, and then got pregnant with no intention of telling me.

Nothing Keeley does could surprise me at this point, aside from her potentially behaving her age, which is twenty-nine, a fact I only know from the marriage license. *Jesus, what was I thinking, and what is she thinking now?* She's so desperate to cut me out of all this and take care of the kid alone when she barely seems capable of taking care of herself.

We reach the counter. It's on the tip of my tongue to remind her she can't have caffeine, but right now, she's holding all the cards. I need her to agree to this plan before I start treating her like the child she basically is.

"I'll have a venti decaf mocha," she says, leaning toward the male barista, who is definitely one of those assholes who moved here hoping for his big break. "But tell me something— do you guys, like, experiment with all the syrups when it's slow?"

He's eating out of her palm. *Of course he is.* The most gorgeous woman he's ever laid eyes on is currently looking at him like he has the world's most fascinating job.

He grins. "All the time. We—"

"That drink has twenty grams of sugar," I announce, placing my hand on the small of her back. "That can't be good for the baby. And I'll just have the breakfast blend, venti."

His eyes widen. *Yeah, asshole, she wasn't gonna date you even if she wasn't pregnant.*

"What the hell, man?" she demands of me once we've moved beyond the register. "I was about to find out all the barista secrets and you ruined it."

"You are five months pregnant and flirting with Criss-with-two-s's while he figures out what to do with his life. Do you really not see anything wrong with that?"

"I wasn't *flirting*, and you have no idea what Criss-with-two-ss's does when he's not at Starbucks."

She seems legitimately peeved, which makes me wonder if she just doesn't understand her own power, doesn't realize that when she smiles, men turn into fifteen-year-old boys again, too overcome by hormonal impulses to make reasonable decisions. And then they marry her, apparently, if the opportunity arises.

"You were flirting."

She groans and turns away from me to face the woman beside her. "Oh my God! Your shoes," she gasps, clutching the woman's arm as if she might fall over from shock. "I absolutely love them."

The woman's face relaxes into a smile. "Oh, I got them at Maxfield over on—"

"Melrose!" Keeley cries. "I'm there all the time! How have I not seen them? Are they comfortable? They look super comfortable."

And that's when I realize Keeley isn't flirting. Or maybe she is, but she's flirting with the entire world. I've spent my life trying to care about as little as possible, and she wants to care about everything and everyone she meets.

She is terrifying.

"Okay," she says a moment later, sighing loudly as she slides into a chair. "Even though you just blew my shot at learning the secrets of Starbucks, I'm in. But we need some ground rules. First, you stay out of my room and I'll stay out of my closet."

"You might want to adjust to the fact that it's never going to be a closet again."

She doesn't seem to believe that. I guess she's still holding out for the Saudi prince.

"Second..." She chews her lip, unable to meet my gaze. "I'm a butterfly. I don't stay anywhere long, and it's best to get that out in the open. So this isn't going to turn into some romcom crap."

"I have no clue what you're talking about." This is something I'll probably say often over the next few months.

"Like, you're not going to be all sensitive and tell me I'm beautiful when my feet are swollen, etcetera, etcetera."

She's going to be responsible for a human life in four months, but this is what she's worried about? "Why the hell would I tell you you're beautiful when your feet are swollen?"

Her eyes roll. "You've clearly never read a romance or watched a movie involving someone who's pregnant. It always involves him reassuring her about her looks and ends with the couple having sex to make her go into labor."

"Have *sex* to make her go into labor?" I demand. She's got to be fabricating this. "Aren't there drugs for that?"

"It's a movie thing. I guess it knocks the baby out or something."

"*Knocks the baby out?*" I repeat. "There is no way you're a real doctor."

"I said *or something*. I was spit-balling, not delivering a Ted Talk on childbirth."

I have to stifle the urge to laugh. "Fine. I will never look at your swollen feet and tell you you're beautiful, though, in my defense...I doubt it was especially likely in the first place."

"Third, occasionally I'm going to eat junk food and you're not allowed to comment."

I glance at her side of the table. She just ordered a scone along with what is essentially a heated chocolate milkshake. "I'm not sure your junk food intake is *occasional*. And I have some rules too."

She frowns. "You're the one inconveniencing me. It doesn't seem like you should get to make rules."

"First, you can't tell me I'm beautiful when my feet are swollen. Any other time you can, but not then."

Her lips curve. "Done."

"Second, you need to tell me when you have prenatal appointments so I can attend, without complaint."

"Nice try, perv," she says, sipping her drink. "But you have seen all you're going to see of my vagina, which, by the way, will not be ruined through the delivery of this child. Julie, my OB, has promised to do a c-section if it's big and to stitch things up perfectly afterward if necessary. But I'm probably gonna push for the c-section no matter what."

I can't believe she's discussing her vagina at 11 a.m. in a public place, but I'm guessing it isn't a first for Keeley. "I'm coming to the appointments. I also want to stay married until the baby's born," I continue. "I know it's old-fashioned, but...I do."

She blinks. I suspect she'd already forgotten we were married. "Fine, but aside from Ben and Gemma, let's tell everyone it was all, you know, *intentional*. My dad would be really ashamed if he knew the truth."

"Has he ever seen your apartment? I'd be shocked if he wasn't already ashamed."

Her mouth twitches. "Don't make me start second-guessing this whole thing."

So it's happening...A spur of the moment suggestion last night—one I suspect I'll come to regret—and it's only hitting me now how huge it was. I haven't lived on the west coast or with another human since grad school. My apartment, my job, my entire life is going to be left behind for four months. And from the looks of it, not a moment too soon. "We'll tell them it was all intentional. I can help clear that room tomorrow if you want."

"*Tomorrow?* What's the rush?"

I glance at her breakfast again. "Given your eating habits, time is of the essence."

She heaves a weary sigh, and another tendril of hair escapes her messy bun. I fight the urge to push it out of her face.

"Since there's nothing left to discuss," she says, rising and gathering what's left of her scone, "I think I'd like to enjoy my breakfast in peace."

13

KEELEY

"*Graham's* the father?" Gemma shouts.

So I guess we *did* have things to discuss. Like when we'd be telling his brother and my best friend.

I sink onto the floor of my closet where an entire emptied rack of clothes now lies. I pick up the Alaia dress I only wore once, trying to think of a use for it, but no...I was in an electric blue phase and it's probably not happening again.

"You can understand my predicament. If I told you, you'd have to tell Ben."

There's a *click, click, click* from her side of the line, which probably means her foot is tapping repeatedly against something. She does that when she gets fired up. "But how? You guys hate each other. You've *always* hated each other."

"Obviously, alcohol was a significant factor. I have no idea how it happened."

Which is sort of true, but also...not entirely true. I remember tiny slivers, and the more I'm remembering, the more real it becomes to me. I'm beginning to suspect I might really have enjoyed everything that led to this pregnancy. Maybe it's for the best that I don't remember.

"And you're letting him move in? The two of you will kill each other."

I rise to look at a white pantsuit that is cut all the way to my navel. Obviously, I won't be wearing this anytime soon. I toss it onto the discard pile. "In all likelihood, only one of us will die. And as long as it's him, there really isn't a problem."

She groans. "It troubles me when I use a metaphor about murder and you take it literally."

The old Gemma would have laughed, but the old Gemma wasn't related to Graham. Which leads me to Ben. I like her husband. He's always been nice to me, even when I grabbed her phone and set her up on a date with someone else because I thought he was cheating.

But our past, coupled with my efforts to exclude Graham from the pregnancy, isn't a great look for me, overall.

"Is Ben...pissed?"

"He's worried," she replies, which sounds a lot like *yes* to me. "You know how protective he is of his brothers. They went through a lot when they were little."

I snort. I've seen photos of his mother's house, and I'm not going to feel sorry for any of her offspring. "Yeah, it was so hard for them, being raised in a mansion in Newport. That one time the electric gates didn't work must have been super traumatic."

She laughs, but it fades quickly. "That house was a recent purchase. You know their dad died, right? He was in a car accident right after Colin was born. Graham was only eight and it was a mess for a long time."

Oh. Shit. I knew their father had died, but I didn't realize it was quite so...tragic. I was half-prepared to let him go through life without knowing about his own kid when he spent most of his life without his dad too.

If I allowed myself to do so, this might make me feel guilty. But life's too short for guilt. My life, in particular.

I WAKE in a good mood on Sunday and feel energetic enough to clean for once—a necessity since my cleaning lady is arriving tomorrow. She'll quit on the spot if she sees my place in its current state. I walk down the street to my favorite bakery and get two Sunday muffins—one for me, one for Mark. It has frosting and three kinds of chips: white chocolate, butterscotch, and peanut butter, but it has cranberries and is therefore healthy. Once I'm done savoring every last bite of it, I get to work. The dishwasher is loaded, and I dispose of this week's donut boxes. I get my luggage moved out of the family room and am dancing around the kitchen with music blasting when Graham walks through the open door.

He raises a brow at the song lyrics. "*Big dick energy*?" he repeats. "What an excellent role model you'll make."

I pick up a half-eaten Oreo and throw it in the trash. "Don't let it make you feel bad about your shortcomings. I'm sure you have other qualities."

His mouth lifts, just a hint, and so fucking smugly as if *that's* the one thing he doesn't have to worry about. I think of how I woke feeling after those two nights with him, and a muscle tightens in my stomach.

Yeah, I suspect he has nothing to worry about.

He walks to the closet—now guest room—and groans when he opens the door. "Keeley, I thought you were going to clean this out."

"I *did*." I point at the two trash bags in the corner. "It's all right there."

I got rid of so much stuff, but the room still resembles the backstage of a fashion show.

He goes to the first rack. "You've got to get rid of this shit. *More* of this shit. I mean, do you really see yourself wearing a leopard-print bodysuit in the near future?"

"If we ever learn how to time travel to the 70s, I plan to seduce Eric Clapton and Don Henley, and that's the outfit I'll wear."

"I'm not sleeping in a room full of clothes you've kept because our species *might learn to time travel*."

I really hope our child does not inherit Graham's relentless practicality. "What if he or she wants to wear it to school for dress-up day?"

"No child of mine, male or female, will be wearing *this* for dress-up day," Graham replies. "Come on. There's not even room for a bed in here, and you *have* an actual closet. At least put this stuff in storage."

"Fine." I start to sort through the rest of the clothes, picking out the few things I'm likely to wear between now and the time the baby arrives. "What's your favorite color, by the way?"

He raises a brow. "Why?"

"Jesus Christ, Graham. I didn't ask for your social security number. I'm just trying to get to know you." I pause, wondering if there's any chance I can still pull off a cross-neck halter dress with an open midriff.

"Black. There. Did that open a whole new layer to me previously closed to you?"

"No. It just confirmed what I already thought was there. Dark, bleak, probably fatal. Mine's red, not that you asked."

"Loud, attention-seeking, unable to blend in with a crowd," he says, grabbing one of the garbage bags. "Yeah, that lines up."

He's wearying me and he just arrived five minutes ago. I'm about to tell him as much when his older brother walks in.

I give Ben an uncertain smile, the kind that says, *"yes, I know I fucked up, but please don't hate me."*

"Welcome to the family," he says, which is generous of him, under the circumstances. He knows both of us pretty well, so he must realize who's really at fault for this whole mess. He turns to Graham, pushing a hand through his hair. "You didn't answer my text about that, by the way. Have you told Mom yet?"

"Not yet," Graham replies, narrowing his eyes at Ben, like he wants him to shut the fuck up. Clearly, it's an issue. *I'm* an issue, or this baby is an issue, or maybe both of us. I don't want that to bother me, but it does.

"I thought she liked me," I say to Graham.

He looks away. "She'll be thrilled. It's complicated."

I was the source of friction between my parents, the source of friction between my father and his wife. And now, it appears, I'm creating problems in a third household as well. I guess I never did do things small.

"I'll let you guys get to it, then," I say quietly.

Ben and Graham spend the next few hours moving my precious clothes to a storage unit, and I wander my former closet—now Graham's bedroom—while swallowing a lump in my throat. It feels like they've taken the best part of me, which probably says something unfortunate about the part that stayed behind.

Graham returns alone that afternoon. "My flight's leaving soon, but I'm driving back later in the week. I plan to be here by Sunday afternoon."

"I'll have to make you a copy of the key." I could hand him the one under the mat, but given how often I accidentally lock myself out, I know I'd regret it.

He nods, and the moment stretches out. It's time for him to leave, and much like his arrival here Friday night, it feels like we should be more than we are, that we should at least hug. He shoves his hands in his pockets. "I'll see you Sunday, then."

"Have a safe trip," I reply, for lack of anything else to say.

He leaves and I flop onto the couch and groan. Four months of awkwardness like this lies in my future. I suspect I didn't think this through, and that doesn't really come as a surprise.

Not thinking things through is kind of what I'm known for.

14

KEELEY

On Monday night, a bed arrives for him, oversized, just like he is. The next night it's a desk and dresser. On Wednesday, I've just carried three Amazon packages addressed to him upstairs and collapsed on the couch when he texts.

Graham: Everything okay?

I suppose he deserves a point or two for not going straight to the real question—*how is the fruit of my loins?* But I'm exhausted and cranky and wondering how much more of an imposition it will be to have him here when he's managing to impose so much from three thousand miles away.

Me: What goes better with pinot? S'mores or Reese's Pieces?

Graham: Keeley.

Me: FFS. It was a joke. Your kid is fine.

But Jesus...if he's this annoying from a distance, what happens when he's actually here? I barely have the energy to put up with myself at the end of the day, much less him.

I wake Sunday, determined to get the apartment together before he arrives—not because I care about making him feel comfortable here, but simply to present myself as a normal, well-adjusted adult who doesn't need his help.

Once I've had my Sunday muffin and forced myself to drink some green juice, I go to the grocery store where I buy a bunch of food that looks awful but with which Graham can't find fault. By the time I've lugged it all from my car, I'm exhausted and sink onto the couch, telling myself I'll put it away in a minute.

I immediately fall asleep, of course.

When my ringing phone wakes me, I have no idea how long I was out, but because I'm on call, I have to go rushing over to Cedars-Sinai, where one of Dr. Joliet's patients has just shown up.

Marissa Anderson is a character actress. Though I can't remember the name of a single show she's been on, you'd think she was Meryl Streep based on how imperious she is when I enter the room. The incision from her Mohs' surgery has split open, and it wasn't my shoddy handiwork that's put her in this position, but she's going to make sure I suffer for it.

"Where's Dr. Joliet?" she demands.

I force a smile. "She's off today. I'm the one on call, but I promise I'll get you out of here fast."

"I was told I couldn't even speak for two days and it still split open!" she says as I inject lidocaine into her nose.

I'd like to tell her that the y-fold on her nose broke open because it was poorly done in the first place and that the next time she needs Mohs surgery, she should go to an expert, not the bitch who does her Botox every three months.

"These things happen," I say instead.

"So now I go for another two days without talking? I can't take the rest of my life off work!"

"Ideally, yes. You don't want to put too much pressure on this until the stitches have done what they need to do." I get the feeling she still wants an apology from me, but I'm not in the mood to provide it. Besides, I doubt she's working all *that* much.

I'm mid-stitch when I feel my phone buzz in my pocket. I know it's Graham, and he's probably at my door, and if I wait even the five minutes this will take to finish, he's going to have a fit.

I ask the nurse to grab it for me. She holds it in front of my face so I can read the text, which is, of course, from Graham. And he does, of course, sound irked.

"Can you tell him the key's under the mat?" I ask.

Marissa's eyes narrow. "You still keep a key under the mat? In LA? Are you sure you're a doctor?"

Sigh. *You, Marissa, are no more surprised than I am.*

Once Marissa's sewn up and leaves, giving me one last dirty look, I go to the nurses' station to chat with everyone.

"I assume Dr. Patel is still torturing residents?" I ask the head nurse.

"Only his favorites," she replies with a grin. "I think he misses you."

I laugh. "Right. Patel *tormented* me my last six months here."

"I don't think he meant to." She must not be much of a judge of character.

They tell me about who's sleeping together and the craziest things that have happened and I realize how much I've missed this. I loved the bizarre diagnoses, the nuttiest patient interactions. I thought I wanted the ease of a private practice—that it meant choosing the kind of cases I'd take, setting my own schedule, and not being at someone's beck and call—but it's none of those things. I've got a full load of patients angry they keep getting pushed onto a new doctor, and they're all the same type of patient. There is no longer any variety to my day, and there is nothing to solve, which is far more boring than I realized.

I'm on my way out when Dr. Joliet calls. I half expect an apology for making me deal with her shoddy handiwork.

"Did you take a call in the middle of stitching my patient up?" she demands instead.

"No," I say flatly. "I did not."

"Well, Marissa said you did. And that you were brusque and unprofessional and appeared put-out that you had to come in. This isn't the kind of experience our patients expect, Keeley."

My eyes sting and it's not because I can't defend myself. It's simply that I miss the hospital, I'm really sick of the job I just started, and I can't do a goddamn thing about any of it.

No one is going to hire a six-month pregnant woman who left her first real job after a month. No one.

"Okay," I say. "Sorry."

Patel was a nightmare. I'm not sure Fox and Joliet are any better.

I order a pizza because I'm starving, and there's no way I'm cutting up kale and grilling chicken now, not that the food would still be good anyway. Nothing about today has gone to plan: no cooking, no cleaning, no getting us off on the right foot. I'm tired, but above all, I'm sad. I hadn't realized how much I enjoyed the camaraderie of the hospital, how much I'd miss the noise, the mild chaos, the intrigue. And...it's Sunday. I just want to eat and relax and watch *The Kardashians,* and now I've got to deal with Graham Fucking Tate instead. At least I was never nice to him in the first place, so he won't expect much.

I arrive home to discover my apartment completely junked up with boxes, a situation I can't say too much about since I completely junked it up with a week's worth of food I never put away. And the clothes I've strewn around here...Oh my God, the clothes. Even *I* am embarrassed, and that's saying a lot. If I weren't pregnant, I'd be racing around right now, picking up the skirts, blouses, and bras that are draped across every surface.

I'd be throwing out the now-spoiled chicken and the now-defrosted supergreens packs. But...I'm just too tired and too hungry, and I can't decide if I want to curl up on the couch and take a nap or demolish a bowl of cereal, so I settle for curling up on the couch with a box of Lucky Charms held to my chest like a favorite stuffed animal.

Which is when Graham walks in.

He's in a t-shirt and deeply in need of a shave. My eyes are drawn, involuntarily, to the bulge of his biceps and triceps as he sets two boxes stacked one atop the other on the floor. I picture those arms braced on either side of my head, his brow damp like it is right now. His jaw tense as he tries not to come.

It must be the pregnancy hormones, but man are they packing a wallop right now.

"Hey, roomie," I say, popping a handful of Lucky Charms in my mouth as he turns to me.

"Hey." His face is stern as his gaze drops to the cereal, no hint of a smile. "Is that your dinner?"

"A, they're healthy because they have the gross non-marshmallow bits. And B, I ordered a pizza, but I'm starving."

Just as his mouth opens to comment on this, the doorbell rings. I start to climb to my feet but he waves me down. "I'll get it."

When he sets my pizza and garlic knots on the table, I grab a slice straight from the box.

"Do you not have plates?" he asks.

I groan around the cheese and bread in my mouth. Nothing has ever tasted better than this first bite of pizza. "Too hungry. Cabinet."

He crosses the kitchen and flings open doors. "You shouldn't let yourself get that hungry."

"I didn't have a choice...I was in the middle of making something when I got called into the hospital." It's sort of true.

He takes the seat across from mine and hands me a plate

before opening the pizza box. He has a burn mark on his forearm, one I never noticed before. Maybe he left his abacus sitting in the sun too long.

"Can't they cut you some slack, given the situation?" His eyes fall to my stomach, the way they do every time he sees me, as if he still can't quite believe there's actually a baby in there.

I reach for a second slice. "They don't know yet. I need them to see that the baby won't change anything."

"Keeley, the baby's going to change *everything*." He leans back in his seat, a beleaguered sigh on his lips. "What do you think will happen when you don't come home on time? No nanny is going to be as flexible as your job seems to demand of you."

The pizza has become a lumpy mass in my mouth, and if he weren't here, I'd just spit it out. A *nanny*? I can't afford a fucking nanny. Just the thought of what that must cost makes me feel like I'm going to throw up.

Am I really going to spend all day at a job I hate, taking endless shit from Drs. Fox and Joliet about my unbelted cardigans and my perceived attitude, just so I can hand the entire paycheck over to a woman who gets to stay home with my baby?

"You'll be on maternity leave," he continues, "but when you get back, you'll need *set* hours afterward. Plus, there are endless pediatric visits with a newborn. You're going to need to—"

"Stop," I whisper. Nothing he's saying is wrong, but I really don't want to think about it right now, and knowing I'll have to face it all—and soon—hammers home how insane this whole thing is.

Maternity leave? Set hours? I can just picture Dr. Fox's face when I attempt to ask for either of those things.

How did I ever think this would work out?

There's no way I'm going to be a decent parent and Graham is here solely to remind me. And probably to document it, too, so the first second we can't compromise, he'll say, *"we'll see what the court thinks"* and produce a long list of my mistakes.

I push away from the table because I'll be damned if I'm going to cry in front of him.

"I'll just clean up then," he says from behind, voice rife with sarcasm.

"Fuck you," I whisper, slamming the door behind me.

15

GRAHAM

The next morning, she's rushing around the apartment, late and frantic.

I open my mouth and she stops me. "It's not my fault."

I doubt Keeley's ever thought *anything* was her fault. But given how mad she was at dinner, and how tired she looks today, I figure I should keep this to myself. We probably need to discuss what happened last night—I'm still not sure what the hell I said that set her off—but this clearly isn't the time.

She swings the bread out from the cabinet. "Can you make Mark his toast?"

I swallow down the unpleasant memory of that name from the night I first came here. For a solid two minutes, I was imagining a man named Mark replacing me, sleeping in her bed, raising my kid.

It felt a lot like jealousy. It still does. I don't want to hear any other man's name on her lips for a good long time, homeless or otherwise. Not when she's pregnant, at least.

"Oh. And this is his paper." She shoves *The Wall Street Journal* into my hands.

"Why is he getting his paper here?"

"Well, I buy it, but I really only want the style section so I give him the rest. You're on your way out, right? Just hand it to him and tell him I'll be down to hang out with him after work."

"Far be it from me to criticize—"

Her eyes roll. "Yes, you've held back admirably thus far."

"But maybe you shouldn't be sitting on a filthy sidewalk while pregnant."

"I'm not," she says, heading out. "He keeps a chair down there for me."

I release a quiet groan as the door slams shut. Of all the women in the world to accidentally knock up, why *her*? After a lifetime of staggering, consummate carefulness, how could I have slipped up with this person who thinks Lucky Charms count as a health food and who has her own chair to sit with the homeless man outside?

I quickly send a text to my second in command, asking him to get the staff researching a new vaccine that looks promising, and head downstairs. The British guy at the front desk, Jacobson, greets me like an old friend, though we only met for the first time last weekend. "Keeley ran late again, did she?" he asks with a fond shake of his head. "She's always telling me to let myself in and move her clocks forward fifteen minutes."

I stare at him. I can't begin to imagine what's led Keeley to tell this man to enter her apartment at will, but that fucking key under her mat is coming in today. For good.

Paul, the doorman, grins, leaning with his hand against the wall. "Keeley's finally settling down. You've won the lottery with that one."

Jacobson lifts his coffee cup to me as if it's a flute of champagne. "She's a great girl. Cheers, mate."

Clearly, these two have very little real-life knowledge of Keeley.

I walk outside, still expecting the chill of New York in April, and LA's sunshine and balmy air hits me like an unexpected gift. I suppose there are a few things about living here I don't hate. Bringing breakfast and the paper to some homeless guy is not among them, however.

Fortunately, there's only one person sitting on the street, using what appears to be a full bag of garbage as a backrest.

"Uh—Mark, right?" I ask. In my experience, the homeless are more likely to grunt at you or expose themselves than they are to read *The Wall Street Journal*, and I wouldn't put it past Keeley to have set this whole thing up as a joke.

He raises his eyes to me and grins. "You must be the father," he says, taking the toast and paper.

I blink. "I didn't realize she was telling people yet."

"Well, I'm not *people*. I'm one of her best friends."

Fifty percent of LA thinks they're Keeley's best friend, I'm guessing. And every last one of them knows where she keeps her key. "Okay...uh, enjoy." I step backward, preparing to walk away.

"She needs a 529 plan," he says.

I still. "Excuse me?"

"A 529 plan. To save for college. If she just cut back by one pair of shoes every month, she'd cover it."

This is the last conversation I ever thought I'd have with a homeless guy sitting on a street corner in downtown LA. "She doesn't even contribute to her 401k."

"Don't even get me started on that one," Mark replies. "I told her when she took that job—'Keeley,' I tell her, 'have them take the money out of your check before you even see it. With moderate growth on the stock market, you could retire in—'"

"Twenty years," I say.

He shakes his head. "Don't tell her that. We've got a few shaky years ahead, and if Keeley sees that money hasn't increased the way you promised, she'll give it a month and decide it's best spent on a trip to Cabo. You've got to keep her expectations low."

It troubles me that he's probably right. "I can't even convince her to tell her office she's pregnant," I mutter. "I don't see her listening to anything I suggest about a 401k."

Mark gives me a sympathetic smile. He has perfectly straight white teeth, incongruous on his very tan, very weather-beaten face. "Give her time. She's overwhelmed right now, and you know how she is...when she's overwhelmed, she needs a second to pretend nothing's gone wrong."

Except I *don't* know Keeley, which means the homeless guy outside the building understands my *wife* better than I do. And I can blame a lot of things on her, but probably not that.

16

KEELEY

O nce again, any hope I had for a lunch break is decimated when I have to take two "emergency" patients, and just as I'm rushing out to grab something, Trinny calls me to say Dr. Fox is stuck in traffic and needs me to take the patients who are already here waiting.

"And she was behind," Trinny warns, "so they might be a little pissed off."

By the time I race out of the office, I'm hungrier than any character in Les Misérables, but every fast-food place has a line around the block and I'm too fucking tired to wait or walk inside anywhere.

I go straight to my apartment without even stopping to pick up the mail, and then grab a bag of Mike and Ikes from the pantry, which is the moment Graham emerges from his room, dressed to go out. I don't want him staying here, obviously, but seeing him looking hot as hell in a button-down, makes me sad too. It's like he's throwing my captivity in my face.

"You're going out?"

"I'm meeting a friend," he says, and I want to grill him the same way he did that night about Mark—*'what kind of friend?'*—but I refuse to be the one of us who turns into my father first.

"Let me guess," he says, carefully rolling up a shirt sleeve, "you didn't get a chance to eat again."

There's a small, stupid part of me that feels sorry for him. For a micromanager like Graham, it must be excruciating to have no control over your offspring whatsoever. Also, he's replaced the burned-out bulbs in all the light fixtures I couldn't reach, and the refrigerator is now full, so he's tentatively on my good side.

"A fetus will draw from its mother as long as she has fat to burn," I tell him, cupping my breasts. "Have you seen the size of these things? Believe me, they are not shrinking."

His eyes dart to my chest, linger a second longer than they should, and then he shakes his head as if jarring himself. "They were hard to miss, yes. But stop going hungry anyway. You got some packages, by the way."

"My bras!" I cry, rushing across the room, all my sadness forgotten. I rip open the first package—three profoundly expensive lace bras in beige, black and red. My rack is gonna look amazing in them.

"And here I was futilely hoping you might be attempting to save money."

I move onto the second package. "Spare me. Hasn't your sperm already infected me with enough enforced responsibility?"

He glances from the mountain of lingerie on the table to the candy I just set beside it. "Yes," he says dryly, "you now appear to be the picture of responsibility."

"*Your* fuck-up does not mean you get to police my spending habits."

"*My* fuck-up? I'm pretty sure I didn't create this situation on my own."

"Look, my vagina is always right here," I say, waving in its vicinity. "It's your sperm that somehow were in the wrong place at the wrong time. I'm not sure how that's my fault."

His mouth lifts with just a hint of a smile, as if he's remembering. And then I am too, though it's simply fragments, like photographs being flipped through at high speed to create a movie—his weight above me, his grip on my hips, his teeth on my shoulder.

"You're right," he says, smirking, "I don't recall you having much to do with it."

Asshole.

"I'm *amazing* in bed. You'd be obsessed with me if you could remember it."

And there it is, in his face again: heat, and a certain knowledge he doesn't plan to share...which leaves me wondering if he remembers more than he's letting on.

17

KEELEY

The next afternoon I get out at a reasonable hour only because the patients Dr. Joliet tried to foist off cancelled when they learned they'd have to be seen by me, which doesn't feel like much of a victory, under the circumstances.

I go to the prepared foods section of Erewhon on the way home. I've just ordered chicken and rice when I hear a polite cough beside me and look up to find Arjun Patel, the worst attending ever.

"Dr. Connolly," he says, raising a brow, "how are you? How's the new job?"

Even if I hate it, I'm not about to let him know, so I plaster a wide smile on my face. "Wonderful," I reply. "Much easier than residency."

"You always did love taking it easy," he replies, and my smile fades. *Easy*? He gave *those* cases to his little favorites. He'd pat them on the back for diagnosing fucking athlete's foot, and then give me medical mysteries straight out of an episode of *House* and pillory me for the tiniest oversight.

I have no idea why he hates me so much when every other

attending *adored* me. Fuck this guy. I no longer need to win him over.

"I don't recall you ever *allowing* me to take it easy," I reply. "You reserved that for Evans and Hutton."

"*They* hadn't batted their eyelashes through their entire residencies. I thought you might appreciate the chance to prove you could get by without that."

The guy behind the counter hands me my chicken and rice. I take it, tempering the wide and possibly flirtatious smile I was about to give him. "I didn't bat my eyelashes through my residency," I snap. "I'm not sure where you got your information."

"I saw it with my own eyes, Keeley. Some women are offended by being underestimated, but you seem to relish it."

I stare at him, my jaw agape. "I don't *relish* it." But even as I say those words, a thousand instances of being let off the hook are coming to mind. I was relieved not to be called on during rounds, always feeling like the kid in class who hadn't done her assigned reading. It felt like a win when I got to leave early or wasn't asked to scrub in. I step past him, my smile sarcastically sweet. "Nice chat."

"When you realize you're capable of more," he says as I walk away, "come see me."

"Whatever, dude," I mutter, getting into line.

When you realize you're capable of more. What the hell did that mean? Does he really think I'd swing by the hospital just to have him tell me how bad I am at everything? So he can once again read me the riot act for misdiagnosing the single case of *Mycobacterium marinum* that ever came through the doors, and demand to know why I hadn't asked what the guy did for a living, a question irrelevant to almost any other diagnosis?

I'm still annoyed when I get home, but the apartment is tidier than it's ever been, and Graham's hung up the large, framed print that fell off the wall during the last party I threw. Maybe he's not all bad, but I hope he stays in his room.

I change into leggings and a sweatshirt, the only comfortable things I can still fit into, then head to the kitchen for my food. I'm so hungry I *want* to eat chicken and rice, which is sad.

Graham has emerged from his lair, unfortunately. One eye narrows on the sweatshirt. "You didn't go to Tulane."

"It belonged to an ex. It's the only one I have that still fits."

His nostrils flare in irritation—God knows why. I take my cardboard container from Erewhon and flop on the couch, only to discover nothing but white rice inside. The idiot behind the counter didn't give me my chicken, and I was too busy arguing with Patel to notice. "Are you fucking kidding me?"

I throw the container on the table and groan. I'm too tired and too hungry to drive all the way back, park, and demand my chicken. *Fucking Dr. Patel.*

"What's the matter?" Graham asks. "Not enough marshmallow bits in tonight's bowl of Lucky Charms?" His brow is furrowed, though, as if he's actually concerned.

I press my face to the couch pillow. "I just wanted to eat. I did my best."

Saying those words out loud has me near tears. I did my best, and I still failed. What happens when I have a small kid to feed? *Sorry, hon, we're just eating white rice for dinner tonight.* Even my mom managed to do better than that, and she was practically a child herself when I was born.

I loved my mom, a lot. But I never envisioned I'd be a *worse* parent than she was.

Graham quietly sets a sub in front of me. "I wasn't going to eat it anyway," he says before he walks into his room.

18

GRAHAM

The next morning, I meet Keeley at her twenty-two-week exam. I'm introduced to Julie, who is theoretically an ob/gyn though I have to wonder, given that we're on a first-name basis.

"Ah, so *you're* the mysterious father?" she asks, giving Keeley a look I can't interpret. God only knows what Keeley has told her.

She leaves and a nurse ushers us into a room and hands Keeley a hospital gown. "You know what to do," she says cheerfully, with a quick, curious glance at me.

It's only when Keeley kicks off her shoes that I realize she's planning to undress.

I scrub a hand over my face. "Should I, uh, leave?"

"Under the circumstances, they probably assume this is nothing you haven't seen before. Just turn around."

I stare at the poster on the wall, which documents the progression of a fetus.

"Our kid…looks like a baby already," I announce, mostly to drown out the sounds of her undressing: the soft slide of a zipper, the jangle of a hanger being used. I have fairly distinct memories of what Keeley looks like naked. I'm trying very hard to forget each of them now.

"Let me see," she says, shoving in beside me. Her bare arm brushes against me, which is when I glimpse a *very* sheer bra and creamy skin, and all my efforts to make this *not* weird go to hell. "Keeley, for fuck's sake, put on the gown," I snap.

"Look at the size of these things," she demands, cupping her breasts. "*Someone* should see them."

"Put on the gown, goddammit." I turn away and subtly adjust myself.

She crosses the room. "It's increasingly difficult to imagine how you could have gotten me pregnant."

I jam my hands into my pockets. "It's increasingly difficult to believe I'm actually the first one who did."

She finishes putting on the gown and climbs onto the exam table just as Julie walks in with a younger guy in a lab coat.

"This is Scott. He's doing his obstetrics rotation. You don't mind him sitting in, right?"

"Gotta learn sometime," Keeley says.

I'm not sure he does *gotta learn*, not given the way he's currently checking Keeley out.

Keeley's feet slide into the stirrups. The gown is bunched around her thighs. I can't see a thing, but this punk has a clear view.

Julie slips on gloves and he does the same. She takes two fingers and her hand slides beneath the gown. "At this stage, we're just checking for dilation and position of the cervix," she says to Scott. "Go ahead."

And then...he's got his fingers inside my wife. If this were all real, I'd be pissed. Actually, I'm really pissed anyway.

"How dilated would you say she is?" Julie asks, and he glances at me and away. *Yeah, I know you're enjoying this, you smug bastard.*

"Uh...she's not?" he asks.

"Right," says Julie and he finally withdraws his hand.

That's an experience we won't be fucking repeating. I'll make sure of it.

"I'm just going to check the baby's heart rate." Julie reaches beneath the gown to press a wand to Keeley's stomach. There's a whirr and a woosh and...it's there, a tiny galloping beat.

My child's heart.

I step closer, almost instinctively, as the sound begins to echo through the room.

And it all becomes a little more real to me.

I came out here to make sure Keeley was up to the task, and to make sure things were ready. But this...is really happening. And if there's anything I can do to make a difference, I need to be doing it.

When the appointment is over, I walk Keeley to her car. "I'll cook tonight," I tell her as we part. "So don't load up on Mike and Ike's or white rice."

She frowns. "Is it going to be gross?"

"Would you consider anything that isn't pizza or Lucky Charms gross?"

Her mouth curves. "Most likely."

"Then yes," I reply, "you'll probably think it's gross."

"FISH," she says flatly. "You made fish."

I look over at her from the stove. "It's nearly ready."

She changes into that fucking sweatshirt and returns just as I'm placing the salad on the table. "No fries?" she asks weakly.

Living with Keeley is basically a trial run for raising a toddler.

She cuts up the fish and disconsolately mixes it with the salad, but nothing more.

"You're supposed to be putting it in your mouth," I tell her.

She grins. "I bet I'm not the first girl you've said that to."

"Most women seem to figure it out on their own."

She blinks in surprise and then there's something between us, a silent, quicksilver moment of tension. Her tongue brushes along her lower lip as if she's picturing the same thing I am, and every muscle in my body tightens in response. *Fuck. Nope. Next topic.* Except all I can think of right now is her on the floor, looking up at me with a gleam in her eyes, as if sucking me off was the only thing she wanted to do for the rest of her life. "Eat your vegetables."

"I had a bunch of Doritos today. The seasoning is full of herbs. It's practically a salad."

"I really hope you aren't the kind of doctor people go to for advice."

"Not yet," she replies blithely. "But I will be soon, once I get my show. What do you think of the name *Kicking it with Dr. K*?"

"Will it be about an old white guy who adopts two inner-city youths and grows more than they do?"

"Okay, what about *Dr. K Knows Everything*? I'll solve medical mysteries."

I lean back in my seat, fighting a smile. "*Could* you actually solve medical mysteries?"

"Of course not. The production team will solve them. They just need me because then viewers will be like 'oh she's pretty and also a doctor, I didn't see that coming'. No one ever believes I'm a doctor."

I glance at her untouched plate. "That might have less to do with your looks than you think."

She clicks her tongue and pulls out her phone. I feel like a dad eating dinner with the teen daughter he's just grounded. I guess, aside from the daughter part, it's not that far from the truth.

"Ugh," she says to her phone. "Fuck you, Shannon."

I raise a brow.

"My stepmother. She's having a party," she explains. "Why the hell would I want to celebrate her son-in-law going to law school at age forty? You know what's worth celebrating? Going to law school *without* taking eighteen years off first."

I focus on my dinner, trying not to laugh since she seems genuinely irritated by the situation. After a moment, I sense her gaze on me. There's something about Keeley's focus. It's a physical thing, one that leaves a mark long after she's left the room, which is the only explanation I've got for the way I followed her all over LA during the weekend of the party we threw. I wanted to shake her off, erase her somehow. I was sober enough to know that it wasn't going to work and drunk enough to keep trying.

"We could just eat in front of the TV," she suggests. "There's a movie about a sexy kidnapper that—"

"I'm not watching anything that involves the descriptor 'sexy kidnapper.'"

We are certainly learning about each other by living together. I'm still waiting for one of those things to be good.

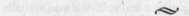

I'VE JUST FINISHED my first conference call of the day with New York when she marches into the kitchen, smoothing balm over her lips while reading on her phone.

"Elijah Wood's house is really kind of small," she says aloud, her brow furrowed.

Trust Keeley to worry that a person with way more money than she has isn't spending enough of it.

"Instead of reading about Elijah Wood, you could actually eat breakfast."

She narrows her eyes, reaching for the muffin she's saved for Mark. "Never too early in the day to start giving advice, is it, Graham?"

I hand her a Tupperware container. "Your lunch."

She takes it, and then her face falls at the sight of the leftover fish and salad from last night.

"Bro," she says. "I didn't even want to eat this the first time. If you think I'm eating it of my own volition, without a single witness to laud me for it, you don't know me very well."

"Keeley, you've got to eat vegetables."

"I know, but the thing is, vegetables are terrible and..."

I wait for her to finish the sentence and she does not. "Vegetables are terrible and...?"

"That's it. I realized I'd already made my point. Vegetables are terrible. Where were all these control freak tendencies of yours the night you knocked me up, anyway?"

Muscle memory takes over, as if we're back in that hotel bed and her nails are digging into my back while she's saying *oh-God-I'm-going-to-come-again-this-never-happens*, her voice breathy and desperate, the way it gets just before she... *Fuck. Stop. You've got to forget all of it.*

I turn away. "This isn't entirely about you, Keeley. I'm not sure how else I can hammer that home."

She stomps out, and suddenly the apartment feels empty, desolate. Maybe it's simply the absence of her incessant noise, which I should be grateful to escape. I send a few emails, then grab my wallet and head downstairs for coffee with no small amount of dread. I lived in my building in New York for five years without enduring a single conversation beyond some patently obvious comment about the weather. Now I can't even get through the lobby without endless small talk.

"Keeley just got another package," says the guy at the front desk. "She said it was just another bra and could wait, but you can take it if you want."

"I'll get it on the way back," I say grimly. Why the fuck Keeley needed more bras or had to discuss *lingerie* with this guy is beyond me.

I walk outside and Keeley's Homeless Friend waves to me. He's got *The Wall Street Journal* open to the trading page. You'd think he'd have more immediate needs than knowing what to buy and sell on the stock exchange.

"Take a look at Press-Kasker," he suggests. "They make a piece of desalinization equipment that's going to be in high demand in the next few months."

Jesus help me. This is what Keeley has brought my life to: I'm back in California, unable to even get a cup of fucking coffee without fourteen conversations and some financial advice from a homeless guy. "I'll look." And because I can think of no other way to escape this conversation, I add, "I'm going to Starbucks. You want anything?"

He shakes his head. "I'm all set. Just ate breakfast, and Keeley brought me lunch."

And he holds up the Tupperware I gave her not an hour before.

19

KEELEY

I know the moment I walk into the office that today's going to go badly.

"Your schedule is totally full," says Trinny, turning her computer screen toward me.

"I blocked off lunch," I argue.

She gives me that combination of a wince and a shrug, the kind that says she was simply following orders. "Dr. Fox had stuff she needed to do."

I swallow. I either nip this in the bud right here or I go home to get scolded by Graham once more. Which is worse?

"I have plans. Dr. Fox will need to reschedule those patients if she can't make it in."

Her eyes go wide. She's scared for us both, now, and it just makes me mad. Completing my residency was supposed to free me from this bullshit—from having no control whatsoever over the hours I work and the cases I take, from having people tell me how disappointing they find me. And now I can't seem to escape it. Not here. Not in my own apartment.

I've just left an examining room when Dr. Fox comes

storming in, her hair freshly highlighted. *Something came up, my ass.*

"Can I speak to you?" she demands. Her voice is thin and high, the voice she normally reserves for support staff who've written something down wrong.

"I've got someone waiting," I reply. "What's up?"

"What's up is that my whole day is a shambles now because I wasn't informed until nine this morning you were unable to see my patients. I need to be able to count on you."

"I wasn't informed until 8:45 that I even *had* your patients. I haven't had a lunch break in over a week, so I actually blocked the time off and I still—"

"Are you serious right now? I'm in here because you wanted a lunch break?"

I should tell her. I should just say, *"I'm pregnant, and I can't keep eating shit from a vending machine because you want to get your hair done."* I can't. Not yet.

"I need to be able to count on thirty minutes at some point in the day. You're not the only one offloading patients on me."

Her left eye twitches. "Don't forget, *Dr. Connolly*," she says, spinning away from me. "You're still on probation."

The words hang over me for the rest of the day, and I can't even plough through a bag of mini Snickers bars to deal with my sadness. I do, however, plough through a quarter of the bag and then throw it in the trash, mad at myself, mad at Dr. Fox, and especially mad at Graham for whom this minor effort at self-restraint would be deemed laughable. When Trinny warns me as I'm leaving that Dr. Fox has scheduled patients during my lunch break the next day, I don't say a word.

At home, I stop to pick up the mail and Paul tells me his newborn grandson won't eat. It could be anything—sensitivities, reflux, or something more serious like pyloric stenosis.

"They've taken him to a gastroenterologist?" I ask, and he says he isn't sure.

It's not my specialty, and I *shouldn't* give him medical advice right now, but the real problem is that I can't do it anyway, and in a few months, I might be the one in his position. I might need to know, and I won't, and I'll have Dr. Fox throwing a fucking fit because I'm taking my kid to a specialist to save his or her life.

All I want right now is to curl up on my couch under a blanket for a while, but I can't because Graham will be there—judging me, angry I skipped lunch, angry that I'm lounging and not stacking gold coins in a safe like Scrooge McDuck or whatever it is he thinks I'm supposed to do in my downtime—so I walk outside to see Mark instead.

"You look tired, Keelster," Mark says. He opens the chair for me and I sink into it. The redistribution of my weight will soon make rising from this thing impossible.

"I think I'm about to get fired."

He's the one person I can admit this to. The one person who won't say, *"Keeley, you're grossly irresponsible and anyone could have seen this coming. You probably deserve it."*

"There are worse things," he replies.

Mark used to be a stockbroker. He's vague on the details, but I know he made a mistake, and a lot of people lost money. I'm still not sure how he got from there to here.

"Your friend with the dumb name seems to be looking out for you," he adds. "I think you'll be fine."

I laugh bitterly. "He's not looking out for *me*. He's looking out for the baby. We're currently in a hostage situation, and he's the police negotiator, acting like we're friends because he has no choice. Once this kid is out, he'll have a SWAT team descend upon me."

"It's interesting," he says, "that you see yourself as the bad guy in this situation."

I swallow. I guess that's the problem. I *am* the bad guy. I'm always the bad guy. It's just been a long time since my actions hurt anyone but myself.

The realization leaves me deeply sad. I've been telling myself this is all a fun little jaunt outside my normal circle of comfort, like the week I spent sleeping on the ground at Burning Man. That's how I get through my life, by insisting things are an adventure and all adventures are good, even when they absolutely suck. What's different is that this time, the outcome matters. If I get stranded in Tijuana or lose my friends at Coachella, it is what it is. But with *this* adventure, there isn't an endpoint. Every decision I make now impacts this kid's life forever, and if I think about it too much, I feel nothing but panic, because *no one* is less well-equipped to parent than I am.

"He's worried about you, too, Keeley." Mark folds the paper over his head to shield his eyes as he looks at me. "Just give him a chance to figure it out."

I push myself to stand and whisper a goodbye, panicked I'm about to completely fall apart.

I just want someone to swoop in and save me from my own stupidity. I want Khloe Kardashian to take me under her wing and give me life advice. I was joking about the Saudi prince, but right now that sounds kind of good. I want my problems fixed, and Mark's as well, and I know neither of those things is likely to happen.

When I get home, I head straight to the Twinkies I hid in an empty container of Greek yogurt at the back of the refrigerator. Graham walks out of his room just as I'm tearing into one, naturally, and I swear to God the look on his face is enough to make me burst into tears if I wasn't already about to burst into tears.

"Don't start," I tell him, holding onto the Twinkie as if it's a sword I may need to yield.

His arms fold across his chest. He looks like Superman

when he does that, except he's way hotter than Henry Cavill. It might distract me on a better day.

"Let me guess," he says. "It's the first thing you've eaten all day."

I'm done. I'm completely over this entire situation. I've been trying to be polite to him, to establish some kind of civil relationship between us, and he is *fucking impossible*. I'm done. "Is this why you're here? So you can sit around in *my* apartment all day, then criticize me for doing my best when I walk in the door?"

He smirks. "Are we seriously claiming this is your *best*?"

"Fuck you. There was nothing else here to eat anyway unless you've got more fish on the grill, *God forbid*."

He raises a brow. "I figured I'd better run the menu by you first so you don't just drop it all off with Mark."

He knows I gave Mark my shitty lunch, and I feel like a kid again, walking home to find my stepmother waiting with the eggs she made me that morning sitting beside her, the ones I buried deep in the trash.

"I don't like fish, Graham, and I don't like breakfast. That doesn't make me a *villain*."

He digs his hands into his hair. "Do you think I enjoy this, Keeley? This situation is a fucking nightmare for me and it's never going away! It's a responsibility I'll take to the grave. So stop acting like you're the victim."

I step backward, stung by the vehemence in his voice, the sheer disgust, and wondering fleetingly, irrationally, if the baby heard this. If the baby is somehow taking in my complaints or hearing her father call this situation a *"fucking nightmare"*. Will he or she come into the world already feeling like a mistake, already feeling unloved? My hand goes to my belly. His gaze follows the motion.

This poor fucking kid. Of all the Keeley messes I've made, this is by far the worst.

I turn, walk straight to my room, and slam the door behind me, climbing into bed and curling up on my side.

My chest aches. Being the center of my parents' fighting was miserable. And being the offspring of me and Graham might be worse. We never cared about each other in the first place.

"I'm sorry, little Bean," I whisper, stroking my palm over my small, rounded belly as tears drip down my face. "I want you. I just don't know what I'm doing, and I'm really scared I'm going to mess things up."

There's a knock on my door and then it opens before I can pull myself together enough to tell him to go away.

The bed sinks under his weight as he takes a seat beside me.

"I'm sorry," he says with a heavy sigh.

"It's okay." My voice comes through a thick fog of tears.

I can feel him shift then turn toward me. "Are you crying?"

"No."

"Keeley—" His hand lands on my hip, so large it feels like it covers half of me. How the hell did this man and I ever have sex in the first place? He's twice my size. "I didn't mean it. I misspoke." He sounds...distraught, which surprises me. It's not something I'd have expected from him, unless he'd just lost money.

"You didn't misspeak," I reply, wiping my face on my pillow before I roll toward him. "You meant every word of it, and I'm offering you an out. Why won't you just take it?"

He stares at the bed between us, and as the moment stretches out, I realize that I want him to agree, but I'm also *terrified* he'll agree. Because I don't want to have to answer to someone...but I also don't want to do this alone. Just a few days of him helping out here—carrying in groceries, dealing with meals, changing the lightbulbs—has made me realize how hard it all seemed before, how daunting. And much of that is only going to get worse.

"I can't just walk away," he chokes out. "I have my own reasons for not wanting kids, but it doesn't have to do with not *liking* them. I grew up without a father, and I can't do that to my own child intentionally. Please tell me how to fix this."

Tears slide down my face once more, because I have no idea what to tell him. This past week has felt a lot like the months after my mom died, when I'd spend the entire school day barely holding it together, and then come home to Shannon and her lectures. It felt as if there was no safe place for me to be. As if nothing I did would ever be enough.

It's still as if it's not enough. I haven't had a drink in months. I haven't had sex once. I haven't even gone dancing. As terrible as my eating is, it's a thousand times better than it was. Every single thing I enjoyed about my life is pretty much gone, and some of it might be over for good, but all I do is mess up, in his eyes.

"This is harder than it looks," I tell him. "You think I'm not trying at all when I'm trying more than I ever have." Tears well in my eyes, but I swallow and blink to hold them in. "I'm returning the bras. And I'm a picky eater...it's just how I was born. I've never been able to eat breakfast. A lot of foods make me gag, literally, and fish is one of them. I'm not trying to be an asshole."

I roll away from him and his hand returns to my hip, giving it a squeeze.

"God, Keeley. I'm so sorry. Please stop crying. You're killing me here. Tell me how to fix this in any way that doesn't involve leaving."

He sounds genuinely desperate to make this right. I'm sure the impulse won't last, but for now, he means it.

"I get treated like I'm barely cutting it at work every single day," I explain. "I can't deal with coming home to the same thing. I really can't. I need to be able to watch some dumb television and eat some crap without anyone making me feel like I'm *less than* because of it."

I brace for him to pull a Shannon on me: to tell me I'm spoiled, to tell me he refuses to coddle me like a child.

Instead, he squeezes my hip once more. "You're exhausted right now, so I'm gonna go to my room and let you pretend I'm not here. And tomorrow night when you come home, I'll make us a relatively healthy dinner and then we'll eat Twinkies and watch some dumb TV."

I roll toward him. "No way *you* are eating a Twinkie."

"No," he says, his eyes lighter as he reaches out to brush a tear off my cheek with his thumb. "But I'll pretend I am and then give it to Mark, which is apparently okay around here."

"Yeah," I reply, smiling through my tears. "That's totally okay around here."

20

GRAHAM

The next morning, I can barely meet the doorman's eye as I leave to get coffee.

If he knew I made Keeley cry last night, he'd attempt to kick my ass and I'd probably let him do it, because Jesus Fucking Christ, I just made a woman who barely reaches my collarbone and is currently carrying my child *cry*.

I didn't think telling her this situation was a nightmare for me would even *matter* to her, but it did because she cares about the baby in ways she doesn't seem to care about herself, and me and my bad attitude aren't what she wants for her child.

When I heard the tears in her voice, when I saw her wiping her face before she rolled toward me, I felt sick. She's more stressed by this situation than she's let on, and I've got to stop adding my stress on top of it.

I'm going to turn this around if it kills me. For my kid's sake, yes. But for her sake too.

And I'll begin by saying, *"hi"* to her friend.

"Going to Starbucks, Mark. You need anything?" I ask.

He holds today's *Wall Street Journal* over his head to block out the morning sun. "You ever sat on the sidewalk before, Graham?"

I knew I'd regret stopping. "I'm sure I have...at some point."

I'm worried he's going to ask me to sit, and I really don't want to. I just fucking showered. I also don't care to have everyone passing by think I'm homeless.

"That's how we met, me and Keeley. She tried to give me that chair because she didn't like the idea of me being uncomfortable. I told her I'd keep it just for her in case she came to visit. You know how many people would have come back? You know how many people of all the millions would come down here, day after day, to check on me? Fucking one, and you got her."

I sigh wearily. "I take it Keeley mentioned we argued last night. Do you have a point?"

He squints. "No, she didn't mention it. But I can see she's stressed, and I'm just wondering...why you? What did she see in you that she didn't see in anyone else? Because I thought when she finally chose someone, she'd be a lot happier than she is."

I rub the back of my neck. "I'm not sure how much she's told you about our wedding."

He laughs. "Oh, yeah, I know the whole thing. But do you think you're the first guy who's suggested running off to Vegas to her? No way. But you're the first one she said 'yes' to."

"It might just be a question of sobriety, or lack thereof."

"Doubtful. She had plenty of non-sober nights out before then too. She saw something different in you—that's why she agreed. I guess what I'm saying is...bro, *find* that thing. It's like the whole world is connected. Can you see that? Can you see the lace patterns in the air? Can you see all those rainbows?"

"Uh...I'm not sure about the rainbows."

"That might be the mushrooms talking. I ate a few grams

just before you came downstairs. But anyway, there's a connection between you and you've got to find it."

I still. "Just out of curiosity, it wasn't my wife who gave you the *drugs,* was it?"

He laughs. "Course not. I ordered 'em."

He pulls an iPhone out of his pocket. It's newer than mine. "Your wife did give me this, though."

"She bought you a phone?"

"My last one got stolen. This is how I manage her investments."

Keeley, who has no interest in investing or saving whatsoever, asked him to manage investments for her because it would make him happy.

She loves people so wholeheartedly.

I wonder what it would be like to be among them.

21

KEELEY

That night when I get home, he has dinner waiting. And he's wearing shorts.

I don't remember seeing Graham's thighs before, but they are corded with muscle and dusted with dark hair. I can picture the way they'd flex as he kneeled above me, rolling on a condom. Maybe that was the problem...maybe I was too busy ogling his thighs to mention he was putting on each of those condoms in some ridiculous way. To say, *"you've got to leave some room at the tip"* or *"you clearly need a bigger condom"* because based on how sore I was, I assume he should be ordering his from a specialty site.

"Grilled chicken," he says. "Does that work for you?"

I nod. "I'm so hungry right now I'd eat it even if it didn't work. And I ate lunch today too. I don't know why, but I'm famished."

"You're getting bigger. It stands to reason you'd need more calories."

"Please never use the phrase 'getting bigger' again," I say sternly.

He gets two plates from the cupboard. "Keeley, you're supposed to pack on weight. It's not a bad thing."

My eyes narrow. "Don't use the phrase 'pack on weight' either."

"Apparently," he says, eyes twinkling, "our conversations are going to be very limited over the next few months."

I change into sweats and return to the table, where he's just placed dinner. Salad again, but there's avocado in it and he made baked potatoes too. I cut into my chicken, spearing it with a bit of avocado. "Thank you for doing this. I know I was a little ungrateful the last time."

"I was being overly punitive the last time. It's not like I'd have cooked that for myself."

"I *knew* no one could possibly like fish!" I cry victoriously, holding my fork in the air, and he laughs. "I promise not to give the leftovers to Mark."

"Leftovers make you gag, Keeley. *Of course* you're giving them to Mark."

I focus on my plate, suddenly bashful. "You've only been here two weeks and you already know me better than Shannon does."

"She's your...stepmother?"

I nod. "Since I was five. She doesn't like me. Never has."

He frowns. "Who couldn't like you?"

I search for the inevitable sarcasm in that statement but don't find it. He seems legitimately befuddled. "*You* don't like me."

"I don't approve of some of your habits." He flushes, suddenly unable to meet my eye. "That's different than not liking you."

I'd assume he was bullshitting me now, but that's the thing about Graham...I'm pretty sure he's physically incapable of bullshitting me, and thus his repeated references to the fact that I'm growing bigger when he should be saying, *"you look exactly the same to me."*

Which means Graham actually thinks I'm likable. It makes me feel weirdly defenseless, hearing this. Vulnerable.

"What are we watching tonight?" I ask. "I think I should get to choose since you made me cry yesterday."

He laughs, deep and rumbly and unexpected. "You sure like to bring that up. Fine, what do you want to watch?"

Maybe I've got a shot with the sexy kidnapper movie this time, if I frame it better. "There's a movie about a guy who kidnaps this woman he's obsessed with and—"

"Veto. If I wanted to watch porn, I'd just watch porn."

My gaze flickers to his face. *Does* Graham watch porn? He seems like the guys I knew at Catholic school who truly believed every word Father Thomas said, the ones who always looked like they were gonna pass out before they went into confession Wednesday mornings.

Then again, he seemed perfectly okay with premarital sex, so he's probably okay with masturbation too. I picture one of those big hands sliding into his boxers, the way he'd swallow hard to stifle his groan. I squeeze my thighs together as I try to drive the image away.

"We'll alternate," I tell him. "My show tonight, because you made me cry, and yours tomorrow. Let's just rewatch *Bridgerton*, I guess."

"The word *rewatch* implies I saw it the first time."

I gasp in horror, my hand going straight to my chest. "How could you *not* have? What the hell were you doing during the pandemic?"

"Preserving brain cells?" he offers, and I kick him.

After dinner, I move to one end of the couch and he moves to the other, as far apart as we can possibly be, though he's sitting up politely while I'm stretched out. If I knew him better, or at all, I'd slide my toes under his thigh for warmth.

I cue up *Bridgerton*, which begins with a sex scene. It's awkward, under the circumstances. Does this remind him that he slept with me? Because it's reminding *me* I slept with him.

I'm relieved when we move on to Daphne, the main character, being presented to the queen.

"Why is her chest heaving like that?" Graham asks. "She barely walked twenty feet to get there."

"She's nervous. It's a big deal."

"I think Daphne needs to do more cardio."

I ignore him, but minutes later he's questioning the distribution of the free gossip rag, arguing that without ads, no one's turning a profit. I tell him he's taking the show too literally and slide my toes under his thigh.

He yelps. "Jesus Christ, your feet are like ice."

"Stop being such a baby. My toes are cold, your thigh is warm. It's a perfect symbiotic relationship."

"I'm not sure what *I* get out of having your dirty feet pressed to my skin."

I guess I really didn't have to warn him not to tell me my swollen feet were beautiful. *I could be a foot model and he wouldn't tell me my feet or any other part of me was beautiful.*

An image of him comes to mind, though, from one of those nights we were together. He was pushing my hair away from my face, about to kiss me, and looking at me like I was the moon and the stars. I think it might have been our wedding. *Huh.*

"And now they're talking about Daphne at full volume and she's sitting right beside them. How is she not hearing this? The duke should run. She needs serious cardio and is deaf in one ear."

I groan aloud. If he's this bad with *Bridgerton,* I can't imagine what he'd say about *365 Days.* "Stop shitting on it and let me enjoy the fantasy of being courted by the perfect man."

"So *he's* perfect? How is the duke different from me?"

I bark a laugh. There is an entire universe between Simon, the Duke of Hastings, and Graham Tate. "He's a *duke*."

"I'd actually figured that out on my own."

"He's—" *Cranky, commanding, intense, smug, fierce, handsome, amusing, intelligent.* All words someone other than me might use to describe Graham, too, dammit. "British."

His lips twitch. "Yes, there's not much I can do about that part."

"It's sort of a dealbreaker, unfortunately."

He laughs. To be honest, he has a pleasant laugh. I've dated men who make a noise that sounds like laughter but doesn't feel like it. When Graham laughs, it's like I've caught it in my own chest, some kind of minor virus that leaves me happy for the rest of the night.

If we weren't going to be forced to share a child, he's someone I might be friends with.

We're at the final scene: Daphne and the Duke's first dance, under the stars. Fireworks explode, the music swells...and Graham speaks.

"Those fireworks are going to destroy that lawn. Seriously. That grass is never coming back."

22

GRAHAM

I meet Keeley in the lobby of Julie's office. It's not her first sonogram, but it's the first I'll be present for, and I'm strangely nervous, though I'm not sure why.

"What do you want, anyway?" she asks as we wait. "A boy or a girl?"

"I don't care as long as it's healthy," I tell her, though that's not totally true. The real answer is that I want whatever won't set my mom off, and there's no way to know what that will be. The stuff that happened when Colin was a baby is always with us, somehow. "What about you?"

"I'd prefer a girl, but given my family curse, I guess I shouldn't. Good news for you, or bad news depending on how much involvement you hoped to have with this kid: the O'Keefe women die really young."

I swallow. She told me this before, though she doesn't remember it. *"If you hate me,"* she'd said, *"at least you won't be stuck with me for long."*

I thought it was a joke at the time, and she's still saying it like it's a joke, but I'm starting to wonder—it's a weird joke to make repeatedly.

"Just because your mom died young doesn't mean *you* will."

She laughs. "What if it's my mom, my aunt, my grandmother, her sister, and my great-grandmother? Does that change your thoughts on the odds?"

She's scrolling through something on her phone as if what she's just said doesn't matter. I reach for her arm to get her attention. "Did they all die of the same thing?"

She glances at me and away. "Everyone but my great-grandmother has died of cancer. *Everyone.* It's the bit your internal medicine doc will gloss over: that you might just be genetically fucked and then all your efforts to stay healthy will be for naught."

Her name is called and we rise to follow the nurse back to a room. "No offense, Keeley," I say, "but I'm not sure you can claim you're making a lot of effort."

"Exactly. Because I watched my mother making green juice every morning and only eating salad, and look where it got her."

I wonder how much of Keeley's attitude toward life—her live-for-the-moment, who-cares-about-a-savings-account brand of *joie de vivre*—is related to this curse she seems to believe she's under. And if that's true, has having a kid changed it?

We are taken to a different room than usual, and this time there's no undressing. Keeley simply reclines on a table and tugs her shirt up when Julie enters the room. Even the sight of her bare stomach is a wonder to me, with that unmistakable swell just beneath her skin.

Julie squirts a gel on Keeley's stomach and starts moving a wand back and forth. An image appears on the screen—at first, it's nothing discernible, just a mass of white and black, and then: a child. A child with long thin arms and legs, a nose—a single hand, fully formed.

Our child. It's absolutely amazing. I never wanted a kid. I never wanted the responsibility of a kid. But I have it. And inside me, already, something has shifted. Something matters a million times more than my fears, my plans, and I'm looking at it right now.

"I'm assuming you don't want to know the gender," Julie says, which is when I realize Keeley is very intentionally *not* looking at the screen.

"You don't want to know?" I ask. She's desperate for a girl, and I'd have thought she'd want to know ASAP so she could blow every penny she makes on baby designer dresses.

"I'm not sure," she says.

I *do* want to know. I want to plan. There's a part of me that thinks the answer will help get it through Keeley's head that this is happening, but there's clearly more going on here than meets the eye. If Keeley isn't ready for this, I'm not going to force the issue.

"Maybe they can write it down for us?" I suggest, looking at her. "And put it in an envelope?"

Keeley smiles up at me as if I've just done something heroic. It makes me wish I really had.

WE WALK to Whole Foods after the appointment because the overlap between healthy foods and foods Keeley is willing to eat is painfully small, and I'm running out of options.

She takes a seat on the patio while I go in to get our sandwiches. When I return, she's holding the envelope up to the sun.

"Cut it out." I snatch it away from her. "If you want to look, we'll look, but you're not going to do that and claim you discovered it by *accident* later on."

Keeley barely seems to have heard me. She's too busy tearing into her sandwich.

"Oh my God," she groans. "It's *so* good."

I flinch and adjust myself. My life would be infinitely easier if she wouldn't make everything sound so goddamn sexual. But maybe it's just that every moan and groan and inhalation triggers a specific, filthy memory of her making those sounds beneath me.

"What do you think of the name Maddox for a boy, by the way?" she asks.

"He sounds like a runaway who's turned to sex work to survive life on the streets."

"So that's a maybe, then," she says cheerfully. "I like Kalamity for a girl. Spelled with a 'k', though."

"At least we won't have to worry about paying for college."

She laughs, but then deflates only seconds later.

I follow her gaze to the girls walking past us in skimpy shorts and half-shirts. "Jesus Christ," I say quietly after they're gone. "I don't want a daughter."

Keeley sets the second half of her sandwich down on the brown paper wrapper.

"What's the matter?"

She glances back at them and her face grows longer. "Nothing."

"You'll lose the weight," I offer helplessly. "I know it's—"

Her mouth falls open. "Oh my God, are you saying I'm *bigger* than those girls?"

And that's when I know I've fucked up and there's really no way to salvage this. "Well, obviously. You're *supposed* to put on wei—"

"I'm not bigger than those girls!" she cries, though obviously she is. *I mean, she must realize*...but that's not relevant right now.

I set my own sandwich down. "Keeley...you're pregnant. It would be worrisome if you hadn't gained...gotten...I have no idea what to say here."

Her face is a storm cloud, eyes narrowed, mouth in a child's pout. "It's not about the weight, which is mostly in my rack and fucking *spectacular* at the moment."

She isn't wrong, but I'm not even going to touch that one. I scrub a hand over my face. "Then why are you upset?"

She stares at the uneaten second half of her sandwich, unable to meet my eyes. "I'm never going to go to Coachella again," she whispers. "I just realized I'm never going to Coachella again. And also, that I have to learn to cook, and I don't want to."

"You can still go to Coachella. I mean, God only knows why you'd want to, but—"

"It's not about Coachella, Graham! It's that I'm never going to be one of those girls again, and I feel like I barely got started being one of those girls."

It still sounds like it's about the weight to me because what else has changed? But I know not to say it aloud.

Now. I know it *now*.

"I don't understand. You will look exactly like those girls in a year. You'll be able to go to Coachella. What's the difference?"

She finally meets my eye. "When I meet Harry Styles and Machine Gun Kelly backstage and they're like, *'hey, let's go to Amsterdam'*, you know what I'll have to say? *'Sorry, Harry Styles. Sorry, Machine Gun Kelly. I have to go feed my baby.'*"

I am at a loss for words. Mostly because I can't imagine that she's serious, and I'm a little worried she is.

"Sorry, Harry Styles and Machine Gun Kelly, but I've got to get home and sew a Pilgrim costume," she continues. *"Sorry, Harry Styles and Machine Gun Kelly, but I have to chaperone a school field trip in the morning."*

"Just out of curiosity, how long would you call them by their full names? At what point do you just call them *Harry* and, uh, *Machine Gun*?"

Her mouth twitches, a reluctant smile at last. "I'm pretty

sure his birth name is not *Machine Gun*. And shut up. You see my point. I'm never going to be fun again."

There's a part of me that wants to say, *"this is what I've been trying to tell you, dammit. Parenthood is serious. It's time to stop fucking around."* But there's this weird, unexpectedly soft thing in my chest that keeps me from doing it.

Keeley has spent her whole life rebelling against the status quo, refusing to let anyone tell her how an adult has to behave, and she still wants to refuse. It's for the baby's sake that she's giving in. Maybe it feels like she's losing her whole identity in the process.

"You're still going to be fun," I say, pushing her chips toward her. "You'll be *too* fun. You'll be the mom who suggests our kid teepee someone's house and gets arrested for providing minors with alcohol. And I'll be the boring dad who has to come bail both of you out of jail."

"You'd only have to bail out me," she whispers with a guilty shrug. "They don't take you to jail for minor in possession. They just write you a ticket."

I laugh, that soft thing in my chest growing a little bit more, though I wish it wouldn't.

Because she has no idea how or why she married me—and she'd never have done it sober—but I've known, all along, exactly why I married her.

23

KEELEY

My father emails, reminding me about the invite Shannon sent last week. As if I want to go to this dumb party for Karl when all I got when I graduated from med school was an *e-card*.

But I suppose this is a golden opportunity to spring my new husband and future baby on them before one of those things disappears, as long as I can get my future ex-husband on board with the charade.

Graham works out every single day at ass o'clock before he joins his extremely loud East Coast Zoom meetings. On weekends he pampers himself with a sixteen-mile run, followed by weights or a few hours of surfing. Whatever he chose this morning, he seems to have returned from it.

His door is open so I walk in. The bathroom door is cracked and I can hear water running—therefore, there's at least a fifty percent chance he's not doing anything embarrassing. I'll take those odds.

I knock. "Are you clothed?"

"What?" he shouts.

Sounds like a *"yes"* to me. I push the door open to find him in nothing but a towel. He's got the razor angled, right along the top of his jaw. The wonderful thing about fit men is that every action, small to large, is a symphony of musculature. He could be lifting a beer to his lips or hunting down Bin Laden with the rest of his SEAL team and it would mostly look the same, the muscles of his back bunched delightfully—rhomboid minor, rhomboid major, latissimus dorsi.

His eyes go wide. "What the fuck, Keeley?"

I shrug. "I *asked* if you were clothed."

"And I didn't answer because, obviously, I didn't hear you."

"It's nothing I haven't seen before."

His gaze meets mine in the mirror. It's another of those little moments of *knowing*. When all the bullshit about *why-are-you-so-boring* and *why-is-all-the-TV-you-watch-garbage* is swept away, and there's just...us:

An intensely handsome man and the woman he was once attracted to.

An intensely handsome man who once had his hands everywhere, who was once inside me and—if my stomach is any indication—sort of enjoyed being there.

"I wanted to know what you're doing this weekend," I tell him, somewhat breathlessly.

"And this casual conversation about my weekend plans couldn't take place until I was dressed?"

"I had no idea you were so prudish," I reply. "I mean, I guess if I'd ever thought about it, I'd have known, but still."

He goes back to shaving. "I think you're, quite intentionally, missing the point."

I groan. "Do you want me to take off my shirt too?" I demand, and it's not a mock threat. If he says, *"yes"* I'll totally do it. "Will that level the playing field?"

He flinches, cursing under his breath. I assume it's the idea of seeing me naked and disgustingly growing a human inside me until I spy the small dot of blood blooming on his cheek. "Oh." I reach for toilet paper just as he turns to do the same. "You cut yourself."

He's frowning as if *I* was the one wielding the razor. I ignore him and press toilet paper to the cut, aware only once it's in place that I'm pressed up against him, his bare arm against my breasts, his warm skin just beside my nose, smelling deliciously soapy and clean and male. The last time I was this close to a nearly naked man was...January. *Him.*

"Keeley," he grunts, "do you think we could hold this conversation once I'm done in here?"

I glance at our reflection in the mirror. His eyes are closed as if he's in pain. Apparently, I've pushed him too far.

"Fine, whatever," I say, weirdly stung by his dismissal as I head for the door. "I just need you to come to dinner at my family's house this weekend and pretend we're in love, okay? Great, thanks, bye."

"Wait. *What?*" he yells, but I'm already walking away.

I'm defrosting a bagel for Mark when he emerges, clean shaven, and braces himself against the counter. "So we're really doing this, then? Your father is going to hate me."

My laugh is a sad bubble of misery and self-loathing as I push the bagel into the toaster. "Have no fear. He'll find a way to blame me for all of it. Well, actually, Shannon will blame me, and he'll nod as if he was thinking it too."

As much as I want them to meet Graham and think *wow, Keeley finally did something right*, when he leaves, they'll just go back to saying, *"Keeley strikes again."* There's no way to win with them.

The toaster dings and I reach for the bagel, wincing as I burn the top of my fingers. I vaguely wonder what the hell I'm going to feed a kid when I can barely manage to use a toaster without injury.

"Have things always been this bad between you and Shannon?" Graham asks.

I shrug. "Yeah, but it makes sense. I'm so much like my mom, and she hates—" I stutter over the incorrect tense, "*hated* my mom."

He slides me the cream cheese. "In what ways are you like your mom?"

I smile. "I look a lot like her. I mean, practically identical. And I guess we're similarly...flighty."

I sort of hope Graham doesn't ask for details because they make her sound a little reckless, even by my standards. I'm sure I only know the tip of the iceberg and yet I know more than a kid should: the way she dropped out of college one week into her freshman year to tour the world with some guy in a band, and left him for a guy in a more famous band, and then returned to college, where she promptly got knocked up by an English professor—my father—who was engaged to someone else at the time.

"My mom was awesome, though," I argue as if I've spoken all this aloud. "She just really believed she was destined for greatness. She thought we both were. She spent every penny she had trying to get me voice lessons so I could audition for *The Mickey Mouse Club*."

His mouth curves, almost as if he can remember her too. "I take it that wasn't successful?"

I shake my head. "No amount of money was going to fix a voice as bad as mine."

I wish he could have met her, though. He'd understand it then. My mother was all sparkle and light. She had the biggest ideas and the biggest dreams and very little follow-through, but it was fun to live in her world. I grab Mark's bagel. "Okay, so we're all set for next Saturday?"

He nods, and then his tongue slides over his lower lip. "Do you still have your ring?" he asks quietly.

I'm a little embarrassed by the truth. "Yeah, I..." I'm not sure what I was going to say, how I was going to excuse it. I'm not sure why I didn't just leave it in the hotel room when I woke.

"I still have mine too," he says.

Neither of us can meet the other's eye.

24

KEELEY

On Saturday night, we put on our rings and take the elevator downstairs to the garage. I come to a complete stop when I realize he's driving a Volvo SUV.

"If you showed up for a date in this car," I tell him, "you'd never get a second one."

"Given how far you apparently go on the first date, I wouldn't *need* a second one."

I laugh. I like that I can give him shit and he always gives it back.

He holds the door for me and carefully shuts it. Being raised by a single mom clearly had its drawbacks, in his case, but he certainly is good about all the dumb little rules.

"It's just a rental since there's no point in owning a car in New York," he says when he climbs in. "It was the only SUV available that was rated high for safety."

"You just made it so much hotter, what with all the concern about your safety."

"It wasn't about *my* safety," he mutters. "It was about yours."

By which he really means the *baby's*, but it's still kind of sweet.

"Okay," I say after I've plugged in the address for my dad's new home, which I've never even seen, "let's get our story straight. How did we meet? I'm thinking we tell them you saw me working in the hospital when I was a resident and became obsessed with me. You followed me all over the country until I gave in—"

"Or we could just tell them the far more likely *truth*, which is that we met through the union of your best friend and my brother."

I sigh. "That's so *normal*."

"Keeley, tonight is going to be hard enough without asking me to keep up with some ridiculous story you've concocted. Besides, I'm too cheap to follow anyone around the country. You know that."

I laugh. This is true. I could be his soulmate and he probably wouldn't even shell out for an Uber from Santa Monica to midtown.

"Fine. What did you fall in love with first?"

He rolls his eyes. "How careful you are financially."

This is going to go disastrously. Graham can't even be bothered to assure me I don't look *big*. There's no way he's going to convince Shannon he's in this situation by choice.

"What do they do for a living?" he asks. "Ostensibly, that's the kind of thing I'd already know."

"They're retired now, but they were both English professors. That's how they met. Oh, and he dumped Shannon for my mom, so that's touchy too."

"Wait a minute," he says with an incredulous laugh. "Did you seriously just tell me that your father and your stepmother were *English* professors?"

"Is that really so hard to believe? It's not like I didn't finish high school. I *am* a doctor."

"The last thing I saw you reading was '*The Cast of Dawson's Creek: Where are they Now?*' So, yes, I did not expect you to be the child of an English professor."

"Well, you'd have gotten a little burned out on reading, too, if every time you picked up a book as a kid you had someone making fun of you for it."

I'd almost forgotten there was a time when I enjoyed reading, back before there were too many instances of Shannon making fun of me. "*Anne of Green Gables*?" she'd say, looking at her daughter or my dad with that gleam of amusement in her eye. "By the time I was your age, I was reading Milton."

Eventually I just gave up. I guess I'd be a little closer to the person Graham thinks I'm supposed to be if I hadn't.

"They're older, by the way," I warn as we pull up to the house.

He gives a low laugh. "Were you worried I'd *announce* that they both look old?"

"Well, I doubt anyone's called you tactful. Barely a day's gone by that you haven't mentioned my weight."

"That's not true," he argues as I climb from the car. "I was trying to console you, and you look fine."

"Right. *You look fine* is exactly the kind of compliment women love to hear. Anyway, since my dad was so much older than my mom, I guess I always felt like I needed to warn visitors."

"How much older?" he asks as we approach the house.

"Twenty-seven years."

He raises a brow at that but says nothing since we're nearly to the door. People—at least the people in this house—always want to cast my mother as this femme fatale. No one ever suggests that maybe it was fucked up for a forty-seven-year-old man to be sleeping with his twenty-year-old student. Maybe it's simply what Shannon has to tell herself, since she's the woman he left behind.

The door opens before I've even rung the bell. I haven't seen my father since the holidays, right before Ben and Gemma's party. He's more stooped and gray than he was the last time, and it makes me sad. As much as I hate the way he hurt my mother, I recognize that somewhere under it all...he actually cared about us both. That, much like Graham, he was trying to do the right thing. He probably got tired of feeling like the bad guy all the time.

I ignore Shannon, grumbling as she approaches, and turn to my father.

"Dad," I say as we step inside, "this is Graham. My husband."

"Husband," he repeats, saying it as if the word is new to him —some crazy made-up thing all the kids are saying and he's not sure he understands.

"*What?*" barks Shannon. "You got *married*?!" The note in her voice is less surprise than it is accusation, and Graham steps closer to me, wrapping his arm around my waist as if he thinks I'm at physical risk.

"Yes," I reply, my gaze flicking toward her before it returns to my father. "We got married last January, actually, but with my training and his job we—"

"*January?!* You've never even mentioned him!" Shannon snaps.

Graham raises a brow at her and the arm around me tightens as he extends his free hand to my father. "Graham Tate," he says, shaking my dad's hand. "It's a pleasure to meet you at last."

I stare at him in wonder. He's so smooth and suave and masculine right now when I expected nothing but awkward silences and uncertainty.

Graham Tate is apparently good at hiding what he feels.

"Jim Connolly," my father says. "I...this is a surprise, obviously."

"I believe you know my sister-in-law, Gemma," Graham continues.

"I don't understand," Shannon snaps. "It's June. How could you have failed to tell us you were married for *five* months?"

I open my mouth to reply but Graham speaks first, squeezing my hip. "Perhaps we could sit? Keeley's been on her feet all day." There's a hint of a reprimand in his voice directed at Shannon. *Do you always make your guests stand in the foyer while you hurl accusations?* that voice asks, and something warm and sweet blossoms in my chest. As long as I'm carrying his child, Graham Tate isn't going to let anyone hurt me.

Sybil, Shannon's daughter from her first marriage, and Sybil's husband, Karl, are seated at the table when we enter the kitchen. "She's married," Shannon says to her daughter. There's a whole world of shade in that flat pronouncement to Sybil, a *can-you-believe-what-she's-done?* With a side helping of *I told you she was crazy.* It's been par for the course with Shannon and Sybil my entire life, toward me and my mother alike—the news that my mother had auditioned for a part could spawn an entire evening's worth of shared glances and snickering at the dinner table, even when I was small. Anytime my mom wanted *me* to audition...the mockery was entirely open. "*I wouldn't hold my breath there, Jennifer Aniston,*" she'd say.

"So, uh, how did you two meet?" my father asks as we take our seats.

My eyes meet Graham's. I still think my obsessed hospital stalker story would sell this better.

"We planned the party for Ben and Gemma together last fall," I reply.

"I had to go back to New York and Keeley was getting ready to leave for DC," Graham continues, "and we didn't want to wait so we took off for Vegas as soon as the festivities were over."

"You got married in *Vegas*?" Shannon says from the stove,

not trying to hide her disdain. In even my earliest memories, she was making me feel like I'd done something wrong and this time, I actually have. I can't wait until she learns I'm pregnant.

Graham tenses at her tone, and then, beneath the table, his hand squeezes mine. A shiver runs through me—he has nice hands. Huge hands, to go with the huge rest of him. I think, once again, that it's a shame I can't remember just how huge the rest of him actually is.

"Not ideal," agrees Graham. "I wish I could have given Keeley the wedding she'd been planning, but it was still very special."

Wow. I don't think Graham can lie to me, but he sure can lie on my behalf. I give his hand a quick squeeze to say *thanks*.

"Well, that's certainly a *Melinda* way to go about things," Shannon says.

My mother has been dead for fourteen years, but Shannon still can't miss an opportunity to trash her.

The topic turns to Karl and his law degree, to Sybil and her crusade to get a speed bump placed in front of her house. For ten minutes straight, she and Shannon discuss how unfair it is that her efforts haven't worked and how the people cutting through her neighborhood are going to kill someone.

When the subject of speed bumps is finally exhausted, my father turns to me. "So how was your thing at NIH?" he asks.

"I can't imagine that's anything we want to hear about right before we *eat*," says Shannon.

Graham's head turns toward her, his jaw locked tight. It's embarrassing to have a witness to all this, but I'm used to it, so I ignore her.

"It went really well—" I begin.

"Let's go into the dining room," Shannon cuts in. "Dinner's ready."

My father winces but follows her to the formal dining room, where a glass of wine sits at each place. People claim that when you're pregnant, the things you're not supposed to have don't appeal to you, but I've never wanted a drink more in my life.

"So, congratulations, Karl, on beginning law school," Shannon says, raising her glass once we're all seated. "And I suppose we need to congratulate Keeley and Graham, for as long as it lasts, anyway."

Graham stiffens, then lowers his wine. "Excuse me?"

"You do know what we call her, right?" Shannon asks, and something sinks in my stomach. *Here we go.*

"Shannon—" my father begins quietly.

"The *baby bolter*," Shannon continues. "It's from this Nancy Mitford novel...the Bolter is this woman who bolts from one man to the next, just like Keeley's mother did. And we call Keeley the *baby bolter* because she never sticks with anything or anyone for long either."

I'm used to this nickname. I barely notice anymore, but I hate that Graham is hearing about it. I hate that it's probably reinforcing every negative thing he's ever thought about me himself.

"She's stuck with medicine for eight years now," Graham says. His voice is sharp—a warning.

"She stuck with *school*," Shannon corrects, turning to me. "You've only been at that job for a few months, right? If the boredom hasn't set in yet, it will."

"Shannon," my father begs quietly, but goes no further in my defense. He couldn't stop her anyway, and she'd manage to find fault no matter what I did.

If I'd chosen to leave med school, I'd have been a quitter, but I stayed and yet I'm still a quitter. I could remain with Beverly Hills Skin for a decade, and when I finally moved on, Shannon would say, *"I knew that wouldn't last."* But she's also... right. I *don't* like my job and would leave if I could and even if I could list a thousand reasons why, I also know how little that means. Every time my mom dumped someone, every time she decided a job just wasn't working for her anymore, she had a whole list of reasons. Maybe mine are no more valid than hers.

I stare at my plate, feeling leaden, and quietly pick up my fork, preparing to ignore what's been said and just get through the night.

But Graham's hand lands on top of mine, telling me not to. I look up to find his shocked gaze on me, and I worry he's just seeing me through Shannon's eyes—all my gross irresponsibility, my genetic ineptitude.

"I'm not putting up with this," he says quietly. "And neither are you." He rises, tugging my hand to join him. "My wife, a *doctor*, has been in the same field for eight years. And, as I believe I mentioned, she's my *wife*, so in the future, I'd suggest you keep the nicknames and comments to yourself. Which you might want to do anyway, Shannon, because they make you look petty...and jealous."

He pulls me out of the room, his fingers wound tight in mine, and I allow myself to be led, stumbling and shocked until he's got me bundled inside the Volvo.

I can't believe we just left when dinner had barely begun. Even more than that, I can't believe he did it to defend me.

"I'm sorry," he says, once we're both inside the car. "But she shouldn't be allowed to treat you like that, and you shouldn't be allowing it, either. I mean, what the hell, Keeley? If I casually suggest you try eating vegetables, I'm waiting for a knife to be thrown, but you let Shannon say whatever she wants."

"You know why I'm a doctor?" I ask him with a sad laugh. "Because on her deathbed, my mom said she wished she'd gone to medical school. And when I mentioned it later, Shannon said, *'as if your mother could have stuck with anything that long'*. How fucked up is that? I chose my career just to prove something to a woman I don't even like, on behalf of a woman who's dead, and it didn't make a dent anyway."

He reaches over the console to squeeze my hand. "Keeley,

people do all kinds of things for the wrong reasons. You think you're the only person who got a degree to prove something to a parent? It doesn't take away from what you've accomplished, and you can't *allow* her to take away from it. No matter whether you stay at that practice or not, you've achieved something many people aspire to and very few attain."

A slow smile tugs at the corners of my mouth. "You called me your wife in there."

"Well, technically you are." Two spots of color grace his cheekbones.

I decide to let it go. I decide not to tell him what I was thinking as it all went down: that he said it like someone who meant it. Like someone who cared. And for a moment I almost thought he did.

25

GRAHAM

The way Shannon treated her infuriates me. And the way Keeley allowed it, when God knows she's more than capable of standing up for herself under normal circumstances, is like a splinter in the center of my chest. I fucking hate that a piece of her seems to think Shannon's right.

It explained a lot, though, about why she's so determined to keep everyone's expectations of her low.

I've heard her on the phone when she's on call—she's clearly good at her job. But then she hangs up and tries to convince me that, *"chocolate sandwich cremes are healthy"* because *sandwich* is in the title, or she asks me how soon we can highlight the baby's hair if it's dark like mine. As if she's scared even the smallest proof of her competence will end up being used against her.

I bet it was used against her a lot growing up with Shannon, and it became easier just to let everyone think the worst of her all the time. No one can accuse you of failing if you weren't trying in the first place. But I need her to start trying, before our kid is born.

"I was thinking tonight we could cook together," I tell her

when she gets home. She's arrived later than planned, undoubtedly because she refuses to tell her bosses she's pregnant.

She wearily blows a lock of hair out of her face. "Can't we just...order in together?"

"Keeley, you told me last week you needed to learn to cook. When this kid is old enough to eat real food, you can't just order in burgers every night."

"I wouldn't get burgers *every* night." Her shoulders sag as she gives in. "Fine, just let me change."

She emerges a few minutes later in leggings and the Tulane sweatshirt. Why does it piss me off to see her in another man's clothes? It's not like we're together, and honestly, I haven't cared less about that kind of thing in the past. Anna was constantly bringing up her ex, hoping to make me jealous, and I almost felt guilty that it had no effect.

"Maybe it's time to just get some new clothes," I offer, a little testier than I intended.

"I'm turning over a new leaf." She holds her chin up. "No more spending."

There's a world of difference between blowing eight hundred dollars on a dress she never even wore and buying some maternity clothes, but this isn't the time to bicker. I glance at the sweatshirt again. *I'll buy her some fucking maternity clothes myself.*

She steps beside me, her nose wrinkling at the raw chicken on the plate in front of her.

"You're just going to dredge it through the egg and then through the breadcrumbs." I grab a chicken breast to demonstrate. "Nothing could be easier."

"Ordering in is easier," she mumbles, but she reaches back to tighten her ponytail before washing her hands, and a memory hits me out of nowhere: It was last winter, after the party, and her hair was falling out of its careful updo for a very different reason, her cheeks flushed, her eyes bright. "*When you kiss me,*" she said, "*I forget how to think.*" I already knew we were more than some drunk hook-up, but that was the moment I hoped she might be figuring it out too.

She grudgingly dredges the chicken in egg, but she's making a disaster of it, so I take over and have her watch the pieces as I move them to the frying pan.

"Have you given any more thought to the name Kalamity?" she asks.

I glance at her. "I assure you, I never gave it any thought in the first place. What about Esther?"

"*Esther*? Isn't that name, like, from the Bible?"

I take the spatula and nudge her out of the way since she's letting the chicken burn. She takes a seat at the counter and watches me work.

"Half the names you know are from the Bible."

"*My* Bible must have been missing the story of Jesus's friends, Keeley and Graham. Did they, like, go on a road trip?"

"I'm not sure road trips feature heavily in the Bible."

"They absolutely do. They just don't sound like fun. Although the one where Jesus walked on water...you can't tell me drugs weren't involved there. I did shrooms at Burning Man and let me tell you...I *saw* a lot of things."

When the chicken's done, we move to the table. Keeley takes her first bite and moans, because she's incapable of eating a meal she enjoys without forcing me to adjust myself.

"When this ends," she says, "I'm really going to miss the way we pretended you were teaching me to cook while I made you do all the work."

My smile fades. "About that...how *does* this end?" I really hate the idea of letting Shannon think she was right about anything. "What do we say to explain when we're not together anymore?"

"Oh, you'll have to dump me. I need to remain blameless.

But don't worry, they'll all still secretly blame me." She tilts her head, struck by a new thought. "Unless I tell them you hit me."

I stare at her in shock. "Keeley, *no*. You're not telling them I hit you."

She sighs. "Then you come up with a plan."

I swallow. "We could just...stay married. If that's something you wanted."

Her fork falls to her plate with a crash. "If *what* is something I wanted? My father's approval?"

I flinch. "No. Marriage. Look, I'd have brought it up before, but you seemed overwhelmingly hostile to...well...every aspect of this, so the timing wasn't right. But if that's something you want—"

Her jaw hangs open. "No. God. *No*."

I roll my eyes. "Well, you managed to handle that with all the grace and diplomacy I've come to expect."

She touches my hand. "It was...nice of you. But it's not 1850. Being a single mother is totally normal and, obviously, I'd make a horrible wife."

"You're aware the qualities that make a good wife are probably the same qualities that make a good mother, right?"

"Like what?"

I shrug. "Cooking, cleaning, laundry..."

"Fuck you. I don't even do those things for myself, so I'm sure as hell not doing them for a *man*. None of that is a wife's *job*."

"So, what do you think a wife's job *is*?"

"Pretend to listen to your boring stories about actuarial tables," she begins.

"I don't use actuarial tables. I'm not sure how many times I have to tell you that." I'm pretty sure she knows it by now and is just saying this to mess with me. At least I hope so.

"Fine, listen to your boring stories about whatever it is you actually do, tiptoe around you all afternoon after your football team loses a big game, provide frequent blow jobs and anniversary anal."

"*Anniversary anal?*"

"You know, like once a year. It's a thing."

"I wasn't aware that was a thing." I'm fighting a grin and failing.

"You can't do it too often or that area might not go back in place," she argues. "So, you know, a few times a year. Anniversary, special occasions."

"I wasn't objecting to the *infrequency* of the anal sex. I was just surprised to hear it offered up so openly," I say, finally giving in to the urge to smile. "But I'm thinking marriage to you might not be so terrible after all. Perhaps I was hasty."

She throws a napkin at me and I laugh.

"Anniversary anal," I say, taking our plates to the sink. "Where the fuck do you get this stuff?"

KEELEY

JUNE

We fall into something of a routine, and I guess I don't hate it. Graham usually cooks, forcing me to help in small ways that won't lead to the actual destruction of our meal. He insists we eat dinner at the table instead of watching TV. "Meals are when you get your kid to talk about his day," Graham says, like he's suddenly *The Today Show*'s parenting expert, but he might have a point. My mom had fond memories of eating on a TV tray with her dad and her sister each night, and so we did it, too, but that doesn't necessarily mean it was ideal.

After dinner, we watch TV together and sometimes we read. When I tell him I want Pinkberry or Froot Loops, he's willing to drive me. And yes, there are nights when I really wish I could just eat Hot Tamales and watch *The Bachelor*, but there's something about this too. I'll miss it when it's gone.

"What are you reading?" he asks. We are on the couch, my toes tucked beneath his thigh.

I glance at my phone. "*'Celebrity Kids who Could Stand to Lose Some Weight'*."

He laughs. "You're making that up."

"You clearly have no idea just how lowbrow my taste is."

He grins. "I got a pretty good idea when you pushed for a movie about a 'sexy kidnapper.'"

I kick him. "Hey, do you want to check out that class Julie suggested on Saturday?"

I'm now twenty-five-weeks along. That we are at the point where we would take parenting classes makes things feel very real to me. I'm going to be responsible for a real, live baby in a very short period of time, and he won't be here for it.

He scratches the back of his neck. "Uh, this weekend is a little busy. My great aunt is coming in from Boston."

There's something cagey in his manner that alarms me. "She's not, like, staying with us, is she?"

He shakes his head. "No, she gets in Friday morning. I figured I'd take her to the Getty and—"

I throw a hand to my face dramatically, as if I'm Scarlett O'Hara in a swoon. "The *Getty*? God. Tell me you weren't assuming I'd come along for this."

He rolls his eyes. "How could I not when you're such a good sport about everything? And what the hell is wrong with the Getty?"

I push myself upright. "No one *really* likes museums or art galleries or churches, Graham. It's just an excuse to get dinner and drinks. You know, '*hey, let's meet at the Getty, and grab a drink afterward.*'"

"I'm pretty sure there are people who actually enjoy museums and galleries."

"Boring people," I reply, grinning at him. "Okay, maybe this all lines up."

His gaze rests on me in a way that looks an awful lot like *interest*, though I can't imagine why. "I can't wait to hear what you think I should do with my *ninety-year-old great-aunt* instead of the Getty, then."

"Does she drink? I'd start there and see where the wind takes you."

He sets his phone down and turns toward me. "So my great aunt is flying across the country, and your suggestion is that I take her to a bar. For the *day*."

I hitch a shoulder. "Well, she's Irish and from Boston. I doubt it'll be the first time she's spent a day in a bar."

His mouth moves as if he wants to laugh. "*That's* an offensive stereotype."

"If I'm wrong it's only because she was too busy spitting out one baby after the next to get a day in a bar to herself."

He shakes his head. "Keeley...Jesus. That's *another* offensive stereotype."

"A, I can say these things because I'm Irish. And B, how many kids did she have?"

"I don't see how that's relevant."

I laugh. "More than six, then?"

He sighs and runs a hand through his hair. "Eight. It's still a stereotype. But anyway...it does involve you a little. She's flying out for a party at my mom's house."

"What does that—"

"The party is so everyone can meet you."

My jaw falls open. "*Me?*" I repeat, suddenly nervous. Because Graham's family is huge. Three brothers, two stepsisters, assorted spouses, and significant others. Including my best friend, who knows exactly how much of this is fake. "Graham, what the *hell*, dude? When were you going to tell me?"

"I just found out." He wraps a hand around my foot, and I wonder if he's planning to hold it hostage until I agree. "Right before you got home. Look, I know it's a lot, and believe me, I hate lying to my mom about all this but...it's what you wanted."

I feel the briefest sting of guilt. It *is* what I wanted, simply because of the grief I'd get from Shannon and the very strong possibility she and Graham's mom will meet at some point in the future. Maybe it wasn't fair of me to ask.

"Fine," I say with a sigh, "but only if I can wear the Tulane sweatshirt."

He glares at me. "One of these days that sweatshirt is going to fucking disappear."

The funny thing is he sounds jealous. As if he cares about me, regardless of whether or not I'm having his child. He squeezes my foot, now pressed to one of his very muscular thighs, and I wonder what it would be like if that was actually the case.

"THEY AREN'T GOING to demand we kiss, right?" I ask on Saturday night, preparing for the worst.

He cuts a glance at me from the driver's seat. "What kind of people would demand we *kiss*?"

"It happens in movies all the time. You can't be in a fake relationship without winding up on a kiss cam or having to kiss because someone's family has demanded it."

"That has literally never happened in a single movie I've watched, nor in a book I've read."

"If that economics book you're reading had a fake relationship trope in it, you'd have finished it weeks ago."

We pull onto the idyllic streets of Newport, which I'm familiar with thanks to abundant reality TV programming, and then arrive at his mother's house.

I've seen it before in photos, but never from the street in all its glory: a massive two story with a Spanish tile roof, a wood door, and a long driveway that is already full of cars. It's far more impressive in person than it was in photos.

"Your mom should be on *Real Housewives*. This is incredible. I'd never have thought you came from this."

His lips press tight. "I didn't come from this. My mom and Walter moved here a few years ago, after his company took off."

I'd forgotten they had some lean years after Graham's father died. Of course they didn't live in a mansion.

"My mom is...sensitive about a few things," he continues. "From when we were kids. We try to avoid talking about childhood stuff as much as possible around her."

There's something in his face that warns me not to ask what she's sensitive about. That same something in his face *whenever* he discusses his mom.

"You know, if we'd just lived a little closer to Newport, your mom might have married my dad instead. We'd have been stepsiblings."

"I think we dodged a bullet, then," he says as he opens my door.

"I'd have been a very good little sister," I argue.

He lifts me from my seat as if I'm as light as a feather, his gaze falling to my face, to my lips, then away. "I wasn't trying to say you wouldn't have been. Come on. Let's get this over with. Pretend you're in labor if this thing isn't over within two hours."

We walk through the wooden door and discover absolute chaos, the kind I longed for as a kid. A football arcs through the air, followed by a woman shouting, *"no football in the house!"* Two of his brothers wrestle over the ball, and his mom gingerly steps past them before throwing her arms around me as if I'm a long-lost friend.

"Keeley, it's so good to see you again!" she cries.

I worry for the first time about whatever conversations she and I might have had the weekend I drunk-married her son.

I hope none of them were about Six Bailey.

Graham is dragged off by one of his younger brothers, while Jeannie Tate leads me through the house, its walls lined with photos of her boys and Walter's daughters. I was hoping to spy baby photos, to get a hint of what our child might look like, but there are none. Instead, I spy Graham as an awkward teen warily staring down the photographer in a family photo, and a more recent picture where he's shaking hands with someone and looking devastatingly handsome. The frame is different than the others and appears to be hand-painted. "I love that," I tell his mom, touching it.

"Oh, right, I should take it down." She blinks, stumbling over her words. Her discomfort is so obvious that it's painful, and I can't imagine why. It's not like I was going to ask her to *give* it to me. "I just got that at Christmas. Err, as a gift, but, um, anyway, let's go out back while Walter finishes grilling."

I'm led out to the spacious terrace, overlooking a large pool. Walter, Graham's stepfather, waves from the grill, and I'm pushed into a comfy chair and surrounded by his stepsisters, Gracie and Noah, and his great-aunt and his mom.

"I can't believe Graham's going to be a father," says Gracie. "Are you going to find out what you're having?"

"We haven't decided. We had it written down for us and put in an envelope."

"How can you stand the suspense?" Noah squeals. "I'd have torn that thing open before I was out of the office."

"Have you thought of a theme for the room?" his mother asks.

"No..." I glance across the lawn to Graham, feeling the first twinges of panic. We should, I guess. We probably need to look at furniture.

"What are you going to do about work?" Gracie asks.

"I—"

"You need to get the room ready, soon," says his great-aunt. "I knew a girl whose baby came almost three months early, and cribs were all backordered. That poor child slept in a Pack 'n Play for two months after being released from the hospital on a feeding tube."

I cough. "Three months early?"

"It was a mess." She leans forward to pat my knee. "Best to be prepared."

"So you haven't bought a crib or a car seat yet?" Jeannie asks. "We should check the safety ratings, especially for the crib. If the slats are too far apart, the baby's head can get stuck."

My chest starts to tighten, and I glance across the lawn at Graham, who's now watching me and frowning. There's so much to do, and when the hell am I going to have the time?

Jeannie claps her hands together, holding them to her chest. "I want to buy your furniture. I'll come to LA and we'll go shop. Though if you're thinking about getting a bigger place, we should wait until you move. You don't want to have to disassemble the crib—they never go back together right, and God forbid it collapses with the baby inside."

Collapses? What the fuck?

I swallow. "We haven't discussed moving."

"They can't move *now*," says Gracie. "Not when they've only got a few months to go. The move alone could send her into labor."

Jesus, they're discussing this like it's imminent, and—oh my God—*is it*? My inhale is shaky. Three months ago, I was taking a pregnancy test and it still feels like yesterday. Three months from now—less than that, actually—I'll be a mother. There will be a helpless human depending on *me*, a person who once let her car run out of gas because she was looking at the wrong gauge. A person who existed for an entire week of residency on grape soda and Swedish Fish.

"Up," says Graham.

I blink at him and then stand.

He takes my seat and pulls me into his lap in one swift move, as if it's something we do all the time. And I immediately feel...better. No matter what lies ahead of us, he'll make sure it's okay.

"You're interrupting our girl talk, Graham," says Noah.

"I got the very strong feeling that your 'girl talk' meant harassing the shit out of my wife."

My wife. I don't know why I get this tiny, sweet thrill when he says that.

"We just wanted to know about a theme for the baby's room. You're going to find out the gender, right?" his mom asks. "Keeley said you hadn't, but it'll make decorating so much easier, and if we throw a shower—"

"Mom, stop," he commands, pulling me closer, his hand spread over my hip. "No more questions."

My body settles, the tightness in my chest easing. I smile at him, and he gives me the barest beginnings of a smile in return, one I mostly see in his eyes.

"Okay, but have you thought about names?" his mother persists.

My smile grows. This morning I suggested Khal Drogo for a boy, and he told me our son would have face tattoos and be serving time before he could drink.

"We haven't figured it out yet," I tell them. "But *Graham* likes *Esther* for a girl."

Their noses wrinkle. "Graham," says Gracie, "*no.*"

He laughs against my ear. "Well played, but that doesn't mean we're naming her Kalamity with a K, either."

The crowd disperses when dinner's nearly ready, which is when Ben and Gemma arrive, full of apologies. Their new puppy, Lola, apparently had a cut on her paw and needed to go to the vet. Ben drags Graham off to the grill, and Gemma and I are told to relax while everyone hustles to get dinner out.

I ask her about the puppy while glancing across the lawn at Graham. He grins at me, and when he makes a show of looking at his watch, I laugh.

"Well, *that's* interesting," says Gemma.

"It's not interesting," I reply. "It's horrific. If we leave

Graham in charge of the burgers, they'll be full of healthy shit, and I bet he won't even put cheese on mine."

"You know that's not what I'm referring to. You guys *like* each other now."

"We *get along*. That doesn't mean we *like* each other."

She regards me, her margarita glass against her lips. "Would it be so terrible if you decided you *did* like each other?"

"It's just a bad idea. That's what leads to people throwing new socks in the fire."

She raises a brow. "That's...I don't even know what you mean by that."

"I mean that if we did anything, it would end and then we'd have to divide up custody, with one of us pissed off and making it all fucking terrible, and we both know it'll be me who's left and Graham who's pissed."

She squeezes my hand. "Some love stories have a happy ending, you know."

Yeah, but I already know mine won't. That's sort of the problem. No love story is assured a happy ending, but any story involving me has way fewer guarantees than most.

We're called inside to the table. I sit next to Noah and save the seat beside me for Graham, who's still outside with Walter.

"He's got it so bad," whispers Noah, glancing at Ben and Gemma. "Look at the way he's watching her."

My gaze follows hers. Gemma is holding forth on the best way to train Lola, and Ben looks almost dopily infatuated as he listens and mentally prepares a rebuttal.

"That's the goal," Noah says. "To be with someone you don't want to look away from, someone who makes you feel like you've been *found*. Those Tate boys love with their entire hearts."

Graham will want someone like that one day, will look at someone the way Ben looks at Gemma, and it won't be me. The idea has me swallowing hard just as he slides into the seat on the other side of me.

"Oh my God, are they still talking about the dog?"

I laugh. "Gemma has a whole lot of theories, you'll be surprised to learn."

"Actually," says Gemma, eyes sparkling with mischief as she looks at me, "I was going to see how you'd feel about housesitting next weekend. Ben and I were talking about going to Santa Barbara."

I'm not sure why she's acting like this is something I'd say *no* to. *A puppy? Her bomb-ass house at my disposal for the weekend?* "Of course," I reply. "I love your house."

"I meant both of you, obviously," she says. "Believe me, you don't want to be dealing with Lola on your own."

Oh.

I turn to glance at Graham. A few weeks ago, I'd have been disappointed to have him along, but I guess I don't feel that way anymore. He's kind of fun in his own rarely-smiling, money-focused way.

"Sure," he says.

Walter stands and raises his glass. "I'd just like to make a quick toast to Graham and Keeley. I'm not sure what's led to this, but we couldn't be more pleased. Welcome to the family, Keeley."

That's when Colin shouts, "Kiss!", *exactly like I predicted*, and the rest of the Tates join in. Even Gemma, my former friend.

"Kiss! Kiss! Kiss!"

God. Nothing like being asked to kiss someone for the first time in front of his whole goddamn family. First time sober, anyway. I *knew* this would happen.

I raise a brow at him to say, *"I told you so."*

Graham swallows, his gaze uncertain as he looks down at me. "We don't have to," he says under his breath.

I let my hand press to his chest as I lean forward. "I've done worse things with my mouth."

There's a tiny flare in his eyes, a spark dancing.

"They definitely weren't *worse*, as far as I recall."

It takes me a second to understand what he's referring to, but there's no time to react because his hand is on my hip and he's leaning toward me. His lips press to mine, full and surprisingly firm and certain, as if he knows exactly what he's doing here and has done it a thousand times. As if it's something he has wanted to be doing.

His mouth is warm and I like the smell of his soap. I let myself lean into him. He's built like a fucking wall, and I have a sudden flash of déjà vu.

We've done this and I wanted it to happen. I *asked* him to do it. I wanted to climb him like a goddamn tree.

He pulls back, and for a fraction of a second, my lower brain thinks *no, wait*. I sit up at last, blinking at him in surprise. His mouth curves as if he knows exactly the effect he just had: that kissing him was like a drug, one that made my mind slow until it barely functioned. Maybe that's what made me want to marry him—he drugged me, sort of.

My mind remains slow for the rest of the night, focused entirely on the wrong things.

People tease Colin about his fiancée never coming to anything and I'm still thinking about that kiss. When there's only one burger left, Colin and Simon wrestle for it, which Simon wins by elbowing Colin in the face. And I watch, thinking about how firm Graham's mouth was, how assured he was. That he kisses like a guy who would know exactly what he wanted in bed and wouldn't be the least bit shy demanding it.

Obviously, this isn't about him. Pregnancy hormones are infamous for increasing sex drive, and I already had an unreasonable one *before* I got pregnant. But God, I wish I could remember the weekend in January with him a little better.

When dinner is over, everyone seems to barrel out of the house at once.

Graham's mother hugs me. "I can't tell you how thrilled I am. He seems so much happier with you than he did with Anna."

Anna? Who the fuck is Anna?

My gaze darts from her to him. Graham is avoiding my eye and this isn't the time to ask, but I bet Anna was the source of the Christmas gift his mom turned herself into a nervous wreck over.

And he married *me* two weeks after Christmas.

ANNA...IS Anna Tattelbaum, a financial analyst named *"one to watch"* by *Forbes.*

And she is the female Graham—tall, lean, intimidating.

There are very few photos of them together online, but enough for me to know she's *that* Anna. Enough for me to hate her—she's gorgeous, but she also looks like the kind of person who uses words like *patriarchy* and *heteronormative* in regular conversation. And I guarantee if I asked her opinion of *Bridgerton,* she'd manage to use both.

That probably explains why I hate her so much.

"So this is her," I say, holding up my phone with a picture of them together at some swanky function.

He takes a quick glance at the photo and rolls his eyes before his gaze returns to the road. "It's interesting the way you can't figure out how to use the stove or washing machine but are able to find complete strangers on the internet with only a first name to go by. It's almost like you're feigning incompetence when you don't want to do things."

"*Obviously* I'm feigning incompetence. I wasn't exactly subtle." I scowl at the image on my phone. "So this is the mysterious Anna. I bet she's fun in bed. She probably says, *'increase intensity seventy percent'* when she wants you to fuck her harder."

He smirks in a way that makes me want to punch him. "I don't recall her needing to ask."

Because he was already doing it. Already pistoning like a man possessed.

A disgusting thought, but my gut tenses in the most delicious way.

"What happened?" I ask. "Why did it end?"

He glances at me, suddenly wary. I'm not sure why he's acting like this is all some dark secret. I'd happily discuss my former sex life if he asked. "It was always very casual, and it just wasn't going anywhere."

He's being weird because it was *recent*, I realize. Really recent.

"*When* did it end? And who ended it, you or her?"

"A while ago, and what's with all the questions, Oprah? It's none of your business."

I nod, smiling like the little brat I am. "Ah. *She* ended it."

He heaves a sigh and pushes a hand through his hair. "No, as it happens, she didn't. I just knew it wasn't what I wanted."

I wonder if he realizes he keeps answering after insisting he won't. I wonder if he realizes my interest in this is wildly inappropriate for someone who isn't even attracted to him.

And then a more sobering thought occurs to me: if this tall, elegant girl in the photo who looks like she was made for Graham wasn't what he wanted, I can't imagine who would be.

But it's weirdly disappointing to realize it would never be me.

27

KEELEY

"We should probably go look at baby stuff," Graham says when I walk out of my room the next morning. He's in shorts and a t-shirt, showered and shaved. Even from across the room I know exactly how his neck would smell if I pressed my nose to it. I know exactly how his arm would feel if I grasped it, how long those fingers of his would feel as I pulled them between my thighs.

That kiss was three seconds at most and I can't shake it off. It's like we opened Pandora's Box, and a whole host of memories that should have stayed repressed have come spilling out: his hand on my stomach when he went down on me that first night; him knocking over a barstool to lift me onto a counter somewhere; his fingers sliding inside my panties, *growling* when he felt how wet I was.

I fake a yawn. "Your mom wanted to do that."

"We probably should just figure it out on our own first." His jaw shifts. "Believe me."

I don't know what's up with his attitude toward his mom.

He acts like she's one step from the psych ward when she seems completely together to me.

I groggily fall into a chair at the counter. "Don't you need to do your whole workout thing?"

It's so unnecessary. Unless you're Anna Fucking Tattelbaum. *She* probably appreciated all his superfluous muscles.

He laughs. "Keeley, it's eleven. I worked out hours ago. Get dressed."

"I need to feed Mark. And get my Sunday muffin."

"I already brought him food. And that muffin is just candy swaddled in a paper lining."

I'll forgive him for maligning my muffin because he brought something to Mark.

"Okay. But I want my goddamn muffin."

WE GO to Buy Buy Baby after he shoots down my suggestion that we start at Saks.

"You can't even walk into Saks for less than a grand," he says. "Their cribs are probably made of white gold."

"We're not going to find a Silver Cross stroller in *here*," I mutter as we walk to the doors.

"Knowing how expensive your taste is, that's probably for the best."

Inside, we are greeted by an employee who hands me a mind-numbing list of "suggested items" and gives Graham a scanner so all our choices will be saved in their registry system.

"This can't all be necessary," I say under my breath. "My God. Even the *bathing* section of this list has twenty things on it."

He glances at me. "We have plenty of time."

"Maybe we don't. Your aunt had a story—"

He laughs. "My aunt has a story for everything." He places

his hand on the small of my back. "I'm not going to let this get fucked up, okay? I promise you...by the time this baby arrives, we'll have everything we need."

I feel my shoulders settle a little. I don't trust myself with any of this. But I do trust him.

We begin to scan things I didn't even know existed until today: infant tub, diaper genie, bottle warmer, nursing pillow, window car shade, video monitor. Will he stay long enough to help me get it all set up? The odds of me correctly putting together a diaper genie or connecting the monitor to my phone are close to nil.

"I think we should find out what we're having," I whisper as we look at the strollers.

I see both hope and worry in his eyes. "You're sure? I thought you wanted to be surprised."

"I'm sure." I'm still scared, but when I look at him, I know he'll make sure things work out. And there's enough we don't know without adding gender to the list.

He reaches into his wallet and removes the envelope—he's been carrying it around all this time, which is sort of sweet—and hands it to me. I take a deep breath before I tear it open.

Girl.

We're having a girl. I stare at it, blinking back tears as he stares at it too.

He swallows. "Well, then," he says, his voice a little rough.

I could make a joke right now, throw out yet another dumb name I don't actually like, but I just can't. We're having a girl, and I already love her.

And God, I don't want to mess this up.

～

THAT NIGHT, I fall into an exhausted, troubled sleep and wake gasping. I stumble out to the living room, and turn on a lamp, needing to escape my thoughts.

I'm curled up on the couch with my phone when he opens his door, blinking at me in the dim light. He's wearing shorts but no shirt, and his abs *ripple* as he walks. My gaze falls to that happy trail of his, just below his belly button.

Fucking Anna Tattelbaum.

"Why are you up?" he asks.

I set the phone down. "I didn't mean to wake you. I had a bad dream and was too upset to go back to sleep."

He hesitates. I'm certain he's going to shrug and go back to his room, but instead he comes and sits at the end of the couch, arranging the blanket so that it's covering my toes. I'd be better off if he'd cover his bare chest because, Jesus, he looks so good right now.

"What happened in your dream?"

I frown. It's going to sound ridiculous to him. "I dreamed I put the baby in the oven."

He makes a startled sound—some combination of a cough and a laugh. "*What?*"

"I put her in the oven. It's not like I was sitting there thinking, *oh, putting the baby in the oven sounds like a good idea, I think I'll go for it.* I just arrived at work and remembered I'd done it. And then I was terrified and couldn't get home fast enough, and I was running and I—"

I can't even continue to describe it. The whole thing was so terrifying.

"And you felt absolutely powerless," he says quietly, wrapping a hand around my foot.

"Yes," I whisper, "exactly."

"It's a lot...to go from being only responsible for yourself to being entrusted with a human life."

"I can barely take care of myself. Who the hell ever thought it was a good idea to entrust me with a baby?"

He laughs. "Well...no one."

I kick him. "And here you were doing so well for a minute. I almost didn't hate you."

He laughs again. "Almost?"

"I don't want to do this alone," I whisper.

He squeezes my foot. "You're not."

"But you won't always be here. You'll go back to New York, and then what?"

He frowns, biting his lip as he hesitates. "I've still got plenty of time," he says after a moment, which is when I realize I was hoping for something else, hoping he'd say, *'I'll stay as long as you need me.'* Or better yet, *'I'm not sure I plan to go back.'*

But he hasn't said that. He *does* plan to go back. And when did it become the case that I didn't want him to?

"Look...I get it," he says. "This is terrifying. And there are so many things that can go wrong, and you have no control over what happens. It's why I was so determined not to have kids— because I didn't want to go through my whole life feeling—" He stops, his tongue darting out to tap his lip before he looks away. "I just never wanted to bring things into my life I couldn't afford to lose. But Keeley...you'll get the hang of it, I swear. We both will."

"You'll stay until you're positive I'm not going to put her in the oven?" I ask.

He laughs. "Yes. Although, by the second or third incident, I think you'll be able to remember on your own."

"Maybe there's an alarm I can set." I reach out to him. "Hey, give me your phone."

He blinks at me and fishes it out of his pocket. "Why am I giving you my phone?"

"Don't worry, I'm not going to try to see all the fetishy porn you've downloaded of Japanese men's feet or whatever."

"Is that actually a category of porn? And more to the point, is that actually a category you think I'd be jerking off to?"

Heat shoots through me at those words.

Does he?

Does he lay there at night with his hand wrapped firmly around what was, as I recall, a pretty significantly sized erection?

Mind, pull thyself from the gutter.

"No, your preference is probably something more like *Girl Takes it From Behind While Balancing Checkbook.*'" I tap on his phone and hand it back to him.

He looks at it and laughs. "*Text Keeley, remind her baby can't go in the oven,*" he reads. "This is like a month after the baby's due. You're sure you want to wait that long?"

I swallow, staring at my blanket-covered feet, his broad hand resting atop them. "I assumed, maybe, you'd stay. Just for a bit." I can't meet his eye, but I hope he hears the plea in my voice, the one saying, *"please, please don't leave right away, Graham. I can't do this alone, and I don't think I want to do this with anyone but you."*

"Yeah," he says, his voice softer and lower than normal, "I can probably stay."

28

KEELEY

The following Saturday morning, we are in Ben and Gemma's kitchen with Lola jumping at our heels, and a ten-page list of directions Gemma's *reading aloud* to me.

"Keeley went to medical school, hon," Ben says. "I'm sure she can comprehend it on her own."

Graham hoists himself onto the counter. "I wouldn't be so sure. The only thing I've seen her read all week is *Ugliest Celebrity Babies* and *Celebrities Who are Bad in Bed*, and they were both mostly pictures."

"I'll have you know I also read *Help! I'm in a threesome with my boyfriend's parents and I don't know how to tell him!* And it had no pictures at all, which was unfortunate."

Gemma laughs. "Okay, we're leaving, but don't baby her the whole time, okay? If you're holding her 24/7, then she's going to want me to do it while I'm at work."

"Are you bringing her to work?"

"Well, I can't leave her here alone."

I laugh. Gemma is probably the most driven, professional person I know. She worked weekends and holidays for years and wore a suit every day of the week. I never thought I'd see the day she'd bring a *dog* to work.

"Oh, and if she sees a dog on TV, she goes nuts, so—"

"Hon," Ben says, his jaw tight, his voice sharper than normal, "I really want to get there."

Her mouth curves. "Fine. Just call if—"

"I know how to operate a phone, Gemma. Go, before your husband kills us both."

They leave and I sink to the floor, pulling Lola on my lap, which is probably exactly the kind of thing Gemma was warning me about. "I've never seen your brother like that before."

He laughs to himself. "He had his reasons."

"What reasons?"

Graham brushes a hand through his hair. "She hasn't slept with him all week," he says. "She said she wanted to make this weekend special. I suspect he's been pushed a little too far."

"Ugh," I grumble. "He's complaining about a *week*? Give me a break, *Ben*. I've been married for six months, and I haven't had sex once. I think that's grounds for an annulment right there."

He stiffens. "So there was no one else...after Vegas?"

I sigh heavily. "You are the only person I've slept with since last summer, and I don't even *remember* it."

Our eyes meet and I feel that shift inside me again, which is occurring more and more. That goddamn kiss was the worst thing that's ever happened to me. I can barely think of anything else half the time. He simply has to walk into the room and my skin is too warm, the lace of my bra is too rough, and I'm wondering what it would take to get him to kiss me again. I'm wondering what it would take to get him to do *more*.

"It's been a while for me too," he says.

What an absolute waste. *Someone* should be taking full advantage of that body and that face. And if he's not sleeping with anyone and I'm not sleeping with anyone...maybe it could be me?

It would be a terrible idea given the baby is coming and we're actually friendly at the moment, but I've never let the fact that an idea was terrible stop me before.

And it would be expedient. Efficient. He'd like that aspect of it. *I mean, we're in the same place and it's not like he can get me extra-pregnant and—*

"Ben asked me to take a look at something," he mumbles, walking away.

"I think we dodged a bullet there, Lola," I whisper, as the door shuts behind him.

Lola and I play for a few minutes, but she's not especially chatty, and the house gets too quiet. "Let's go see what Graham is doing," I tell her, and we walk out the back door to find him on his knees, looking muscular and competent while he messes with an outlet. There's a screwdriver held in his teeth and a toolbox at his knee. I never imagined I'd see him with a toolbox, and I never imagined how appealing I'd find that. I've always been more the type to find men hot when they're...you know, on stage. Or ignoring me. I suppose Graham *is* mostly doing the latter.

"You love all this, don't you?" I ask. "A house, a garden, all the family bullshit."

He gives me a slight, sheepish smile. "Yeah. I guess I do." He shrugs. "Who knows if it'll happen? I'm gonna have some baggage."

I think about the way women look at him when we're out, and out of nowhere I feel leaden.

"You'd get snatched right up, if that's what you wanted," I tell him.

His gaze lingers on my face. "What makes you say that?"

"You're adorable, obviously." I flush and scuff my shoe along the patio's edge. "I mean in a really gruff, stern, 'those shoes are overpriced' kind of way."

He smiles, but there's something wistful in it. "You mean in a way you personally hate."

"I don't hate it," I reply. "Well, the commentary on my spending, yes. But the rest of it is just fine."

His mouth quirks up a bit. "You'll appreciate the commentary on your spending later on, when you're ready to retire."

"I'm not sure that's true," I reply, and we both laugh. "I'm going to take Lola for a walk."

"Are you actually walking her or are you just planning to carry her the whole way? Because you haven't put that dog down once. Our kid isn't gonna learn to walk 'til she's five at this rate."

"Ugh, you're not the boss of us," I say, hugging Lola closer. "We don't want him to come anyway, do we?"

Lola and I walk to the pet store, and I wind up carrying her most of the way because she keeps just sitting in the middle of the sidewalk. And she's very little, after all. I then buy her more dog treats than she should eat in a year and feed her half of them on the way home, but again, she's very little and probably needs food.

Just as we reach the house, though, she vomits.

Because of me.

Is this the kind of mother I'll be too? Will I let my kid eat until she vomits? Will I ignore completely rational advice because I like my own way better and ruin her?

Lola falls asleep in my lap once we're inside, and I just feel guilty. If I'm a terrible dog mom, I'll probably be an even worse regular mom.

I go outside to look for Graham, hoping he can somehow make me feel better without me admitting what I've done. He's at the far end of the yard, shirtless and tugging God knows what out of the ground, his taut, ripped shoulders glistening in the sun.

Ugh. Why does he have to look so goddamn good without a shirt?

He glances up as I approach, and his face is clear and untroubled for once. He's in his element here, fixing shit and pulling up weeds. Working hard and being responsible—my polar opposite.

"I just saw your future," I tell him. "You'll settle down with some nice little wife who grows her own vegetables, loves to cook, and worries about getting your shirts done just right."

He rises, studying me. "You sound like you don't approve."

I swallow, staring at the ground as I blink back tears. "It's all fine until you decide our kid should stay with you permanently because it's a better environment."

"Jesus, Keeley," he whispers, closing the distance between us. "Stop. I would never, ever do that to you."

My eyes fall closed, my heart aching so much it's hard to speak. "But you'd be right," I whisper back. "She'd be better off with you."

He nestles me against his firm chest, his arms wrapping tight around me. "Bullshit," he says. "You'll feed her endless amounts of garbage and she'll get expelled at least once for saying something wildly inappropriate, but no one will love that kid more than you do, and make sure she knows it. And what could possibly matter more than that?"

I can almost see myself the way he sees me: a version in which my gross irresponsibility is merely a quirk and my heart isn't jaded at all.

"I made Lola vomit," I whisper. "I gave her too many treats."

He laughs. "That sounds about right. But it'll be okay."

29

GRAHAM

In the afternoon, there's a knock at the front door. I open it and a little girl comes rushing into the house. Hayes, Ben's best friend, stands on the front stoop.

"Sorry," he says, "Ben said it was okay if we stopped by? My daughter is obsessed with Lola."

I glance toward the kitchen where Keeley, Lola, and Hayes's daughter are all on the floor, and two of the three are giggling. I'm pretty sure Keeley has found her peer group.

"Audrey's grown so much since I saw you guys in January!" Keeley exclaims. "I didn't even recognize her. How's the baby? Callum, right?"

"Sleeping in ten-second intervals. He and Tali are finally resting after a very long night and morning, so I thought I'd keep Audrey out for a while."

He pulls out his phone to show us pictures of the baby, and she coos over them while I fret. What happens if our daughter isn't a sleeper? I doubt Beverly Hills Skin is going to be okay with Keeley coming in late or stumbling through a day on no sleep if they won't even let her eat lunch.

"We should get out of your hair," Hayes says. "Come along, Audrey. It's time to go to the store."

"I would like to stay, actually," says Audrey, so prim that Keeley and I both laugh.

"Can she?" Keeley pleads. "You could go to the store and get her on your way home?"

I fight a smile, watching her. Keeley has no idea what she even brings to the table, but here she is begging for time with a little girl she will cuddle and care for as if her life depends on it. What she brings to the table are the things that matter most.

"You're in *deep*, my friend," Hayes says as I walk him to the door. "It's written all over your face. I bet she's got you running out at eleven at night to get her obscure foods."

I think of the last Froot Loops incident. Yes, I drove to the grocery store at midnight because she wanted Froot Loops. "They're not *that* obscure."

When I walk back inside, the TV is on, and Keeley and Audrey are curled up together on the couch with Lola across their laps.

"So here's the deal," Keeley is saying. "The duke doesn't want to have kids because his father was abusive, but Daphne does, and now they're married and happy but it's about to go downhill. If people are happy at the midpoint of *anything*, whether it's a movie or book, you know you're in for it."

Keeley points the remote at the TV. "Oh, we're probably going to have to forward through some of this based on the look she's giving him. Cover your eyes. *Ugh*, kissing in the rain." She pauses the show. "You can open your eyes because this is important: don't let a guy do this. It's not romantic at all, and seriously...no mascara is *that* waterproof. You just wind up cold, and you'll look like a clown afterward."

She picks up the remote again and I finally step in. "Keeley, what are you watching?"

She narrows her eyes at me. "We don't need your help."

"Clearly, you do." I attempt to snatch the remote and she slides it under her thigh. "Audrey, what's your favorite show?"

"This," she says. "They all talk like Daddy."

"Keeley," I beg.

An unwilling smile slips over her face as she pulls out the remote and changes the channel. "Fiiine. We'll watch something else. Have you ever seen *Charlie and Lola*, Audrey? They talk like your dad too."

I'm relieved to see it's animated. I would not have been at all surprised to discover *Charlie and Lola* was a documentary about two British prostitutes.

AFTER HAYES RETURNS for his daughter, we walk to Brentwood for dinner. We bring Lola, in theory to get her some exercise, but Keeley spends most of the walk cradling her like a baby.

For the past two blocks, she's been telling me about the sexy kidnapping movie because, as it turns out, she wants us to watch the sequel together.

"I don't understand how there can be a sequel," I argue.

"She gets kidnapped again," Keeley says, just as the restaurant comes into view. "So, what happens is—"

She suddenly falls silent at the sight of the guy only feet away from us, the one staring at Keeley like he's seeing a ghost.

Ethan Kramer.

He's the founder of a tech start-up and worth millions. He *was* someone whose public opinions I respected, but it's clear from the look on his face that he knows Keeley *well*—which means she dated Ethan Fucking Kramer—and my respect turns to jealousy in a moment's time.

He walks toward us, frowning as we are introduced. She asks how he's been and if he's taken his boat out. His answers are distracted, and his gaze is on her stomach the entire time. "I thought you didn't want kids," he finally says.

Her cheeks flush and her long lashes lower as a lock of hair falls across her face. If she wanted to torture this guy with what he's lost, this was a good day for it: she is glowing, and in tiny shorts and a fitted tee, she makes pregnancy *hot*.

She shrugs, apologetically. "Accidents happen."

He glances at me again, eyes narrowed as if I'm at fault. I guess I might be looking at him similarly if our positions were reversed.

Keeley turns toward the restaurant and tells him goodbye, and even after we've stepped into the foyer, he's still standing outside, staring at the door.

"I take it you dated him," I say. "*Recently*."

She bites her lip. "It ended last summer. It had kind of run its course."

I glance outside. He's walking off fast, angry. "He seems like he's not over it."

She rolls her eyes and shrugs. "I told him at the start I didn't want anything serious. Rich guys always think they'll be the exception."

"I guess he's the source of your Birkin bag?"

Her eyes narrow. "If you're about to accuse me of having an 'arrangement' with men again, we are going to have an extremely loud and public fight."

I wince. I'd forgotten I ever said that. To be fair, however, I had no idea she was dating guys like Kramer. "I'm surprised you let him go. I thought your greatest dream was to be kept by a Saudi prince."

She rolls her eyes. "Jesus Christ, Graham. Do you not know me better than that? My greatest dream is to make my own money and be alone for the years I've got left." She offers me a forced smile. "I'm a butterfly, remember?"

She thinks she doesn't want to be grounded or kept by

anyone, yet she didn't want to stay inside alone today for five seconds. She follows me around the kitchen in her apartment every night like I've got her on a leash, and I've even seen her following the cleaning lady around to chat. She doesn't want to be alone, ever. So why is she telling herself the opposite?

When we return, it's bedtime. Lola cries when we put her in the crate in Gemma and Ben's room, and Keeley's eyes well. "I can't stand it."

"Go stay in the guest room," I tell her. "I'll sleep in here."

"Or we could just, you know, *not* make her sleep in the crate. She could sleep in bed with me."

"They're trying to train her, Keeley. You can't just undo their hard work. Go to the guest room."

She does so reluctantly, and I settle into bed, ignoring Lola's pathetic little cries. This is going to be an issue with me and Keeley once we're parents: she will give in, and I'll always be the heavy. She'll have our kid eating Lucky Charms and sleeping in her bed and watching *Bridgerton*, and I'll have to be the bad guy coming in to ruin everyone's fun. But I guess it's good that she's bothered by the crying. Despite all the things that will go wrong, our child will never doubt she's deeply loved.

Eventually, I fall asleep. I'm vaguely aware of a noise in the middle of the night—Gemma warned us that Lola gets up to pee around four—but it stops before I've even opened my eyes. I figure if it's really an issue, Lola will let us know.

I wake to discover the sun coming through the windows and Lola and Keeley in my bed, Lola between us, Keeley's hand on Lola's stomach.

Keeley's loose waves cover half her face, but I can still tell she's smiling in her sleep.

God, the sight of her like that burns in my chest. It's all the things I wish were different and all the things I wish we could have been, wrapped into one.

30

KEELEY

O n Sunday morning, Lola and I play while Graham is very Graham: making himself a healthy breakfast, going for a run, checking on work, telling me to stop holding Lola.

When he's finally exasperated by my inability to follow directions, he suggests we take her for a walk. We head toward downtown Santa Monica, and since Graham refuses to let me carry her, Lola spends the walk begging every person we pass for attention—and getting it.

"You should get a tattoo," I say, glancing back at the tats on the guy who just finished cooing over her.

"Tattoos are ridiculous," he replies. "I can't imagine caring about something enough to permanently disfigure my body over it."

"Well, I think that's sad."

"Yeah, so sad. What are the deeply meaningful things Six Bailey has written on his body?"

I reach for my phone and look up *Six Bailey* and *tattoos* because I'm certain Graham's wrong. He takes my phone, flinty-eyed, and expands the picture.

"A marijuana leaf. How touching. Then there's a bird, I suppose to signify his desire for freedom? A shark. I'm not sure what the fuck that's for. Oh, and it looks like McGruff the Crime Dog."

"You don't know that," I mutter, rising onto my toes to see the picture again. "I'm sure there are loads of St. Bernards who wear a trench coat with the collar popped."

He laughs to himself. "Well, you've definitely proven your point. It's deeply sad that I don't care about freedom, drugs, sharks, and McGruff the Crime Dog enough to permanently disfigure myself."

"Well, I think—"

Graham's hand wraps around my hip as he presses my back to a storefront, his body shielding mine as a kid on a skateboard blows past us seconds later.

I blink up at him, at first in surprise, and become aware—not for the first time—of his lovely sharp jaw, already in need of a shave, and his lovely mouth, slightly ajar, and his bright blue eyes, which are currently focused on my lips.

For a half second, I can't imagine wanting to look at anything else.

For a half second, I'm certain I know why I married him, I *definitely* know why I slept with him...and I think he might want the same thing I do.

"I'm gonna—" I ramble, breathlessly. "I'm gonna pop in this store."

"No shoes, Keeley," he warns.

I give him the finger, but once inside I'm not looking at the shoes at all. I'm wandering blindly, trying to sort my shit out.

I want him. I have never wanted to sleep with anyone in my entire life the way I do him. The pregnancy hormones are out of control, clearly, and they're making this situation fucking untenable.

Maybe we could just sleep together once, to take the edge off.

Keeley, you know that's a terrible idea.

Yes, I know. But still...

I turn to glance at him out the window. Two women are there now, pretending to gush over Lola when they're really hitting on him.

I know that trick. I fucking *invented* that trick.

One of them places her hand on his bicep and I see red.

I burst out the door. "Hi!" I say, my voice overly bright.

They look me over, assessing how expendable I am. I lean against Graham and place my hand on my belly. *Not expendable, bitches.* They move along quickly after that.

Graham looks down at me with a brow raised. "What was that?"

"You can do a lot better than those two. The brunette looked like your friend Anna, by the way."

He glances back at them and shrugs before he starts walking. It's an insufficient response. I wanted him to say, "*I barely remember what she looked like*" or "*Anna is a monster who hates animals, children, and the poor.*" Instead, he's given me nothing.

"So what happened with you guys anyway?" I ask.

He shoots me *that* look. The one that says, "*what are you really asking me, Keeley?*" I seem to be getting it from him on a daily basis, of late. "I told you this. It was just a relationship of convenience and it ended. That's it."

"*When* did it end, though?" I ask. "I mean, the girl sent your mom a *Christmas* gift."

I wait for him to deny it. Instead, he scratches the back of his neck, stalling. "It ended in January," he admits.

I come to a stop, something sinking in my stomach. "*Before* we got married, or after?"

He winces. "Look, we weren't serious. She met my mom and Walter when they came out to New York last fall, and she struck up this friendship with my mom because...I think because she wanted it to be more. And I ended it the second I met you because I realized she and I were never going anywhere."

He seems cranky now, and I'm not sure if it's because I asked the question or because I ruined something for him. Maybe he ended things with this girl because, for a few hours, I was *Drunk Keeley*, the version of me who is endlessly fun and makes big promises she can't fulfill. Except...I wasn't endlessly fun with him. Not at first anyway.

"It was over before I ever slept with you, if that's what you're about to ask."

"I don't understand," I whisper. "I remember being pretty awful to you."

"I guess you weren't awful enough." A half-smile tugs at his lips. "And later that night you weren't awful at all."

A sharp spike of lust hits me. "But I was always calling you boring, and cheap, and not fun."

He steps closer, his eyes resting on my face. "There's something in the way you lob an insult, Keeley, that makes it sound an awful lot like foreplay. Every single time you call me *boring*"—his gaze falls to my mouth for one long moment—"it feels like you're hoping I'll pin you down and fuck you, simply to prove you wrong."

Fuck. My core clenches hard at those words. Even if he has wildly misunderstood me.

I do think he's boring. Well, somewhat boring.

But I also like the way his nostrils flare when I say it. I might like the way it leads to that slow perusal of his and the cord it tugs inside me.

I might think he's boring, but that there's an opposite side to him, too, something fierce and overwhelming, and I want to set it free.

He walks away, so I straggle after him, wanting to tell him how wrong he was and wondering, increasingly, if he had it right on the nose.

EVERY SINGLE TIME you call me boring, it feels like you're hoping I'll pin you down and fuck you, simply to prove you wrong.

We're back at my apartment and I'm disconsolately flipping through channels on the TV. I no longer have Lola to distract me, so all I can think about is him and those words falling from his pretty mouth. And then I picture him acting on it, with someone other than me, and I'm turned on and angry all at the same time.

"You're in a bad mood tonight," he says, sitting beside me. "Do I need to agree to watch *Bridgerton*?"

"I don't feel like watching Daphne get laid right now," I mutter. "Fucking Daphne."

"Is this about the duke again?"

"No."

"Then what is it?"

I know I'll be ridiculed for my answer but I'm beyond caring at this point. "I haven't had sex in six months, Graham. That's the problem. Even when I'm not pregnant I...I want it more than other people do. And now that I *am* pregnant..."

He winces and leans forward, burying his face in his hands. "More than other people," he repeats flatly.

"I knew you were going to make me feel bad about this."

"I'm not." His jaw locks. "I'm just trying to understand." He raises his head to look at me. "What do you mean by *more*? How much?"

I hitch a shoulder. "Ideally, uh...several times a day."

"Jesus," he whispers.

"I knew—"

"I'm not complaining," he hisses. "You have no idea how hot I find it that you...*fuck*. Never mind."

"How hot you find it that I *what*?"

He glares at me. "What do you think, Keeley? The idea of

you, spending your entire day wanting to get laid...what sane man isn't going to hear that and be tortured by it?"

I freeze, wondering if he's joking. Based on how pissed he is, he's probably not. "*Lots* of men aren't into that," I reply. "And with the way I look now, I think the odds of me ever attracting anyone again are painfully slim anyway."

He laughs, but the sound is rueful and unhappy. "With the way you look now? What's wrong with the way you look?"

I stand and flip my shirt up. "Look at my stomach, Graham! Look at my stretch marks!" I let my shirt fall. "I've got *veins*."

"Any man would give up a year of his life to fuck you, Keeley. Supposed veins or not."

My breath stills. I'm good at equations, and this is a simple one:

Any man would with sleep me + Graham is a man = Graham would sleep with me.

"You *could*," I suggest.

He blinks. "What?"

"You heard me."

His eyes fall closed. "Keeley...I'm not sure that's a good idea."

It's not like I thought he'd be *thrilled* with the offer, but I wasn't prepared for outright rejection either.

"Of course you don't want to," I reply. My voice grows quiet. "I can't even blame you. I wouldn't want to fuck me either."

He laughs—the sound low and menacing—as his hand wraps around my wrist. "You can't be serious," he says, and then he rises, too, stepping close to me—the heat of him along my chest, his breath against my forehead.

I swallow. *Pull it together, Keeley.* "Yes, I'm serious. I—"

He presses my hand to his cock. "Does it feel like I don't want to?"

Beneath my hand he is thick and long, and very, very hard.

And I remember this: standing close to him, just the way I

am now, and feeling the sharp edges of his hunger, and being simultaneously terrified and compelled by the depth of it. He seemed safe from a distance, but now I realize how wrong I was; there's nothing safe about him. He's been like a feral animal kept on a leash, and I just suggested removing it.

He lets my hand go, but it remains anyway, instinct urging me to try to wrap my palm around him through his shorts.

"Keeley, stop," he says. "I wasn't trying to—"

I keep my hand right where it is. "You don't want my hand here?"

"Of course I fucking want your hand there. I just meant...I wasn't putting it there for that reason."

"Graham," I say quietly, "what else do you want from me?" And then I grasp him again, harder, and air hisses through his teeth.

"Everything," he grunts, moving away. "But not when you're offering it as a one-off."

He walks into his room and I remain behind, breathless.

He just turned me down, but it's not because he doesn't want me. It's because he knows he will want more than I will. He's probably right.

I've never hated his practicality as much as I do right now.

31

KEELEY

I expect things to be weird in the morning, but they're not. I'm running late, he's cranky—business as usual. He offers to make Mark breakfast and suggests that it wouldn't take me so long to get dressed if I'd just tell the office I was pregnant, though I'm completely hidden by a lab coat these days.

It's like last night didn't happen...except it did. And I can't stop replaying it in my head. Big, lovely Graham with his sharp tongue and his constant disdain.

I never dreamed he'd want more than once from me. I never dreamed I'd want more than once from him.

And, goddammit, maybe I do. I doubt I could *ever* tire of having sex with him, and I like having him around. These weeks with him have been comforting and fulfilling in a way the weeks and years preceding him were not. But there are so many ways it could go wrong.

Anna Tattelbaum had him for months, probably. How many months? And how will she ever recover from the memory of it, when I simply stood next to him for thirty seconds and already know I won't move forward?

"Will you be home at a reasonable hour tonight?" he asks, turning toward me from the blender, in which he's crafting something I want no part of. "I was gonna grill steaks."

I hesitate. "Not tonight. I've got a thing."

A muscle flickers in his cheek. "What *kind* of thing?"

I wonder if he realizes just how often he *growls* his questions. Because it's a lot. And I don't owe him an explanation, not after he shot me down last night, but I don't have the time or energy right now to bait him, either.

"It's my mom's birthday."

He turns fully, bracing himself against the counter. "You must know it sounds weird when you say it like that, under the circumstances."

"It's a séance. I've got her skull right here." I pat my tote bag. I wait until he laughs before I shrug. "I'm going to her grave. It's a pain in the ass because she's buried all the way up in the Valley, but it is what it is."

He prods the inside of his cheek with his tongue. "I'll drive you. You shouldn't be in your tiny little car on the highway."

I open my mouth to object, but I like having Graham around. "I guess if you're driving, I can finish telling you about all the people on *Glee* who dated each other in real life."

His mouth curves. "Something to look forward to then."

I laugh and I'm pretty sure only Graham could make me laugh on my mom's birthday. It's probably for the best that he turned me down. I might get more attached than I already am.

I GET a lunch break for once, and I spend it online, reading about Anna Tattelbaum. She is everything I am not—she likes art and doesn't go to fancy galas simply for the free booze. She is British, something I can't even fake, and I know this because I've tried several times.

The sentence that stops me in my tracks, though, is this: *Anna Tattelbaum, rumored to be dating hedge fund manager Graham Tate, one of the city's most sought-after bachelors.*

Graham is one of NYC's most sought-after bachelors? *How?* Sure, he's good-looking, but that kind of status is reserved for royalty or heirs to fortunes and he is neither. Which means it's time to do something I've avoided for months.

Looking a man up online, especially one you really want to have sex with, is the slippery slope that leads to the Pit of Obsession. You learn one fact and you want to learn another. You see one photo and you need to see more. I sense, even before I begin my search, that my slide into the pit will be long and painful, and that I will thoroughly regret this later on.

The first thing that comes up is an article on "NYC's Sexiest Male Singles". They've got a photo of him looking bored and ridiculously hot at some charity function.

Graham Tate, the reclusive founder of Tate Capital, leads our list. With a net worth estimated at over a hundred million, we'd date him even if he didn't look like the face of the next Tom Ford campaign. But he does. Therefore...Graham, give us a call. *Any* of us.

What. The. Hell.

The guy who was too cheap to get a chocolate fountain or tequila luge for our party is worth a hundred million. The guy who doesn't own a car. The guy who bitched about the cost of the green juice I wanted this weekend and keeps telling me I don't need both Netflix *and* Hulu.

I've known loads of millionaires and every last one of them flashed his wealth somehow. More importantly, I've never known one who didn't think it made him special, who wasn't under the impression his money exempted him from taking out the trash or carrying his own plate to the sink.

I slam my laptop shut and bury my face in my hands. I thought success was an attractive quality in a man, but it's got nothing on the discovery that Graham has it in spades...and couldn't care less.

NYC's SEXIEST Single is forced to wait for nearly forty minutes outside my office, because I'm so backed up...and that's *with* me telling Trinny I couldn't take Dr. Joliet's six o'clock.

"I'm sorry," I say, rushing out to the car, still in my lab coat.

"You've got to tell them," he says as he pulls into traffic. "Seriously. This is insane."

I sigh. "I know."

"I mean it, Keeley. What's the worst that can happen if you tell them? You don't even like that job."

I frown at him. "Oh, maybe I hadn't mentioned this, but I'm actually about to have a child. It's not a great time for me to be *unemployed*."

"I'm not Jeff Bezos, but I can afford—" He circles his hand over me and my stomach. "—all this. If you want to just quit and wait until you find something."

I laugh. I spent every free minute today researching Graham Tate. I now know he's the guy billionaires entrust with their finances, and that there's an entire subreddit devoted to *What Graham Tate is Buying*. I'll continue to imply he does something with insurance, though. It keeps him on his toes.

"I appreciate the offer," I reply, "but I think that would go poorly."

He rolls his eyes. "*Why*?"

I can't believe he's arguing. Only a fool would offer to support me while I look for a job. He's got to know I'd just sleep in until eleven and shop all day.

"Because then our power isn't equal. The second you're paying the bills, you'll be like 'No, Keeley, we can't buy a Silver Cross stroller.'"

"I already *told* you we're not buying a Silver Cross. Fourteen hundred dollars for a fucking stroller. It's ridiculous."

"Yeah, but right now I still can say, 'oh, screw you, Graham, I just bought one.' If you're footing all the bills, I can't do that."

"I'm guessing you'd still manage to do that," he mutters.

When the cemetery comes into view, he pulls into the spot closest to the gates. "I can just wait in the car," he says. "Take your time."

I reach over and unclip his seat belt. "Nah, come on. It takes two people to operate the Ouija board I brought."

He laughs and climbs out, following me across the rolling hills to my mother's headstone.

"So, this is it," I say brightly. "Pretty exciting stuff. And that's my aunt." I point to her grave, which is right next to my mom's.

He reads each headstone, his gaze growing darker by the minute. It's different, seeing it in person. "They were my age," he says quietly.

I nod. "My poor grandfather. He outlived his wife and both his daughters. I can't even imagine."

He glances over to my mom's grave. "Is he the one who left the flowers?"

"No, those are from Dillon, the guy my mom was dating at the end." I shake my head. "He still brings her flowers for every occasion. It's kind of fucked up."

"What's wrong with that?"

"He was twenty-eight when she died. He had his whole life ahead of him but never moved on, and if she'd lived, well, she probably *would* have moved on. I don't know. Maybe it's just easier to think she would have."

He takes my hand and pulls me over to the bench on the other side of the gravel path. "Why is it easier to think that?"

"Because can you imagine going through your whole life only to find your soulmate a few months before you get diagnosed with stage four cancer? Can you imagine leaving that person and your teenage daughter, knowing you've hurt them and they won't ever, ever get over it?"

His brow furrows. "Wouldn't you just be glad you were missed? That, to me, seems like a sign you did something right."

I shake my head again. "I *never* want to do that to anyone else. I don't want my daughter to spend her whole life missing me. I don't want a guy coming to my grave every month, unable to move on."

He grips the edge of the bench. "That's why you didn't want kids, isn't it?"

I force a smile. "I mean, Coachella was a factor, too, I'm not gonna lie. But yeah, that was most of it." I pat my stomach. "Anyway, what's done is done, and now you're screwed. The parent who dies first gets all the worship. No one is going to talk about the times I drank too much or really fucked something up and all my flaws will seem charming. *You'll* be the parent who has to be multidimensional."

A muscle flickers in his cheek and his hands curl into fists.

"You're so goddamn sure you're going to die young, Keeley," he grits out. He sounds *angry*. "Even if your mom had some genetic thing that made this happen...she only contributed half of your genes. Why aren't you even considering the possibility that you'll be fine?"

I stare out at the descending sun. "It just seems easier than getting my hopes up and discovering I was wrong. My mom was so *shocked*, Graham." I swallow hard and my voice grows quiet. "When she got that diagnosis, she was so shocked because she thought she'd done everything right. I'm just trying to be realistic."

He wraps an arm around my shoulders. "Was it that she was shocked, or was it that *you* were shocked? You realize being prepared wouldn't have fixed anything, right? She wouldn't have wanted you to go through your whole childhood panicked you were going to lose her."

"Yeah, I know." But I think of my mom's last days of consciousness when she knew what was going to happen. She was devastated. Anytime Dillon or I walked into the room, she cried. And that made it harder for us. It was just this horrible, inescapable circle of grief.

"I guess it's just...if it happens, I don't want it to hurt me the way it hurt her. I don't want it to be so hard to say goodbye to everything, and have it be so hard on them."

He pulls me closer, and I rest my head on his shoulder. It's a nice shoulder, broad enough to hold me up, perfectly firm.

"The only choice is to love everything a little less, Keeley. I'm not sure that's a better option."

He might be right. More importantly, I'm not sure it's even possible. Because I already love our daughter. And I'm starting to like her father an awful lot too.

"I WANT DESSERT," I announce on the way home. "Like I don't even want dinner. I just want dessert. And because I just cried, you have to give in and coddle me."

He laughs. "We could make a pie."

"Do you know *how* to make a pie? Because I sure as hell don't."

"Of course I do," he says, and his eyes are light. "I think we probably have all the ingredients too. I just bought apples yesterday."

Making a pie sounds like a pain in the ass, the kind of thing that will lead to a barely edible mess neither of us will want to eat or clean up. But when he's like this, all twinkling eyes and dimples, I'm incapable of telling him *no*.

"Okay. But if it's inedible, you're taking me to Pinkberry."

"Deal," he agrees with a quiet, confident laugh.

When we get home, I change into one of the new maternity t-shirts I bought after Ethan's Tulane sweatshirt disappeared, which Graham *claims* to know nothing about.

He sets me at the counter to peel and slice the apples while he works on the crust. I watch, mystified, as he scoops flour and sugar into a bowl and mixes it with the butter he set out to soften. He never has to check a recipe once.

"How do you know how to do this?" I ask. "I can't even boil eggs without looking up the instructions."

With his hands he kneads the dough then shapes it into a ball. "My great-aunt taught me when I was little," he says, only glancing up briefly.

"And you remembered it? All this time?"

He hesitates. "My mom was...sick. After my dad died. She had really serious postpartum depression that got missed with everything else going on. Anyway...things went bad for a while, and then my great-aunt came to get us all back on track, and she told me the pies were my job."

He doesn't seem bothered by this story at all, but I am. He was *eight*, which was too young to be given a job of any kind. "I'm not sure an eight-year-old should be using a stove."

He shakes his head. "It helped, knowing there was something I could do, some way I could make up for things. Anyway, until I left for college, I found myself making a lot of pies."

"I still wish you hadn't had to," I tell him quietly. Our eyes meet and I have to look away. "The apples are ready."

He says nothing, just starts dumping sugar and cinnamon and—weirdly—jelly into the bowl. "Now we mix it up." He smiles when I reach for the spoon. "Just get your hands in there. It's the only way."

"My bare hands?"

"They're clean. Come on, doc." He tugs my fingers into his,

placing our joined hands atop all the fruit. "You've put your hands into worse things than this."

Together we mix, our hands sticky, brushing against each other. His hands are large, and rough, and all this wet fruit sliding through our fingers makes me think of other things entirely— of his fingers sliding beneath my thong, pushing inside me in some semi-public place.

"Come on my fingers, Keeley," he crooned. *"Just once. Then I'll kiss you again."*

I remember the heat between my legs, the ache that felt almost like pain as my thighs braced. The sounds as I got wetter and wetter were exactly like the sounds we're making right now.

I look up and find his eyes on my face, on my mouth, the same way they were that night. My nipples tighten beneath the smooth fabric of my t-shirt, and the memory has left me soaked. If he would just close the distance between us and kiss me, if he'd just reach beneath my panties with those filthy wet fingers, I'd go off like the grand finale of a fireworks show.

God. No fucking wonder I married him.

I'd probably do it all over again.

32

GRAHAM

JULY

"Can we eat out?" she asks when she walks in the door Thursday night. Her eyes are dreamy. "Dinner out. In a restaurant. Steak, maybe. Or, no, wait...chicken tikka. God, I want chicken tikka so bad."

Porn stars wish they could moan as convincingly as Keeley does at the idea of chicken tikka. I have my most important meeting of the week early tomorrow morning, but I can't seem to say no to her.

"Then come on," I say, rising. "Let's go."

Her eyes are wide, as if I've told her a Birkin bag is being delivered, made especially for her, which is definitely something I will never tell her, having learned what they cost.

"I've got to get dressed!" she shouts. "Ten minutes. No! Twenty!"

She runs toward her room faster than I realized she could move. A man would wind up paying for a whole lot of shit if he was with Keeley, because pleasing her has the strangest rebound effect. I feel something open inside me every time I manage to make her smile.

Thirty minutes later, I'm about to start growling when she emerges from her room in a bright red dress and lips to match.

It's not a maternity dress, but stretchy enough to contain her...barely. The creamy swell of her breasts threatens to overwhelm the low-cut neck. I'm going to have a really hard time not staring all night. Every other man we pass is going to stare as well, which is the part I have a bigger problem with.

Her hand rests on her stomach. "Is it okay? I...don't have much I can get into anymore."

"Maybe it's time you bought some more maternity clothes."

Her face falls. "So that's a *no*, then."

"You look fine." Which is the vastest of understatements. Keeley doesn't look *fine*. She looks like the kind of woman you'd see on a billboard and find yourself stopping in place to gawk at. The kind of woman you'd never fucking move on from if you had her once. "People might stare at your breasts."

She cups them with a grin. "Are you saying *you* want to stare, Graham? Stare away! They're not gonna last forever so someone ought to get some enjoyment from them."

I swallow, heading for the door. "I don't need to stare at your breasts, Keeley." *They're already burned into my brain.*

"Don't worry," she says cheerfully as she searches her purse for her keys. "I've taken so many photos of them. Maybe I'll give you one as a birthday present."

I choke a little at the idea. "You give away photos of your breasts as a *gift*?"

"Just to friends. You, Paul downstairs, Mike the UPS guy—"

I come to a dead stop and she laughs.

"No, I don't give away pictures of my breasts. But to be fair, they only turned into showstoppers this year. I bet I could make more on *Only Fans* right now than I do as a doctor."

I just keep walking toward the elevator. But Jesus Christ, a daughter like Keeley will put me in an early grave.

~

WE ARRIVE at Keeley's favorite Indian restaurant.

She doesn't seem to notice the way the host's eyes slide over her, the way the kitchen staff look up and lean over. She's too busy trying to convince me she needs two orders of chicken tikka.

"Just for me. If you want some, too, we'll need three orders. But you have to order all of it so I can continue to look like a delicate flower who's only here because you wanted Indian food."

The waiter takes our order. Our meal should be free in exchange for the amount of time he's spending looking at Keeley's cleavage.

"You know what we should do?" she asks once he's gone. "We should get to know each other."

"Haven't we been doing that all along?"

She gives me one of her baleful looks, the kind that says, *"stop being a buzzkill, Graham."* They used to annoy me. Now they make me laugh.

"Fine," I concede. "You can have dinner with any person, past or present. Who do you choose?"

"Can it be a person made of chocolate?"

"I'm referring to a dining companion you do not intend to *eat*, Keeley." She really must be starving if that's the first place her mind went.

"Gandhi," she replies. "Or Khloe Kardashian."

"Gandhi is rolling in his grave right now."

"Gandhi was cremated, so I doubt he's doing much *rolling*. And Khloe is cheerful in the face of adversity and nice to everyone she meets. You could learn something from her." Keeley looks toward the kitchen. She's been watching every tray that emerges, hoping one is ours. "Who would you have over?"

"John Locke or Paul Krugman, this economist from—"

"Oh my God. Really? Trust you to find the one person more boring than yourself to invite over for dinner." As soon as the word *boring* comes out, she blushes, and I know she's remembering what I said.

I still can't believe I said it, though it was entirely true.

"What's your obsession with economics, anyway?" she asks. "No one else in your family seems into that kind of stuff."

I shrug. I never gave it much thought before. Maybe it's just that bad things happen to people without the resources to fight back when they're under siege, and I never want to be among them again. "I like knowing I'm financially secure. I want other people to be in the same position."

"You sound like such a *dad* when you say things like that."

I think she intends it as an insult, but her eyes are shining and her smile is soft. She likes it, even if she'll never admit as much.

Our tray approaches at last and her excitement is palpable. She claps her hands together and squirms in her seat like a kid who has to pee.

"Are you like this on *dates*?" I ask, mildly horrified.

"Whatever. I'm adorable. You love my childlike appreciation of the world."

A bowl of basmati rice is placed between us, and through the steam I take in Keeley's wide eyes, her unrepentant grin. The last time I ate out with Anna, we were at a Michelin-starred restaurant, and she spent the whole meal finding small flaws in the food and the service.

Yeah. I guess Keeley's childlike appreciation of things isn't all bad.

She serves herself a steaming plate of rice and inhales, her eyes closed as if this is the most erotic dream she's ever had. Then she opens the first bowl of chicken tikka and groans low, in a way that cuts straight to my groin.

She spoons the chunks of chicken and sauce into her bowl,

and just as she picks up her fork with a blissful sigh of anticipation...shouting begins.

A chef comes out of the kitchen at a run. "Is there a doctor here?"

I look at Keeley. The fork is still in her hand, poised to begin.

She frowns. "I doubt they need a *dermatologist*."

"Keeley, you went to medical school. You theoretically know about other things."

"Goddammit," she says with a sigh, pushing away from the table. "I really wanted that chicken tikka. And this is sexist. They wouldn't ask a man to give up his chicken tikka."

"I'm fairly certain they would, under the circumstances." I rise with her. "And it'll still be here when you get back."

"I wanted *hot* chicken tikka," she replies, stomping across the room toward the chef. "Is it so much to ask that I get hot chicken tikka to make up for all the vegetable eating and not-sex-having I've endured?"

I'm praying she doesn't ask the chef this. He stares at the two of us as we approach, and then looks at me, with relief. "Thank God," he says. "You're a doctor?"

Keeley groans audibly. "Because any emergency would be handled better by a man, right? No, *I'm* the doctor. He's just here to hold my healing crystals. What's going on?"

The chef's eyes widen a little. He looks at me as if to say, *"Is she serious?"*

I shake my head, though you can never be too sure with Keeley. "Graciela, one of our line cooks, went into labor," he says, still addressing me. "It's bad. I think the baby's coming out. We can...see it."

Keeley stiffens. "Did you call an ambulance?"

"We did but they said it'll be a while and—" He flinches as a female scream cuts through the air.

"Jesus Fucking Christ," Keeley says, pushing past him like

she owns the place. "You guys owe me some fresh chicken tikka."

"Is she really a doctor?" he asks me as we follow.

"It shocks me too."

The kitchen is at a standstill and most of the cooks have abandoned their posts to stare with horror at the woman now lying on a tablecloth on the kitchen floor.

Her legs are spread, and the top of a human head is visible between them. That's terrifying enough, but it's the bloody fluid beneath her that makes my pulse rise. Maybe it's standard, but it has me remembering that first episode of *Bridgerton*, the one where a woman died in childbirth. Yes, it was a couple of centuries ago, but is this any different? With no ambulance coming, is there a single tool at Keeley's disposal that wasn't available three hundred years ago? And if this woman dies... what happens then?

Keeley skates through life as if nothing matters to her all that much, but if this goes badly, it will weigh on her every fucking day. She wept because she made the dog throw up. What would something like this do to her?

The woman cries out, and her pain sends a chill up my spine.

"Sink," barks Keeley at the manager, who looks taken aback. She kicks off her heels and her precious Birkin is thrown to the ground as she crosses the kitchen while tying her hair back. She washes her arms all the way to her elbows, her brow furrowed...someone else entirely. Someone serious, focused. She dries her hands with paper towels and sinks to the floor between the woman's legs.

"I'm Dr. Connolly," she says. "Looks like you're having a baby in a kitchen."

The woman replies in rapid Spanish, and Keeley replies in kind. Again, I'm surprised. I pictured her as the sort to learn something like French simply because Paris has a better Fashion Week.

Keeley sounds...different, speaking Spanish. Assured, authoritative. I don't even know what she's saying, but I believe her. I'd believe anything Keeley said to me right now.

"I need a knife," Keeley tells the manager. "The sharpest knife you have, and I need rubbing alcohol. It might not be necessary, but I want it here in case I do. And please, for the love of God, don't come in here *brandishing* the knife so she can see it. Wrap it in a towel or something. And find out where the fuck that ambulance is."

The woman screams as another contraction takes over. I flinch, but Keeley is steely-eyed, utterly calm, her voice alternately cajoling and forceful as she urges Graciela on.

Her hair is starting to escape the bun, clinging to the sweat on her forehead, which is the only signal I've got that Keeley isn't completely relaxed. Well, that and her shoulders, which are tense as she reaches down to get a grip on the baby. Someone deposits a pile of towels beside her—she doesn't seem to notice.

"*Él está casi aquí,*" Keeley says, her hands clasped on the baby's shoulders. "*Una vez más.*"

The woman pushes, wailing, and I flinch. One of the men across the kitchen quietly opens the back door and pukes in the alley.

The woman cries out and then...the head emerges fully. Keeley works to get the top shoulder out, then the bottom and suddenly the baby just seems to slip free. A boy, covered in blood, his cry a shrill little bleating sound. A cheer echoes through the room but Keeley's still focused, clearing his mouth and nose, checking his pulse, murmuring to herself, "Pink, one twenty, vigorous response, active." Satisfied at last, she leans forward to hand the baby to his weeping mother.

Her expensive dress is ruined. The shoes she kicked off are

sitting next to a mousetrap, and she's smiling as if all is right with the world. There is so much more to her than she lets anyone see. There's so much more to her than even *she* seems to see.

I just fell more in love with the mother of my child than I already was. Which is really inconvenient. I was already a little too far gone.

33

KEELEY

Surprisingly, now that my dress is covered in blood and afterbirth, I don't have much of an appetite for chicken tikka. We remain until the ambulance arrives and then I'm ushered out the back door, into the alley. Graham steers me around the vomit just outside, and I throw my ruined shoes in a dumpster.

"Keeley, you can't walk barefoot. There's probably glass out here."

"Did you see those shoes? They were sitting in an inch of mouse droppings. I'm pretty sure the pavement can't be worse."

I squeal in surprise as he swoops me into his arms, carrying me like I weigh no more than a coat or a small child. "If I'd known you were this strong, I'd have made you carry me *everywhere*."

"I should have kept it a secret for longer, *Dr. Connolly*." He smiles. "I've never heard you introduce yourself like that, by the way."

"She was panicking, and the whole doctor thing reassures people. Though, obviously"—I point to myself—"it probably should *not*."

He carries me in silence, allowing me the space to marvel at how fucking fit he is. With my arms looped around his neck and my body resting against his, it's impossible not to notice that his chest and biceps are like carved stone. I think I see why women look so dazed when Superman rescues them, and it has very little to do with the part where they didn't die.

But I suppose I was already moderately obsessed. Ever since that night when he shot me down, I've been struggling to turn this thing off. I don't know how to stop picturing him when he's not in the room—the broad set of his shoulders when he's on my couch, his narrow hip leaning against the kitchen counter, the way he rubs a hand over his jaw when he's thinking, and how every fucking time he does it I think *I want to be that hand.*

I don't know how to stop imagining I smell his soap in places I know it isn't. How to keep my pulse from racing anytime I see a dark head in a crowd.

I don't know how to stop thinking about him so fucking hard beneath my hand and him saying, "*does it feel like I don't want it?*"

"What are you thinking right now?" he asks. His mouth curves upward, almost as if he already knows.

"That I want a big, juicy steak." It's not entirely a lie. I *do* want a steak. He doesn't need to know everything in my head.

"Your wish is my command, *Dr. Connolly*."

~

BY THE TIME I've stripped out of my ruined dress, showered, and put on pajamas, Graham has somehow acquired steak and baked potatoes for us. He even says we can watch TV while we eat. Of course, the show we're watching is *Dr. Who*—his choice, which seems a little unfair. I mean, did *he* bring a life into the world tonight? I think not.

"So are these people ever going to have sex?" I demand.

"We're only ten minutes into it. But there are no sexy kidnappers, if that's what you're after. You'll have to wait and see for the rest."

I groan. "That means *no.*"

He pauses the show and glances at me. "You impressed me tonight, you know. Everyone in that kitchen was a wreck, and you were the center of the storm. I felt like anything could have gone wrong and you'd have known what to do."

"I do way cooler things than that. I can tie a cherry stem with my tongue. And you're giving me too much credit. It just happened to be a very easy and uncomplicated delivery. If anything had gone wrong, I'd have been up shit creek."

"For someone who compliments herself incessantly, you sure can't take a compliment for shit. Can you at least admit you did something good tonight?"

My laughter is a trifle exasperated. "Everyone underestimates me, but I *am* actually a doctor, Graham. I'm *supposed* to be able to do that."

"I think the one who underestimates you, Keeley, is *you.*"

There's something in the way he says it that hits a nerve. Maybe it's just that he sounds a lot like Dr. Patel right now.

GRAHAM'S WORDS echo in my head all night, and they're still there the following morning when I walk into work and Trinny has that worried look she gets before she tells me I'm double booked all day and have patients until seven. Why am I still putting up with this? Yes, I know I need this job at the moment, but why am I not even putting out feelers for something else?

The one who underestimates you is you. Maybe Dr. Fox didn't solely hire me for my looks. Maybe she also liked my utter lack of self-respect, that I came across as someone who would take all the garbage they wanted to shovel out and *keep* taking it because she didn't think she deserved more.

I will brag about my breast size and charm to anyone who will listen. Would I ever consider bragging about my skill, though? No. Of course not. I skated through medical school and my residency doing the bare minimum.

Maybe Dr. Patel had a point.

"Let me guess," I say. "I'm not getting a lunch break?"

"Well, no," she says. "But...I'm just wondering—is this you?" She turns her phone to me. It takes a second to realize that the girl in the red dress, kneeling on a kitchen floor delivering a baby...is me. The caption reads *Hot Pregnant Doc Delivers Baby.*

I had no idea someone was filming me last night, and for a second I'm merely irritated that they're calling me *pregnant*— it's not *that* obvious. They sort of made up for it by calling me "hot", but still...

Then a more serious concern overshadows it: this video is out in the world, saying I'm pregnant before I've revealed it to most of the people I know.

"Where did you find that?" I whisper.

"It was on TikTok this morning. You're pregnant?"

I swallow. Dr. Fox and Dr. Joliet don't seem like the type to go on TikTok much, so what are the odds they'll see it? Shannon and my dad aren't even on Facebook so I'm not too worried about them.

And honestly...there are millions of videos out there and this one isn't even all that interesting. "Can you, uh, not say anything about it just yet? I have to tell Dr. Fox still."

She glances at the video again. "You look *really* pregnant though."

"I don't look *that* pregnant," I argue.

One hour later, a nurse leans her head into my office. "Congratulations!" she cries. "I suspected but I didn't want to say anything."

I'd almost forgotten about that fucking video, but it comes back to me in a rush. "Congratulations?" I whisper.

"You delivering that baby is *international* news."

When she leaves, I look it up. The video has garnered six million views. I scroll through the comments—a third of them are disgusting, and a fair number insist that I'm definitely not a doctor. A handful claim my Birkin is fake, and those are the only ones I reply to because *fuck that*. I did not get my hands on that bag to have some twenty-year-old manicurist claiming it's fake because *her aunt has a real one and she knows*.

But a lot of them are...impressed. Just like Graham was. They like that I spoke Spanish to Graciela. They like that I remained calm and in control while the men in the kitchen looking on were—literally—losing it.

Regardless of which way public opinion is swaying, though, it's clear that the jig is up. I start typing an email to Fox and Joliet, telling them I'm pregnant, but I'm not finished before Dr. Fox is barking at me over the intercom. "My office. *Now*."

I rise from my desk with a heavy sigh. As someone who's never *not* gotten told off by her principal, dean, or chief resident, the position I'm in is a familiar one. Today, however, I'm annoyed at the same time. I haven't done anything *that* wrong. There was nothing in my contract stating I needed to provide them three months' warning before I had a baby. There was, however, plenty in my contract referencing California's labor laws, which they've definitely been violating.

And Dr. Fox needs me every bit as much as I need this job, so fuck it. I'm done being scared of this woman. I'm done acting like I'm in the wrong when she's the one consistently doing a *hundred* things she shouldn't.

She turns her phone toward me as I walk in. The article's headline is *Stunning Pregnant Doctor Delivers Baby in Restaurant*.

"Care to explain this?" she asks.

"I don't know that I would have gone with the word

stunning," I reply. "In New York, maybe, but in LA? I'm a seven. Maybe an eight with makeup."

She stares at me, incredulous. "Are you under the impression that being a smart ass is going to save your job? I was obviously referring to the fact that you are *pregnant*."

"I did not know I was pregnant when I accepted this job. It wasn't planned, and it is what it is."

"*It is what it is*'?" she demands. "Have you forgotten you're still on probation?"

I clench my hands in the pockets of my lab coat. She's been skating off every day for hair appointments and shopping while making a pregnant woman skip lunch to cover for her, but she's too fucking self-centered to see past the handful of weeks I'd need for maternity leave.

The handful of weeks she'd have to work as hard as *I've* had to lately, covering for her.

"If you're going to fire me, go ahead and do it." I pull my hands from my pockets and place them on her desk as I lean toward her. "But I should mention to you that my best friend is one of the leading workplace discrimination lawyers in the country—look up Lawson versus Fiducia and see for yourself —and getting fired when my pregnancy becomes public knowledge sounds like a fucking slam dunk to me."

I sound like Gemma right now, in the best possible way. But I have no idea if what I said is true...and Kathleen Fox doesn't look all that scared.

THE ONLY PERSON I want to discuss it with as I drive home is Graham. Yes, he's been on me for a while to tell them the truth, but I also know he'll have my back.

I park in the garage and skip my normal chat with Paul, Mark, and Jacobson to get upstairs faster, coming to a stop just inside the door to the apartment when I find Graham in jeans and a black button-down, clearly on his way out.

And he looks good.

He looks really, really good.

I'd forgotten he had some bachelor thing for Colin tonight. Apparently, there's tension over the fact that Mandy won't set a date, and they're trying to cheer Colin up. I'd like to suggest that cheering Colin up with lap dances and girls jumping out of a cake isn't going to help the situation, but I guess I'd sound a little jealous.

"I didn't realize you were leaving so early," I tell him. There's a plaintive note to my voice, one I wish wasn't there.

He glances at the clock. "It's seven-thirty, Keeley, and we're meeting for dinner. It's not that early."

"So...are you *just* going out to dinner?"

He's focused on rolling up his sleeves, his watch gleaming in the light. At least he's too cheap to buy a Rolex, so he won't have women throwing themselves at him for his money.

Everything else, yes. But not money.

He shakes his head. "Simon did the planning, so I doubt it'll end there."

His shirt looks soft. If I were a girl seeing him out tonight, I'd walk straight up and run my fingers over it and ask him where he got it. He'd tell me he didn't remember and ask if I wanted a drink, and I'd smile at him—a small reward for playing along because we'd both know I didn't give a flying fuck where he bought that shirt.

He catches me watching him and crosses to where I'm standing. "Are you okay?" He tips my chin up as if he's observing me for signs of illness.

"I'm fine," I reply, batting his hand away. "But don't think you get to bring someone home just because you're paying the rent."

His eyes brush over my face, searching for something

before a smile tugs at the corner of his mouth. "I'll keep it in mind."

He grabs his keys, hesitating.

"I'll be fine," I tell him. "Though I'd be better if I could just find my Tulane sweatshirt."

"It wasn't yours anyway." A hint of a smile creeps onto his face again. "But yeah, it's a real mystery, that sweatshirt's disappearance."

After he leaves, the apartment just seems empty. I change clothes and *consider* eating my weight in junk food—Lucky Charms, washed down with Doritos and Oreos and maybe some guacamole if I need a vegetable—but I don't do it. When this pregnancy began, it was like being held hostage by someone or something I didn't have to listen to. Now, though, the baby matters more to me than anything I crave, so I wind up eating a boring salad, and it sucks that Graham isn't here to pat me on the head like a child for making a good choice. I'm getting texts from friends and acquaintances about the video, but work is my concern and Graham's really the only person I want to discuss it with. I guess there are other people I could call—Gemma would bring both guns blazing to *that* fight, I'm certain—but I know it won't be the same. She might reassure me, but she won't be able to comfort me the way he would. No one could.

I put on *Bridgerton* and turn it off. It's no fun without Graham there to comment, and I wonder if it's always going to feel lonely like this after he's gone.

I thought I loved living alone. I thought I loved being free. Maybe it's just what I told myself so I wouldn't get tempted to want anything more.

~

I WAKE on Saturday morning and scroll through the texts on my phone. Every friend has seen the video by now and it just makes me wish I'd been doing something slightly more spectacular—some kind of crazy roundhouse kick to fight off an intruder while pulling the baby out. Perhaps a John Wick-style pencil to someone's eye.

I have no idea why this video is even a *thing*. Would anyone want to watch a video of a guy catching a frisbee? Because that's basically what I did, only the frisbee was covered in amniotic fluid and briefly wedged inside a vagina.

Okay, I guess I *would* watch a video of a guy pulling a frisbee out of a vagina.

I skim through the texts until my eyes catch on an unfamiliar number.

Hi Keeley. My name is Trevor MacNulty. I'm a producer at *Mindy and Mills*. Hope you don't mind but I got your number from a mutual friend. Saw your video and would love to talk to you about working together. Please give me a call as soon as possible.

This is it. My shot at fame has arrived at last. I'll begin as their medical expert before moving onto a show of my own—something where I diagnose really cool, rare skin conditions but with a personal element: viewers will see me in business mode, but also watch me and Rihanna heading to Pilates together, or me and Jennifer Garner making scones in her kitchen.

"Graham!" I scream, running to the kitchen, still clad in my pajamas. "Graham, I'm gonna be rich!"

My words echo in the empty apartment. His door is wide open, the same way it was when he left last night.

I grip the counter, staggered by the unexpected wave of sheer fury sweeping over me.

He stayed out all night. I told him he couldn't bring someone home and he followed my dictates to the letter and stayed with her instead.

You son of a bitch. You goddamn son of a bitch.

I picture him with someone else, someone more like Anna than me—tall and elegant and, you know, *not* pregnant, unbuttoning that black shirt he wore. Unbuckling his belt. Him beneath her, allowing her to take charge.

And I hate her, but more than that I hate *him*. I hate him so fucking much.

I don't even know why I hate him, and I guess he hasn't *technically* done anything wrong, but my thoughts are rage-filled and irrational. I picture kicking him out. Changing the locks, dumping his files and computer outside the door. And he *has* done something wrong. We are, *technically*, married.

I pick up the phone, my only goal to actively ruin whatever he currently has going with someone else in whatever way occurs to me. *I'll tell him I've gone into labor. Explain THAT to your one-night stand, Graham.* But before his phone's even begun to ring, I see a note he's stuck to the bananas: **At gym. Try not to eat all the fruit while I'm gone.**

I hang up, and then stand for a moment, letting this sink in. Letting the relief hit me, and then the realization I'm relieved when I shouldn't have cared in the first place. This is potentially the biggest moment of my life. How could I have forgotten that simply because Graham wasn't home?

Whatever. I still need to talk to him. I want him to listen to all the side businesses I'll spin from my future reality show. He'd probably know all about syndication rights too. That's where the money is, or so I've heard.

I dress as fast as I can, then take the elevator to the top floor, where the building's plush gym looks out over the city through a million windows.

When I walk in, he's doing dead lifts, so it's his arms I notice first—massive, rippling with extra muscles that don't even exist in real men. And not to brag, but I've seen a lot of men naked, so I'd know. Sweat glistens on his brow, his eyes so focused and determined that lust hits me like a bolt of lightning.

Lust has also hit the chick on the treadmill, however. She is surreptitiously taking photos of him, which I find deeply irritating. I mean, she doesn't even *know* him.

"He's married," I hiss as I pass. "*FYI.*"

I continue on, wondering what the hell led me to say that. Graham will soon be gone, but I might be sharing an elevator with that woman for years.

Well, she shouldn't be looking at a married man. Even one who isn't wearing a ring.

He sees me and sets the weight down, his brow furrowed in concern. "Are you okay? I assume only an emergency would bring you to a room where people exercise on purpose."

"I'm up here *all the time*," I reply primly, though I've not been here once since my tour of the building, two years prior.

Treadmill Stalker is still watching, so I walk closer than I normally would and press my hand to his chest, the way I might if he were actually mine rather than simply pretending to be. His gaze falls to my hand, and he raises a brow.

"I'm checking your pulse," I tell him. "For the life insurance policy I'm taking out on you."

"That's not where you find a pulse, Keeley."

"Oh, I forget...which one of us went to medical school, Graham? Was it you?"

He smirks. "I wasn't convinced it was either of us until quite recently. So what's up?"

"I'm about to be really famous and I need you to help me figure out what my reality show should be called."

"Reality show," he repeats flatly. "Is this an actual thing or are you just spit-balling again?" He runs a broad hand over his head and it holds there. My nipples tighten simply at the sight of his armpit. This is what I'm reduced to after six months without sex—a woman whose nipples tighten at the sight of male armpit hair.

It's a new low.

"I just got this text," I say, brandishing my phone.

He reads it but fails to swing me in the air with the ecstasy of a lottery winner, which I guess lines up—even if Graham won the lottery, he'd just put it all in a mutual fund and go on about his business.

I reach for my phone. "I didn't call him back yet. I don't want to look too eager."

"Let's hope no one caught you running all the way up here to tell me about it, then." He frowns. "That's really what you want?"

"Of course. It's what *everyone* wants."

I can tell he'd like to argue, but he somehow refrains. "Then I guess you'd better go give the guy a call."

I blink. I wasn't done discussing this with him. I want to get his thoughts on merchandising opportunities, the likelihood that the skincare/makeup world is too oversaturated for yet another celebrity line (A Dose of Dr. C, Dr. C's Corrective Cream...the names honestly write themselves). But he's dismissing me, and he isn't happy, and I hate that his unhappiness is taking away a little of mine.

I return to the apartment and dial Trevor MacNulty's number. I leave a message, sounding politely interested at best.

When Graham finally returns to the apartment, I'm still irritated that he didn't drop his stupid workout to discuss this with me. He is gloriously disheveled. That annoys me even more.

"You look disgusting," I say sourly.

"Oh, do I?" He crosses the kitchen toward me then very intentionally reaches above me for a glass, pressing his sweat-soaked chest to mine, his damp arm grazing my face. I smell his soap, feel his exhale dance over my skin.

He's trying to gross me out but instead, a memory hits me out of nowhere, so sharp I can barely stand it: his weight above mine, his breath on my neck, a low, guttural moan—*Keeley, I'm gonna come, fuck.*

A shiver races up my arms while my stomach tilts and flips, as if I'm a roller coaster hurtling toward the ground.

It definitely happened and I never, ever wanted it to end.

"You okay?" he asks, pulling away. "You suddenly look terrified."

"That was more sweat than I've ever come in contact with at once."

"That says more about you than me. By the way, I chatted with the woman in apartment 701. You apparently told her I was your husband?"

I grab a paper towel and begin brushing his sweat off me. "I'd have said you were my brother but that would make the whole pregnancy bit a little weirder than it is."

His tongue darts out. He is...ever so slightly amused. "I'm not sure you really had to say *anything* to her."

I'm not sure you had to say anything to her either. Why the hell would she tell you what apartment she's in?

I move away, pretending I don't care. I can't believe I'm on the cusp of getting everything I want, and all I can think about is...Graham.

34

GRAHAM

Keeley is pacing the room, talking to MacNulty. She's come alive during this conversation, all laughter and wildly gesturing hands he can't see. When she's like this, she could draw blood from a stone. She could persuade you to give her a TV show. She could persuade you to give her an entire *network* if you had one at your disposal.

She seems to be persuading MacNulty, anyway. The interview time is set, and when she tells him she's got nothing to wear, he says he'll have a stylist send some things for her. It's exactly what Keeley wants—fame, stylists, adulation—and I hate everything about it. I guess that makes me an asshole, but I never believed for a second I *wasn't* one, so the revelation doesn't make much of a dent.

"Our daughter will be famous," she says to me, eyes gleaming. It's one fucking interview, and she's already spun this out into a future as a talk-show host. "Can you imagine? She could, like, be on the Kids' Choice Awards and go glamping with all the little Kardashians in a private jet."

"Yes," I say dryly. "That sounds like just the recipe for developing into an intelligent, emotionally mature adult."

She frowns and stomps away, already casting me in the role her father played...the bad guy, ruining all their fun.

And I will be.

Keeley dreams so vividly she can persuade everyone around her it's real. She makes you believe in a world entirely different from what it is, and then you wake up in a hotel room thinking your whole life has changed and discover you've been ditched with nothing but a marriage certificate and the bill for two wedding rings to show for it.

I imagine it's one more thing she inherited from her mom, that ability to spin things so vividly.

When this interview occurs, they're going to love her. The whole world will love her. How could they not? Keeley lights up every room she enters until she's the only thing you can see. And when all that happens, she'll be endangered. There will be fans and photographers and strangers stopping her in the street. She and our daughter will no longer be safe, and I'll be helpless to stop it.

It feels like history is repeating.

35

KEELEY

I t all happens so fast.

There's a live taping of *Mindy and Mills* Sunday afternoon, outside at The Grove. They bump a child violinist to fit me in, which I should probably feel bad about but...that kid's got his whole life ahead of him while with the O'Keefe genes, I've got another ten years or so if I'm lucky.

A rack of dresses is delivered to the apartment by a stylist, who quickly rules out everything loose because of my height, and everything dark because of my coloring. In the end, we agree on a bright pink dress that has a bit of sixties flair to it— sleeveless, with a rounded collar and a built-in belt that loops just above the baby bump.

Graham is in a foul mood throughout, ignoring me and grunting at the stylist when she greets him. And I've had it... mostly with the being ignored part.

It's late by the time the stylist leaves. He's sitting at the kitchen table on his laptop, acting like I've left too.

I ask if he wants to see the dress we chose, and when he grunts, *"I'm good,"* I finally explode.

"What the hell, dude? My dreams are coming true and you're being a dick."

He shuts his laptop and leans back in his seat, letting his eyes fall closed before he looks at me. "Has it occurred to you how hard life is for celebrities? And how unsafe? Drew Bailey wears a disguise everywhere she goes and still can't walk out her door without getting photographed. A guy scaled a twelve-foot fence and hid in their backyard, for God's sake. If this goes the way you hope, you'll spend the rest of your life in danger."

I laugh. "I'm not going to be Drew Bailey-level famous. Doctors don't get stalkers."

"*You* would," he says morosely. "You're the type of female even someone mentally stable marries on the fly. Imagine what you'd unleash in someone who *wasn't* stable."

I'm tempted to suggest he's not acting all that stable himself at the moment, but I manage to refrain. "Drew manages just fine."

"*Drew* doesn't want to chat with every person she meets," he counters. "She's not hanging out at the bakery for twenty minutes catching up with the cashier. She doesn't stop complete strangers to ask about the meaning of their t-shirts or where they get their hair done."

My eyes sting. "I'm not that bad."

He sighs as he rises, tucking his laptop under his arm as he turns for his room. "I never said you were bad, but I worry every time you walk out the door, and it's about to get worse."

I WAKE on Sunday less excited for what lies ahead than I thought. It's not because what Graham said worries me. My plan is to attain the exact right amount of fame: the sweet spot where I get pretty clothes and Khloe and I are workout buddies, but where I can still do whatever I want and talk to whomever I want, and I'm only recognized when it's convenient for me—like when I need to cut in a line or get a table somewhere.

But—though it was fun having the stylist here and dreaming about it all—the reality is that today isn't going to be especially interesting. I'm not going somewhere to diagnose a crazy skin condition. I'm not even talking about what I know. It's just going to be all about catching a baby on a kitchen floor, and that's a story I'm already tired of.

Graham is off doing one of his extensive, unnecessary, workouts while I putter around in the morning, but when it's time to leave for the studio, I find him waiting.

"I'll drive you," he says. He hasn't shaved since Friday and is in a button-down and jeans. He looks rugged, like an off-duty Secret Service officer.

"That's okay," I tell him. "I have to get hair and makeup done and it's a whole thing."

"I know. I'll stay."

"It will be hours—"

"Keeley, do you *want* to do this alone?"

"No," I admit. I'd feel a little better if he was with me. I think, perhaps, *he'd* feel a little better about it too.

"Then let's go," he says.

HE PLUGS in the address and drives us slowly, safely across town to The Grove. I stare out the window, wondering what my mother would make of this moment and when it's going to feel the way I thought it would. Because I pictured the excitement and the clothes, and I pictured the compliments, like the stylist telling me I was adorable a thousand times yesterday, but what I didn't picture was this strange discomfort that's present at the same time. It's nerves, yes, but it's also this...disconnect. I thought I loved attention—I'm *known* for my love of attention —but this is the wrong kind.

Graham parks and walks me to the back door of the building, which temporarily serves as a hair and makeup/greenroom. We take a glass-walled elevator upstairs, through which we can see the entire crowd waiting.

"Wow," I whisper.

"Are you okay?" Graham asks.

"That's a lot of people."

I wait for some kind of admonishment from him, but it doesn't come. Instead, he reaches over and wraps his hand around mine. His palm is large and warm and dry, while mine is sweaty and cold and small. Nothing has ever felt better.

"It's all going to be okay," he says.

I blink back tears. He's going to be a really good dad. He's going to make someone a really good husband.

I can see clearly the life he'll have with her, this mystery female he'll one day marry. It will be intensely boring. They'll eat in all the time and she won't buy an olive-green suede trench coat that costs as much as their mortgage on a whim. They won't go to Cabo for the weekend. They'll live in a house like Ben and Gemma's, and they'll grill in the backyard while our daughter plays in the pool.

It's the childhood I would have had, probably, if my mom and I hadn't been so busy dreaming about fame and fortune. How strange that I might be on my way to those things at last, only to find myself dreaming about the boring life Graham will have with someone else.

Upstairs, everyone gushes over me: *"your hair is so thick, your lashes are so long, your baby bump is so cute."* Ice water and snacks are procured. Both Mills and Mindy pop by on their way outside, bubbling over with excitement about the interview, and my video, telling me how impressive I am.

I gush back, of course, claiming I'm thrilled to be here. But out the windows I see thousands of people, and when I close my eyes for the makeup artist, I dream of being anywhere else.

Graham is sitting far across the room, reading on his phone, probably bored and irritated. I send him a text.

Me: You can go.

In the mirror our eyes meet. Whatever he sees in my face makes him smile as he texts me back.

Graham: I want to stay.

Thank God. I need him here and I have no idea why. It's as if this whole experience is a stormy sea, and he's my one bit of dry land.

The roar of the crowd as the show begins is deafening. My head jerks and the makeup artist laughs. "Don't worry. They get worked into a frenzy when we do these shows on location. It's crazy."

I'm not sure why she thinks I'd find that comforting.

When I'm finally allowed to get out of the chair, one of the producers is waiting to lead me to the stage.

Graham crosses the room to us, determined to stay by my side as long as possible, and I don't know if I want to smile or cry. I'm scared if I do either, I'll ruin my makeup.

I wish he'd grab my hand like he did in the elevator, but that moment seems to be over.

We make our way downstairs, through a hall, and then... outdoors. The walkway to the stage is cordoned off, but just to the other side of the barricade is a solid wall of people. I realize they're not here for me—they simply want to say they saw Mindy and Mills in person and perhaps get on camera themselves—but none of this is what I wanted. I don't like what I'm doing here, but I wouldn't want to be the hosts either, facing a massive, faceless crowd of people they'll never get to meet.

I turn to Graham, swallowing down my panic. "I guess I'll see you afterward."

He hears the uncertainty in my voice, and though he's clearly tense, he leans down, his lips right beside my ear. "In an hour, you'll be back home. I'll order us both steak frites and we'll watch the movie about the kidnapper. You'll think it's sexy and I'll be horrified by your taste but a little turned on. Focus on that."

Warmth rushes through me. There are ten employees here whose job is to make me feel cared for, but it's this, it's Graham knowing just what I need to hear—or maybe the idea of Graham turned on—that actually succeeds.

"Will you give me back my sweatshirt?"

"Now you're pushing it," he growls, and when I laugh, he does too.

I climb the stairs to the stage as I'm introduced and there's a roar from the crowd, which is so vast I can't even stand to look.

I make it to my seat without tripping. Mindy and Mills both exclaim over the video again and then start asking questions: *Was I scared? What went through my head? Do I now get free chicken tikka for life?*

I chat away, smiling, making jokes, but I feel like I've been kicked into a higher gear than I'm meant to go in—electrified, but not in the *"this is where I was always meant to be"* way I expected. It's more like my body is flooded with something toxic, something that can't be good for me or my daughter. I'm sweating, my heart is racing, my core temperature way above normal.

This is what my mother wanted for us: the attention, the adulation, people saying some version of, "Keeley, how are you so amazing?" and all I want in the entire world is to get the fuck off this stage, to have it behind me. Even if they were lauding me for something that warrants it—my current breast size, for instance—I still would hate this. And if I hate the thing I thought I wanted most, then what, exactly, is left?

"Guess what?" asks Mindy. "We found a *second* video of you."

I stiffen—if I got married while drunk and forgot, I could easily be on film doing a whole lot of stuff I *wish* I could forget. I breathe a sigh of relief when the clip plays on the screen behind us and Zuma Beach comes into focus. We were surfing there when this guy got a nasty cut on his shin—clear down to the bone. I used the leash of his board as a tourniquet, which was really all I could do until the paramedics got there.

So it's fine that they have the clip, but I had no idea I was being filmed, and I wish I hadn't been. They're making me out to look like some doctor superhero who runs around LA looking for people to assist, rather than what I am: a very lazy girl who just wanted to surf and eat chicken tikka masala in peace and was compelled to intervene because of a medical degree she sort of regretted possessing on both occasions.

"Honestly, it was just a very uncomplicated delivery," I tell them. "And anyone could have done what I did with the leash."

"Isn't she cute?" Mills asks the crowd. "You're so *humble*."

If she had any idea how many times I've thought my ass looks amazing in the Zuma Beach video, she'd *know* I'm not humble.

At last, it's over. I step off the stage, sweaty and dazed, over-wrought. I used to drink when I felt this way, and I'm not sure what to do with it now that I can't.

No, I *do* know: I want Graham. He's waiting at the other end of the walkway, but before I can reach him, Trevor is standing in front of me.

"You were fantastic!" he says. "Come with us to La Piazza. There's a private party afterward for the cast and crew, lots of Mills's celeb friends coming too. It'll be a good chance for us all to talk about the future."

I have no desire to talk about the future, but I know I should go. I can't abandon my mother's dreams for me based on a five-minute interview. But Graham and I had a plan, and the truth is...I sort of wanted that too. No, *not* sort of. I *really* wanted that too.

"Sure," I say. "Let me just talk to Graham."

He pulls out his phone. "I'll call over now to put your name on the list."

I make my way through the chute to where Graham stands. He's got a brow raised as if he already knows what I'm going to ask. "There's a party at La Piazza," I say. "Trevor invited us."

He glances out across the square toward the restaurant. "How the hell are you even supposed to get there?"

I shrug. "We'll just cut through the crowd."

His nostrils flare. "Keeley, are you serious right now? You were just on stage. You can't just go walk through that crowd."

He's being ridiculous. If I can make my way all the way from the main stage at SXSW to the back without my top on, I can walk through a crowd of middle-aged tourists who've already forgotten me. "Graham, did I suddenly turn into Beyoncé? No one is going to care."

"This is a *really* bad idea."

"Come *on*," I groan. "It'll go fast. I don't even want this job, but if I miss a chance to meet Khloe Kardashian, I'll never forgive you."

I head toward the main exit, certain he'll follow. As I walk through the doors, I hear Mindy and Mills wrapping up the show, which means I'll barely even have to push—the whole crowd will be leaving in a second anyway. I begin to cut through and someone says, "Oh my God, you're the doctor!"

I smile. "That's me!" I'd love to keep chatting but there's a fifty percent chance of Graham having a public tantrum if I actually stop. I keep moving as the show comes to its end, waving to people who recognize me, and I'm over halfway across the plaza when someone jumps in my path.

"Can I get your autograph?" the woman asks. She's so

excited and eager that I don't have the heart to remind her I'm no one.

"Um, sure? Do you have a pen?"

She starts to fish through her bag, but the mere act of us stopping like this has drawn everyone's attention. They were all in *agreement* that I was a nobody, and now the crowd is rethinking it based on one woman's bad judgement. God, what must life be like for Mindy and Mills? They can't walk to Starbucks in the morning without makeup. They can't go to a grocery store and buy donuts and Froot Loops. They can't chill with a friend who sleeps outside their building.

A circle forms around us, and someone else says they want an autograph, too, and then behind them the people who were dispersing suddenly turn to surround us, hoping to see someone famous.

It could turn bad really fast—which is precisely why Graham didn't want me to do this. I'm no one, but there are hundreds of people here who can't even see me but will push and fight simply to find out for themselves.

I look behind me for Graham but he isn't there. Some part of me was assuming he'd fix anything that went wrong, and he probably knew that. I put myself in danger, I put our baby in danger, and then I told him he had no say in the matter...while expecting him to magically extricate me if things went awry. It was so stupid, and so unfair.

The crowd keeps pushing as I sign the first autograph, and the second.

I see no way to get to the restaurant now. I'm surrounded on all sides. My hands drop to my stomach as if that can protect my daughter when it obviously can't. If the crowd keeps pushing, we'll be crushed to death, and these idiots will still be shouting, "*Who is it?*" and pulling out their phones.

I turn again. "Graham?" I shout, and it's only when I hear

the panic in my own voice that I realize how scared I am, how desperate I am to be out of here, away from all this. Two seconds later, he's knocking people out of the way with a violence I didn't know he was capable of, and when he reaches me, I press my face to his chest.

I half expect him to respond poorly, to say, "*I told you this would happen!*", but instead his arms band around me as if he knows. "Are you okay?" he asks against my ear.

I shake my head. I'm not and this right here—his chest under my nose and the smell of his skin and his soap—feels like safety, better than everything else I thought I wanted combined. "Make this go away," I whisper.

"Okay," he says, and then he's got me against him and we're shoving through the crowd.

A guy grabs my arm and Graham's got the guy by the throat with his left hand while still holding onto me with his right.

"Drop her arm," he barks in a tone no sane man would defy, and the guy does. Holding me close, he continues to move us forward, ready to extinguish anything that gets in our way, and when we finally near the restaurant's entrance he glances at me.

I'm still shaking. I couldn't show up like this if I wanted to, and I don't even want to. "Let's just go," I whisper.

He pulls me over to the side of the building where a few limos are idling, and throws the door open of the first one we reach.

"Hey!" shouts the driver. "You can't—"

"She's pregnant," Graham barks, "and this is an emergency. So you can drive, or you can call the cops, but we're not getting out of this fucking car the way things are at the moment."

I bury my head against his chest, thanking God he came with me and that he was so...so *Graham*. So fierce, so protective, so unrelenting.

And some ancient part of me says, *"Keeley, you knew this is who he was. You chose him because of this."*

"Thank you," I whisper.

"Of course," he says, then he gives the driver my address.

"We still need to get your car," I remind him.

He swallows. "I just want you home first, okay?" His hand stretches over his eyes as his thumb and middle finger press to opposite temples. "Fuck, Keeley. That...could have been bad."

He stares out the window for the rest of the ride home, his jaw locked tight. I've never seen him this stressed, not even when I told him I was pregnant, and I don't know how to break through the ice surrounding him right now.

I'm quiet too, because the one thing I thought I wanted...I definitely don't want. Did I blindly adopt my mother's hopes and dreams? I think maybe I did. And then I blindly pursued medicine simply to prove Shannon wrong. I probably could have used some therapy when my mom died, because as it stands, I don't know if there's anything I've done in my life that's actually authentic, that wasn't inspired by spite or sorrow or sheer childlike enthusiasm.

When we get to the apartment, I kick off my heels and go to the kitchen. "Are you hungry?" I ask. "I can make a mean grilled cheese. Well, I can start one and you'll take over when you smell it burning, but my intentions are good."

His smile is so small it's barely there. "I'm fine, thanks. Go to bed."

Except he's not fine. I can tell he's not fine, and how do I insist? How do I convince him that if he'd just let me in, it would all be better? That's never been how he operates.

He goes to his room and I sit on the couch, feeling like a failure in every possible way. I just risked our child's life. I made Graham so upset he can't even look at me, and I have no idea what I am even supposed to dream about now that I don't want the things I did. How am I supposed to swing for the fences when I don't even know which fence I'm swinging toward?

I stare at Graham's door. I can't fix what I did tonight, and I'm not going to solve my career issues in the hour before bed, but I can at least apologize. Because none of it would have happened if I'd just listened to him.

I cross the room, tapping on his door before I enter. He's fully dressed, and appears to be pacing.

He stares at me as if he's furious and lost at the same time.

"Graham, I'm sorry," I whisper.

He regards me for another moment. Probably only a second but it feels longer.

"This was all my fault and I know you're mad, but if you'll just tell me how to fix this, I—"

He takes two long steps, moving toward me so fast my words stop short and I instinctively step back.

And then his hands are on my face, cradling my jaw then sliding into my hair. I expected him to be mad, to punish me for this, and I have no idea what's happening right now.

His mouth lands on mine, his kiss demanding and desperate at once, and I am no longer confused. He was scared, and this is what he needs to reassure himself.

He needed *me*. And I needed him too.

He groans, his hands sliding down my sides to grip my ass and pull me closer.

His mouth, his grip, his urgency...it shuts down everything in my head but the most primitive impulses. I want him so much that my hands are shaking, and my breath is coming in small pants. If there was a magic spell to undress us both, head to toe, I'd already have released it.

My palms land on his chest then slide up around his neck, and I know I've lived this exact moment before: the moment of realizing how much he'd been holding himself back and feeling overwhelmed by it, feeling as if there was just...*too much of him,* and wanting it anyway.

I untuck his shirt.

He breaks the kiss only long enough to wrench it overhead and hurl it to the floor. "Take off the dress."

I think of my body the way it is now—the stretch marks, my swollen breasts lined with fine blue veins, the seven-month swell of a human being pushing out from beneath my skin. "I—"

Before I can think of an excuse, his hands are on my hips. "Take off the fucking dress," he growls. "I want to see."

That edge in his voice, that barely restrained desire, makes me bolder. Even if I'm not the girl I was last winter, I get the feeling it doesn't matter to him. That, impossibly, the current version of me is every bit as hot to him as the previous one might have been.

I lift my dress overhead and his eyes fall to my sheer lace bra.

"Fuck," he groans. "You didn't return the bra."

I glare at him. "Are you seriously bitching about my spending *now*?"

He holds my breasts in his hands, as if taking stock of their weight. "No." He bends lower. "I want you to buy a hundred more." His mouth closes around my nipple, and I let out a strangled moan.

It hurts and feels amazing in a way it never has before, and I'm not sure if it's pregnancy or him, or the fact that I haven't had sex in many, many months, but I'm pretty sure I could come from this alone.

"God, Graham, I want you to never stop doing that."

He laughs against my skin. "No? You're sure?" And then one hand is slipping between my legs.

"*Oh*, maybe not," I whisper.

My skin is hot. His palm is cool and rough, drawing goose

bumps as it slides up, up, up to find me wet, already close to coming.

"Jesus Christ," he growls. "Get on the bed."

That he isn't being *polite*, that he's simply taking the things he wants, has me clenching, desperate for his fingers...or something else. The second I sit, he's on his knees, spreading my thighs. He pulls my panties off to the side and then there's one slow, glorious slide up to my clit, his tongue moving in small tight circles as two fingers push inside me.

"I want you to pull my hair when you come," he says.

Not *if* you come. *When.*

He's got not a moment's doubt about the outcome here, nor do I.

My palm slides into his hair. "God. Keep doing that."

My panties are removed, and then his flickering tongue becomes harder, more pointed against my swollen clit. His fingers inside me curl inward, and I'm gripping his hair not because he asked but because I'm already *close* and he's barely begun.

"I've come a hundred times thinking about this," he growls against my skin.

Oh God. The idea of him coming while imagining this makes me feel like I've just been kicked up another gear.

"*Ohhh*...that," I whisper. "With your fingers. That's—"

He moans, the sound clearly involuntary, and I just explode, throwing my head back, the entire world disappearing. I want to tell him how good this is, how much I needed it, and how badly I want him inside me right now—but all I can do is tug at his hair. "Graham," I groan, "*fuck.*"

It's a long minute before my eyes open and I realize how entirely selfish I've been. He has the feral look of someone who's been pushed too far.

I love it.

"Stand up," I command, and he does, watching as I tug on

his belt and then slide to my knees, pulling his boxers and pants down as I go. He hisses as I take him, swollen and throbbing, in my hand. *No wonder I was so sore.*

"Jesus, you're big. It'll be like trying to put my lips around the head of a Coke can."

His quiet laugh is cut off by the first flick of my tongue, and as I pull him into my mouth and moan, he stiffens and gasps. "Keeley, stop."

I release him. "You don't want me to?"

He winces. "Just the sight of you on your knees asking me that question is enough to make me come."

"I thought that was the point."

"The point is for me not to come in two seconds flat, which is something you'd never let me live down."

I fight a smile. "That does sound like the kind of thing I'd dwell on, yes. Do you want me to talk about the patient I killed when I was a resident?"

His gaze holds mine. "Yes, but not now. Also, if I remain hard while you describe someone dying, I'm going to creep us both out."

My gaze drifts to his lovely, sizable cock.

"I'm going back in," I warn him. "Think about something unsexy. Calculate how much I could have invested if I hadn't bought all those designer bags."

He gasps again as I slide him into my mouth. "I've already done that calculation in Excel."

I laugh against him, my hand rising to cup his balls then slide around his shaft.

My mouth will definitely require some help here.

"Do it hard," he says, wrapping his hand around mine for a moment. The bossiness in his voice is sudden, sparked by hunger. He's no longer reticent—he's hell-bent on coming, and this burst of selfishness from him has me soaking wet. This is the real Graham, unrestrained and demanding and laid bare for me.

I give him what he asks for, my tongue laving him while I let the pressure of my mouth suck him in, farther and farther until he's jerking his hips forward, involuntarily, hitting the back of my throat. My gag reflex triggers, and I ignore it.

"Fuck yes," he says. "God, I just felt the back of your throat. I'm never going to recover from this."

His thighs tense and then shake. I increase the strength of my grip, which is probably how he grips himself when he's alone, and the thought of it has me so wet I'm now desperate.

Inexplicably, he seems to get *bigger*.

"Oh Christ, Keeley, I'm gonna...I want—"

I get the briefest hit of salt on my tongue and then he's pulling out, grasping himself as he paints my chest and neck.

He's breathing heavily, eyes barely open, just taking in the sight. "Sorry," he says.

I laugh. "Yeah, you look really sorry."

He grins. "Okay, yeah, I'm not. I've jerked off many times, picturing that."

My head tilts and I smile. "I figured you for the type who'd want me to swallow."

He gives a low groan. "Yeah. That too. I've pictured a whole lot of things. Let me clean you up."

I climb to my feet while he goes to the bathroom, returning with a damp washcloth to gently wipe up the mess he made.

"Did you really kill someone when you were a resident?" he asks.

I laugh. "I failed to revive someone. Does that count?"

"I wouldn't have lost my erection."

I smile. "I'd probably bring that up on occasion."

"Publicly."

"Not, like, into a microphone at your brother's wedding. Maybe at lunch with your mom, though."

He gives a quiet laugh. "About what I expected."

My nipple tightens as he brushes over it, and his eyes flutter closed. I'm not done. I wonder if he isn't either. I'm thoroughly clean, but he's still sliding the washcloth over my skin. My body arches toward him against my will, but I guess I should politely extract myself and—

His hand slides between my legs. "You're so goddamned wet. Don't even try to tell me you're done."

I want to open my eyes but his fingers are *perfect*. "No, but I assume you are."

He pulls my hand to his cock, which is already hard again. "What do you think?"

"I think you must be subbing out with an identical twin because there's no way you got hard again that fast." I grip him tight, the way he likes, and air hisses between his teeth.

"You clearly have no idea how many times I've thought about this. I want to come inside you. Is that okay?"

The question alone has me clenching around his fingers.

"Nothing you haven't done before, apparently." I glance down at my stomach. "Though I'm not sure how we do this, under the circumstances."

He gently pushes me onto the bed, his mouth curving on one side. "Believe me...I've given this way too much thought."

He crawls between my spread thighs, leaning over me to grab a pillow. "Raise up," he commands before wedging it beneath me.

He grasps himself, staying on his knees as he lines up with my entrance. If he hadn't just made me come, I think the fit would be too tight. But he slides in slowly, inch by inch, bracing himself over me with his eyes squeezed shut.

It's exquisite.

It's too much.

I want more.

"You don't have to go slow for me," I whisper breathlessly. "I'm okay. I'm not going to come again."

His laugh sounds pained. "Keeley, you're definitely coming again, but I'm not doing this for you. I'm doing this so I don't lose it way too fast. I just want it to last."

I hold his gaze as he pushes in again, more quickly. And again. I clench around him as my muscles tighten.

"Fuck," he gasps. His eyes fall closed. "I'm going to come so fucking hard, Keeley."

Oh *God*.

There is nothing more thrilling to me than watching Graham fight for control. His thrusts take on a rhythm now, faster, as if involuntary. And he was right; I am going to come again. Like a car without brakes, there's only one outcome left for us both. I become distantly aware of my own voice whispering to him, urging him on. Breathy, desperate. *Yes, God, just like that. Oh, God, don't stop, Graham I'm close and—*

I fall apart with a sharp, sudden cry, and he gasps again, grunting as he lets go at last.

He's still inside me when my eyes open, his eyes studying my face as if I'm a favorite photograph he's saying goodbye to. As if he can't stand to look away.

My heart squeezes tight. Were it up to Graham, we might happily stay like this for the foreseeable future. And *oh my God*, I can picture that, all too easily: the two of us continuing on the way we have, making dinner, watching TV, and taking care of a baby while having endless, increasingly athletic sex. It's more delicious, more compelling, than any dream I've ever had. But that would just make it all harder in the end; if we break up or if I succumb to the O'Keefe curse, it'll just make it all harder.

"You need to stop thinking," he says, his hand pressing to my cheek, commanding me to look at him. "Which is something I never thought I'd have to ask of you."

I laugh, biting down on the words I want to say: *"Do you promise not to hate me now that this has happened? Can we make things go back to normal?"*

He pulls out at last and falls to the other side of me, his palm on my stomach. The baby kicks, right beneath his hand, a tiny fluttering like a butterfly edging along the sides of a hedge.

"Was that her?" he asks. He's felt this before, but never just...spontaneously. And not when I'm this far along. He pulls himself up onto his elbow, staring at my stomach.

"Little Kalamity does not like being woken from her slumber, I guess."

He laughs. "You're *not* naming her that."

I wish I could stay here and suggest increasingly outlandish names, names—I've been keeping a list on my phone for just such a moment. I wish I could doze off with his hand on my stomach and wake to find him still asleep, face sweet in repose. I'd just stare at him, the way I did the night I climbed into his bed with Lola, and marvel at the perfection of his nose, how boyish a face as angular as his can look at rest.

I'd like to wake in the morning to find us tucked together like two spoons so I could rub up against him until he couldn't stand not to slide back inside me. Afterward, he'd want me to eat something gross, and I'd whine until he went to the bakery and got me a muffin.

But that's the life of a different kind of girl—the kind who stays around—and it would hurt one or both of us so fucking much when I couldn't do it.

I fake a yawn and stretch before I slide away from him and start gathering my clothes. He watches me and doesn't argue. Which is good. I don't want him to turn into the tedious guy who argues.

"I'm gonna go," I tell him.

His eyes drift over my face, a half-second of indecision. I guess I wouldn't mind if he argued a *little* bit.

"Sleep well," he replies.

I go to my own room and climb into bed, wishing I could have stayed. And suddenly a memory hits me out of nowhere:

sometime, during our first night together, he'd pulled me against him and asked if I was thinking about how to sneak away.

"Actually," I'd said, *"I'm thinking you should marry me, and we should have a billion kids."*

It was me. This whole fucking thing was my idea. Possibly even the kid.

36

KEELEY

I wake, worried sick over what I'm in for this morning. Yes, there's the question of whether or not I'm about to get fired—especially once they hear I went onto *Mindy and Mills*—but my most pressing concern is Graham.

I've been in this position before and I know how it unfolds: men laud you for being "laid back" about sex at *first*. *"Yeah, I'm not looking for serious either,"* the guy says, but then he randomly shows up where you work, or texts you forty times in a row while liking every one of your Instagram posts, and has his publicist or assistant call for him when you haven't replied. Eventually, when you realize he's not getting the hint, you politely explain to him that you're just really busy right now— that's when he freaks out and calls you a fucking whore.

So, yes, I'm expecting the worst when I walk out of my room dressed for work. Perhaps not the texts, or stalking, but at least some puppy-dog eyes and tension. A terse *"when will you be home?"* at the very least. And he still needs his car—the long drive to the studio will almost certainly entail some dreary talk about feelings, blah blah blah.

Graham is just getting off one of his East Coast calls—I hear mentions of artificial organs and Russian wheat futures—as I'm finishing up with Mark's toast. He walks in, clean shaven, wearing a button-down and tie. The man was *made* to wear a tie. If I weren't so desperate to avoid him, I'd yank his mouth to mine with that tie and pull him down to the floor seconds later. The sounds he made last night—him saying, *"do it hard"* and *"I've come a hundred times thinking about this"*—play in my head, and I squeeze my thighs together as I try to forget.

He moves toward me and puts the butter and jam in the fridge as if it's any other day. I see no hint of strain in his face whatsoever. I focus on his long, capable fingers before forcing my gaze away.

"I know we need to get your car," I begin. "If you can wait until lunch I can—"

He shakes his head. "I picked it up a few hours ago, but take a lunch break anyway." He moves to the other side of the counter and pulls Mark's toast toward him. "I can take it down today. I need to tell him he was right about shorting Tesla."

I watch, astonished, as he leaves with Mark's toast and paper. I'm still waiting for...*something*. A longing look, some tension or upheaval. There was nothing at all, as if he forgot, and who could forget *me*? I'm amazing in bed.

At least I used to be. *No, I'm definitely still amazing in bed.*

That it ended too quickly for me to show off any skills is hardly my fault. But I can't believe we recovered from it all so easily. I guess we were both just scratching an itch, and that it was fucking fantastic isn't even relevant. No matter how good it is to scratch an itch, you're better off just, you know, not having an itch in the first place.

And I don't. I'm all squared away, and so is he. I mean, maybe I'm not a *hundred percent* squared away, but whatever.

I should be ecstatic.

I *am* ecstatic, I'm sure. It's just buried under all this disappointment.

~

ON THE WAY TO WORK, I swing by the bakery and get three Sunday muffins—one for myself and one for Mark since we missed out yesterday. A third for Trinny because she's probably earned one by now and will likely endure a whole lot of attitude from our bosses this week.

As will I.

A *Mindy and Mills* appearance is probably the kind of thing I was supposed to run by them first. I knew it even at the time—it's just that I wanted what Trevor MacNulty was offering more. And now I don't, which leaves me stuck at a job I hate with two bosses who are going to be very, very pissed off. I can't believe I might be forced to grovel to remain there now.

I deposit the muffin in front of Trinny but she looks more concerned than pleased.

"What's this for? Oh my God, this thing is...is it a muffin or is it candy?"

"Don't judge," I tell her. "But if we call it a muffin, we can pretend it's healthy."

"I wouldn't say muffins are—"

"Don't ruin this for me," I warn, waving a finger at her.

I send an email to both Fox and Joliet, notifying them about *Mindy and Mills*, which airs this afternoon, relieved neither of them will be in for a while so I don't have to hear about it. It's eleven before Dr. Fox appears at my office door.

"Are you serious?" she demands, holding her phone aloft. "You went onto a nationally televised broadcast as a representative of this practice without running it by us first? You had no business—"

"Where I work was never discussed," I reply, enjoying the irritation on her face far more than I should.

"So you just lost the practice a very valuable opportunity to get some good publicity."

I meant to grovel. I really did. But I've seen ten patients already and she's just walking in, and I know for a fact that she'll be cutting out of here long before rush hour, leaving me to handle all the last-minute additions this afternoon. "If it's a problem to say I'm with the practice and a problem if I don't, what did you want? Is there any way I could come out of this having *not* displeased you?"

She stares at me, her arms now folded across her chest. She expected an apology and isn't sure how to react in its absence.

Her brow raises. "Since you don't seem to care about this job, you should probably start looking for a new one," she finally says, glancing at my stomach. "Good luck finding anything *now*."

Great. Just fucking great.

Why didn't I grovel? I sigh as I rise from my desk to see my next patient. I should probably be calling Gemma, but the truth is Graham is the only one I want to talk to. To vent, and possibly to rest my head against his chest the way I did last night. Perhaps, even, to climb into his bed and pick up where we left off, though obviously I'm not going to do that.

I spend the rest of the day counting the minutes until I can talk to him, but when I get to the apartment, he is on his way out. "Dinner's in the fridge if you're hungry," he says, distracted. "Colin and Mandy had a fight so I'm meeting him out."

I stare at him, feeling lost. I wanted him to solve *my* problems, to make it all better. I wanted him to act like a boyfriend, basically, while refusing to give him any of the benefits of actually being one. "Is there anything I can do?" I ask.

He glances up at me from his phone. "Just eat something, okay?"

"Sure," I reply, pretending to be nonchalant.

I was so busy worrying about Graham's reaction after we slept together...it never occurred to me I might need to worry a little bit about myself.

I ignore dinner and go downstairs to bring Mark his muffin. "Sorry it's a day late," I tell him.

He grins. "You know how many carbs are in this thing? You should be apologizing for getting me addicted to them in the first place."

"How have you been, anyway? I feel like ever since Graham moved in and work got busy, I barely see you."

He smiles. "Things are real good, Keeley. Seems like they're good for you too."

My eyes widen. Graham wouldn't have told him we slept together, would he? That's the kind of oversharing *I'd* be prone to, not him.

"What do you mean?"

"You and Graham. I can tell it's changed. The things you used to tell me...you now tell him. Which is exactly how it should be."

"It's not like we're a couple," I say quickly. "He's still leaving for New York once the baby's born."

Mark glances at me through one eye. "You're definitely a couple, whether you're calling it that or not."

"We aren't. You know I don't want that."

He nods, staring off into the distance for a moment. "Did I ever tell you I used to own a '59 Les Paul?"

I put my chin in my hand. "I don't know what that is, but it sounds exclusive so now I want one."

He laughs. "It's a guitar. A really good guitar. But the fucked-up thing was I barely played guitar. I didn't need to blow two hundred grand on anything, much less that, but I was trying to convince myself that...it was all worth it."

"That *what* was worth it?"

"The hours I worked, the pressure. This panic begins anytime the market dips. Your investors get scared and start calling you, and if enough of them call and you can't talk them down, you're fucked. Or you take some gamble, certain it's going to pay off, and discover you've lost billions. So anyway, buying stuff—stupid stuff I didn't need—was how I convinced myself it was worth it."

I love Mark, but he's a little heavy-handed with the allegories. *Irrelevant* allegories, as I wasn't even talking about shopping for once.

"Is this your way of saying I wanted that Birkin because I'm empty inside and trying to justify it? Because I love my Birkin. Every time I carry it, I feel like a shiny little jewel on my way to better things."

"I loved my guitar too. Same reason. But you know what the most freeing moment of my entire life was? When I stood on the ledge of my building and realized I didn't *have* to jump. That I could just fucking walk away."

I blink. Sure, I realized Mark's life hadn't been a bed of roses leading up to this moment, but I kind of thought he'd *grown into* the person he is. Like a man who figures shit out and joins a Buddhist monastery, with this busy corner of central LA his ashram.

"I don't understand what you're trying to tell me," I reply. "I can't walk away from anything. I'm having a kid."

"But that's just it, Keels," he says. "You've spent your whole life jumping because you're so terrified of what happens if you don't. And now you're stuck on that metaphorical ledge, telling yourself you want to jump when maybe you just need to ask yourself why sticking around terrifies you as much as it does."

"Sometimes I think you're too smart for us to be friends. If you'd explain stuff using examples from reality TV, I'd probably understand you better."

He laughs. "You'll figure it out. But I'll try to come up with an example using the Kardashians for next time."

I go back upstairs, sadder than I was and no less confused. I don't entirely understand what he was saying to me and yet...I sort of do. I have spent many, many years trying not to get too close to anyone, but now it's happened, almost by accident. I love this baby. And I think I might love Graham.

If I gave him the baby and walked away simply to avoid being devastated later on...I'd be devastated anyway. If I discover in a year that I've got cancer, am I going to be *glad* I didn't spend that year with him? Will it be a relief that he never knew how I felt? That I never allowed myself just to fall head over heels for him?

No. Of course it won't.

I want him with me, for every second I've got left. And I guess this is what Mark was saying: maybe my path is simply to step off the ledge and face all the pain that's going to come with living a life I love. In the end, I might be glad I did.

But I don't even know if that's what Graham wants—he's sure not acting like our night meant much to him—and the not-knowing is so awkward, so painful.

I'm glad he's not on Instagram. I'd probably be on there, liking every one of his posts, until I could figure out how to ask.

～

HE COMES IN LATE. I stumble across my room in the dark, half-asleep, wanting to see him and check on him and maybe tell him all the things I fell asleep thinking. He's standing by the sink, drinking a glass of water. His Adam's apple—which is actually just thyroid cartilage surrounding the larynx—bobs as he drinks.

It's my favorite thyroid cartilage in the entire world.

"Hey," he says, looking up, frowning. "Sorry. I didn't mean to wake you."

You can always wake me, Graham. I want to see you. I miss you when you're gone.

I'm not telling him that. Especially when he looks so wary, the way I do when I know a guy is about to say too much and

I'm thinking *please don't do this. Don't profess your feelings when I'm about to ask if we can take a break.* "It's okay. How's Colin?"

He runs a hand over his head. "Not great. He thinks she's got cold feet."

The old Keeley would come alive at drama like this. I'd race to the counter and climb on a stool, placing my chin in my hands as I said, *"tell me everything!"* I'd pry and pry, doing my best to get Graham to admit he doesn't like Mandy, or to reveal something shady Colin did that brought this on. I'd suggest Mandy is cheating, and he'd accuse me of enjoying other people's tragedy too much, which is completely true and about which I would be wildly unrepentant.

But the realizations I've had over the past day or two about myself and Graham have thrown me into internal disarray. I find myself tongue-tied, a big tub of awkward as I try to find a path between being the old me and being the girl who begs a guy to like her back.

"The crib's being delivered Friday," I say, struggling to meet his eye. When have I ever struggled to meet someone's eye? "They left a message. Can you let them in?"

He stills. "I'm actually leaving for New York Friday. Did they give you a window?"

"*New York?*"

He never goes to New York. He's been here for months without going back once, but suddenly *now* a visit is a necessity?

"I have a few loose ends to take care of, and as we get closer to your due date it'll be harder to go." He's looking off to the left, which is a sign of evasiveness. I learned this from *Criminal Minds*, not med school, so it's definitely true.

And what loose ends? With technology, no meetings actually *have* to take place in person, and the only loose ends I can think of that demand a face-to-face are personal ones. Is it Anna? And is he doing this for closure, or is he doing this because she's a loose end he might want to pick back up, now that the end is in sight?

God, did sleeping with me make him realize how good he had it with her?

My mouth opens but I can't think of a way to ask without sounding like a jealous harpy.

"Go back to bed, Keeley," he says softly. "It's late." Even hearing the word *bed* fall from his lips is a turn-on for me.

My gaze lingers on him for a moment, and something shifts between us. His eyes are suddenly hazy in a way that looks a lot like interest. But he's turning toward his room before I can even say a word.

Maybe I can pretend I'm going into labor so he misses his flight. That, to me, sounds like an entirely reasonable way to handle this situation. And a lot easier than admitting I don't want him to go.

37

GRAHAM

"**W**e've got a problem," says Ben on Tuesday, and I want to put my fist through a wall.

I've got enough problems as it is, thanks. My second-in-command just quit, which means I've got to leave for New York in the morning rather than Friday afternoon...at the exact moment when it feels *vital* that I stay here and get shit straightened out with Keeley. I could see it on her face last night—she is ready to pull the plug on our arrangement. The crib's coming and she needs me out to get the room ready, and what the hell happens then? It feels like my life is about to implode, and I don't need more Tate family bullshit on top of it all.

"What's up?" I ask.

"Colin and Mandy broke up, and the idiot told Mom already."

Fuck. Tate family bullshit it is.

Colin was a newborn the first time things in our life went sideways, and he wasn't around the second time because his *departure* was what made them turn that way. It was the incident that would eventually help him straighten his shit out, but running off with a girl when he was eighteen and getting thrown in a Colorado jail seemed like the end of the world at the time, especially to our mother.

She never wanted him to know how badly she fell apart. Maybe we should have told him anyway.

"Is she okay?" I ask, pinching my nose. Keeley and I need one normal evening, just to get us back where we were. I have to at least tell her I'm leaving in the morning.

"Of course she's not okay," Ben says. "She's blaming herself. Walter wants her to check in somewhere and she's refusing because she wants 'to be there for Colin this time'. Can you go see her? I can't get back to California until Thursday."

I agree, of course, because the idea of my mom suffering is unbearable to me. She's already suffered so much, and most of it was my fault.

38

KEELEY

I want the phrase *"no good deed goes unpunished"* to be written on my grave.

Here's the score, so far: I stopped drinking and got a real grown-up job. I started saving money and eating salad. I missed out on some well-earned chicken tikka and ruined a very nice pair of shoes to bring a life into the world. And I'm pretty sure I'm now in love with the father of my child, which doesn't necessarily sound laudable but is way less villainous than previous Keeley iterations.

What do I get in exchange for all this virtuousness? Graham, probably rekindling his relationship with Anna, and Fox making work so unpleasant that no sane person would stay. I'm double-booked all day. I've got no lunch break, and my last scheduled patient is coming in at seven-thirty, which means my last *actual* patient will be arriving an hour after that.

And the really shitty thing—well, there are several really shitty things, of which this is one—is that we are flooded with calls from new patients asking for me. If I'd planned for all this in advance, I'd have gone off on my own before *Mindy and Mills* ever aired. I doubt any sane bank would have given me the start-up money for office space and equipment, but I picture it anyway: something modern and glamorous, where I've stolen Trinny and my favorite nurse and we all work reasonable hours.

But that's an ideal scenario...and it still falls flat. Even in a perfect situation, I'd still be stuck seeing one patient after another whose greatest complaint is that she's starting to look old.

There's nothing wrong with those patients. But they are the grilled chicken and salad of dermatology, and what I want is the chicken tikka and spanakopita. They are the boring parts of *Real Housewives* where everyone is sober and being polite. I want the part where they're drunk and accusing each other of shit.

I need a little delicious and exotic and unusual. The occasional guy who turns out to have agyria or ichthyosis vulgaris. I want skin turning blue. I want a kneecap covered in fish scales. I want the cases Dr. Patel pushed me front and center to treat, always finding fault and upbraiding me no matter how well I did.

And I want to discuss this with Graham, along with all the things I'm still not ready to say to him—I don't *know* that I can do a relationship because I haven't really done one before, and I don't know if he wants one because he's sure not acting like it —but the one problem I can't flesh out with him is the one he's the subject of.

Maybe I'll try anyway.

Me: Will you be home tonight?

He normally responds fast, but it's over an hour before I hear back.

Graham: Sorry...had to go to Newport for a family thing and heading to NYC early. Leaving for the airport at four tomorrow morning.

At *four*? How am I supposed to fake going into labor before he leaves at *four*? It's like he did this on purpose to foil me. He knows I won't wake willingly before seven-thirty, not even for childbirth.

And a family thing he didn't even invite me to...he's ghosting me with a level of commitment I'd admire if I wasn't the recipient.

~

I CALL Gemma because I need work advice. I'm also wondering what exactly I wasn't invited to.

"Let's get dinner," she suggests. "Ben's in Seattle tonight and I'm at loose ends."

"You're not...going to the family thing? In Newport?"

"There's no family thing, as far as I know. Jean has her book club on Tuesday nights."

"Maybe I misunderstood," I say quietly.

Except it's *in writing*. I didn't misunderstand. He lied.

We meet at a restaurant between her office and mine. I order a salad to start and asparagus and chicken as an entrée, though I'd really prefer risotto.

"So what's up with Mandy?" I ask.

Gemma shakes her head. "I can't believe she dumped him. It was so sudden."

I blink. "She *dumped* him? The last I heard, Colin was just worried."

Her brow furrows. "Oh, yeah, last night after Colin got home, they had a talk and she said she wanted him out."

Why didn't Graham tell me this? I mean, I realize that him not telling me isn't the most important story, but still...why didn't he tell me?

"Poor Colin. Is he upset?"

She nods. "Yeah, and I guess the last time he went through

stuff with a girl he wound up in jail, so they're all a little concerned."

"Colin? In jail?"

She shrugs a shoulder. "He was eighteen. It's not like it was last week. I'm surprised Graham hasn't told you any of this."

"He isn't telling me anything, apparently," I reply, my voice quieter than it was.

"What happened? You guys seemed to be getting along so well."

I trail a finger over the condensation on my glass. "We *were* getting along. And then we slept together."

"*Wow*," she mouths. "I take it that went badly?"

"No," I moan, pressing my face to my hands. "It was amazing. But, you know, I was the one who didn't want anything and he's respecting it, and now I kind of wish—"

"That he wouldn't?"

I nod. I hate how it makes me sound. "I'm not trying to jerk him around. But you know how I am. I *leave*. That's just what I do."

"With all due respect," she says, "that's absolute bullshit. You didn't leave me, even when I refused to go out and only returned calls sporadically. You haven't left your dick of a father or your awful stepmother, no matter how much they deserve it. You haven't left your career, even though you work crazy hours and aren't doing what you want. You've stuck with the things that mattered to you. And no offense, but most of the guys you've dated until now...*deserved* to be left. They were douches. What's happening here is that you're starting to believe all the shit Shannon has said about you, and do you really want to let the opinion of a woman who's had a bone to pick since you were an infant be the one that sticks?"

I swallow. No. I don't want anything Shannon has ever said to stick. "But what if she's right?"

Gemma smiles. "Keeley, she just...isn't. Trust me."

"But what if Graham doesn't want what I want?" I ask, and she laughs, and only stops when she sees I'm not laughing with her.

"Oh my God. You were serious?" she asks. "Since when are *you* worried someone doesn't want you?"

"I don't know." I guess it's just the first time I've wanted someone back.

39

KEELEY

Though I'm listening for him, I don't wake when he gets in, and he's gone when I get up. I check the kitchen for a note from him, perhaps sarcastically asking me not to eat all the fruit as if I'd ever willingly eat fruit, but there's nothing.

He's just gone, and the apartment has never felt so empty. I didn't realize how much I liked hearing him demand projections and bark orders I don't understand as I got ready for work.

I take Mark his breakfast, something Graham does at least half the time now and stop for a second though I know I'm going to be double booked all day.

"Did Graham get out okay this morning?" Mark asks. "That was a tough break, Prescott leaving like that."

"Prescott?" I repeat weakly.

"The guy running the New York office. We'll see if Jody can step up but I kind of doubt it. And not because she's a woman. I just don't think she's going to be forceful enough for *that* crew."

I know none of this, yet Graham knows all about Dr. Fox and her weekly appointment to get her roots done, and how

Trinny was doing a juice fast and got the runs. Is it Graham's fault for not telling me, or my fault for not asking? It's not as if he greets me at the door every night saying, *"tell me everything."* I just do, and he does not.

"How do you know about all that?"

Mark shrugs. "I had the same job, you know, and it's stressful as hell. Graham's a young guy with a good head on his shoulders. I'm just keeping tabs to make sure it stays that way."

"Maybe I should have been asking more questions," I say quietly.

Mark shakes his head. "You're already performing the most important role, and it's the one thing I really needed back then."

"What's that?"

"You give him a reason to wake up in the morning, Keeley." He laughs when my mouth opens to argue. "No, not the baby. *You.*"

~

I GET through another long day at work, followed by a lonely night without him.

By Thursday, I miss him so much I can barely stand it. I walk into his room—the door is open, it's not like I'm prying—and sit on his bed. The pillow smells like his shampoo. On the right wall, he's begun to consolidate his stuff so there'll be room to place the crib on the left. It's already beginning, this process of him separating himself from us. Maybe that's part of the reason he went back to New York.

I lie down on my side and cry, realizing far too late that my mascara is all over his pillowcase. "Well done, Keeley," I sigh. Rosa's not even in for the rest of the week, and I'm never getting that stain out on my own. I'll blame it on the crib delivery guys, I guess.

Once I've pulled myself together, I call him. He's out, though it's late there—I hear glasses clinking and laughter.

"Is everything okay?" he shouts over the din.

I briefly consider claiming my water has broken, but that'll be hard to play off when it breaks a second time later on. "It's fine!" I shout back. "I had a question about the crib but it can wait!"

A text comes through only a second later.

Graham: Sorry about that. You said something about the crib?

Me: I figured it out, but thanks.

Graham: Is everything okay?

I hesitate. No, nothing is okay. I'm sad, and I miss him, and I don't know why he hasn't told me any of things other people seem to know. Graham is the type of guy who keeps it all close to his vest, or so I thought, but if he can tell Mark something, surely he can tell me?

Me: Why didn't you tell me Presley quit?

Graham: Prescott? How do you even know who Prescott *is*?

Me: Mark. You can tell me that stuff, you know.

Graham: I thought you said everything about my work was boring.

Me: It is. It's super boring. But I still want to know.

Graham: I feel like this isn't really about Prescott.

Me: Ignore me. I've had a hard week. You have, too, apparently.

I wait for him to ask how my week was hard, because he'd usually ask, or to tell me something more.

I wait and wait, but he doesn't even reply.

～

FRIDAY FEELS like the world's longest day, though I leave at a reasonable hour for once.

When I get to my building, I stop by the front desk to thank Jacobson for letting the delivery guys into my apartment, and he waves me off. "I didn't need to. Graham took care of it."

"He's here?" I ask, my heart racing.

Jacobson raises a brow. "I figured you'd be the first to know."

I'm never the first to know, but he's here and I'm too excited to be sad about that. I walk-run to the elevator and then down my hall, bursting into my apartment with no couth whatsoever.

He's in the kitchen, in shorts and a t-shirt, making a pie. I don't know why the sight of him makes my trachea feel half its normal size.

"You're home," I say, then swallow hard. *Oh God, do not let me cry over this. Do not.*

He gives me an uncertain smile. "*You're* home. Hours early."

"I lied about a doctor's appointment so I could leave," I admit, and he laughs. "What happened? You said you'd be gone until Wednesday."

"I've got to head back in the morning. I just thought—" He looks at me, his tongue prodding his cheek. "You said you'd had a hard week. I thought maybe I ought to be here."

I open my mouth to tell him he didn't need to do that, and instead burst into tears.

In seconds, his arms are around me. "Keeley, what's going on? Is this just a pregnancy thing or is it something else?"

I sob against his chest. "You haven't been weird at all," I cry. "Ever since we slept together, you haven't been weird at all."

He laughs quietly. "Isn't that a good thing?"

"*No.* Why hasn't it been weird for you? Because it's been different for me, but you're just business as usual. It's like it was meaningless."

He's quiet for a moment, and then his arms tighten around

me. "Keeley, if I don't seem any different...it's because I'm not. I've been trying to get over you for months, and...I'm still trying. I'm going to be trying for a long while. This is just what it looks like."

A tiny flame ignites inside me, flickering at first and then growing stronger. He wants this. He wants us. And it's incredibly risky and doomed to failure, but I want it too.

I place my palms on his chest as I look up at him. "I don't *want* you to get over it, Graham."

He swallows, hope and uncertainty dancing in his eyes. "You once said you were a butterfly who couldn't stay in one place for long."

I take a deep breath before I answer. "Maybe I just needed a safe place to land."

He searches my face just long enough to make sure I mean it, and then he leans down with a quiet groan and kisses me.

He smells like cinnamon and soap; he tastes like apples and mint.

His arms—not too tight and not too loose—surround me in a wall of muscle he'll use to shield me from the world if necessary. His mouth on mine is urgent and *perfect*. For five days, I've missed this and dreamed about it, and it's even better than I remember.

It's messy, desperate, and when his hand finally slides inside my panties I gasp in relief. "Fucking finally," I say, and his laughter is strained.

He pulls the shirt over my head and pushes my skirt around my hips. When I reach into his boxers and palm him, exactly the way he likes, air hisses between his teeth, and then he lifts me onto the counter.

"I've *got* to fuck you now because I can't stand not to," he says. "And I apologize in advance for its brevity."

His mouth tugs at one nipple as he shoves his shorts and boxers down and steps close.

When he pushes inside me, my teeth sink into his shoulder. "This is another really good position," I gasp.

"I told you," he says against my ear, his voice tight, "I've given it a lot of thought."

He's careful with me, more careful than he is in those slivers of memory from January. He moves in and out slowly, his jaw flexed as he tries not to come. I know he's scared about the pregnancy, being gentler than he otherwise would be. I wish I'd paid more attention during my obstetrics rotation...maybe I'd know enough to assure him it isn't a concern.

His brow is damp, his eyes are dark and drugged. "Are you close?"

"I am. Just do it harder," I beg. "Stop holding back."

"Fuck. I shouldn't," he says, but everything about his clenched jaw, his tight grip on my hips, tells me he wants to. "Just for a minute." He gives in with a muffled cry, as if some part of him has finally been set free.

In seconds, he has me going off like a bomb.

"God, I love that," he hisses and then his thrusts come fast and sharp, and he lets go, too, throwing his head back, his eyes squeezed tight.

When they finally open again, I reach up to his throat. "You have my favorite thyroid cartilage in the entire world."

He laughs. "That's probably the weirdest compliment I've ever received."

"All the blood may have rushed from my brain. I'm not thinking all that clearly right now."

His mouth curls into a hint of a smile—a smug, smug smile —and then he lifts me up, wrapping my legs around his waist as he carries me.

"What are you doing?"

He walks into his room and deposits me carefully on the bed. "Making sure you keep not thinking clearly. Traditionally, that's worked out really well for me."

The second time is long and luxurious, and he refuses to do it hard, the way I ask, but goes down on me instead, and I guess I really have no complaints about this in the end.

When it's over, though, I'm not sure what I'm supposed to do. If he's flying out in the morning, he might want the room to himself. Maybe he's got to repack. Maybe he wants to do laundry.

"Well," I begin, sliding away.

"Keeley," he says. "Don't."

I'm not sure what he's telling me not to do, at first, but then he pulls the blankets over us both and his hand lands on my hip.

Ah, I think, smiling. *Don't leave.*

He tugs my back to his chest, his knees sliding into the curve of mine, his arms around me so that I am covered in him, as close as we can possibly be. And like that we remain for the entire night.

It's the best night's sleep I've ever had.

40

KEELEY

When I wake, the bed is empty.

I'd be lying if I said I didn't find that disappointing, that there wasn't a part of me hoping maybe we'd pick right back up where we left off, or that maybe he'd even just...stay. I don't know what any of this means for when he gets home on Wednesday.

I walk to the kitchen, glancing at my clothes strewn around the room and walking past them to his discarded t-shirt, balled on the floor. He'll never notice it's gone, and even if he does, he wouldn't accuse me of taking it. He'd sound crazy.

I bring it to my nose and breathe him in as I slip it over my head. He was so...*him* last night. So feral and restrained and hungry and unleashed all at the same time. Like a delicious package I only got to partially unwrap.

I'm taking another sniff of his shirt when the door swings open and he enters, carrying two cups and a white paper bag.

He didn't fly back to New York...He went to get us breakfast. What a ridiculous thing to make my heart swell ten sizes.

And then his gaze lands on me, on the t-shirt I'm wearing, and I feel heat climbing up my neck. *Fuck.*

He crosses the room to me and pulls a cup from the tray. "It's decaf," he says and I hold the mocha latte to my nose, letting the steam rise in a delicious waft of fresh roasted beans and chocolate before I take a sip. He holds the bag aloft. "And I got your disgusting muffin."

He bought the muffin he doesn't approve of. For me. Instead of forcing me to eat some gross concoction of protein powder and eggs and peanut butter like he does.

"Thank you," I reply. "I assume you snuck quinoa into it, but that was sweet of you."

"It's quinoa-free." His eyes lower now to his t-shirt.

Fuck. Again.

"I, uh…" I begin, and my mind suddenly is empty of all plausible excuses for stealing his shirt when I had to step over my own clothes to reach it.

His gaze raises to my face, and there's a hint of a smile in his eyes. "I like it." He steps closer and, removing the coffee from my hand, kisses me.

"You can't kiss me," I argue, though I'm making no effort to back away from him. "I haven't brushed my teeth."

"You taste like coffee, which happens to be one of my favorite things."

His hand lands on my hip and I'm suddenly breathless. "I didn't know that."

He pulls me close then, close enough to feel the bulge in his gym shorts—which is pretty much all the foreplay I need. "Would you like to know some of my other favorites, Keeley?" His lips graze the shell of my ear, and before I've even begun to nod, his hand is sliding beneath the t-shirt and over my skin.

"Yes," I whisper.

"You're not going to tell me this is a terrible idea?" His hand runs along my rib cage, his wrist brushing the underside of my breast.

"I'm going to think it but keep it to myself."

He laughs then picks me up like I'm feather-light and carries me back to bed.

❧

THERE SHOULD HAVE BEEN a whole chapter in *What to Expect When You're Expecting* on the dangerous combination of pregnancy hormones and Graham Tate. Because I'm pretty sure that if one of us wasn't a vaguely responsible adult—hint: it's not me, but it's barely him either—we would fuck until we died from lack of sleep or starvation.

We do manage to talk, a little. I tell him about the way Dr. Fox is trying to force me out and how I'm not sure if this is even the kind of dermatology I'm interested in. He tells me about Prescott, the dick who is leaving to manage a competitive hedge fund, and how he thinks Jody, the new second in command, will rise to the task.

Most of our conversations are slightly less intense, of course. I haven't changed *that* much.

"I like the name Blossom for a girl," I muse.

"She can't be secretary of state with a name like Blossom," he argues.

"She's got half my DNA, Graham. She was never gonna be secretary of state anyway." I smooth my hand over my bare stomach. When I'm lying on my back as I am now, I can't even see my legs anymore. "I don't think I look *that* pregnant. There was a model in Australia who had a baby when she went to the bathroom and never even knew she was pregnant. All her clothes still fit."

He chokes on a laugh. "Keeley, when was the last time you could claim that all your clothes still fit? You've been bragging about your new breast size pretty much since I got here."

I cup them. "Aren't they amazing? I hope that part sticks around."

I wait...for him to say he hopes it does too. Or to say it doesn't matter to him. Something to allude to what happens after the baby is born, when he's in New York with the elegant Anna and I'm here—sleep-deprived, covered in spit-up and quite possibly a B-cup again.

But he just laughs.

Which I guess is okay. Your first weekend as a couple isn't the time to have a whole "*where is this headed?*" conversation under normal circumstances. Then again, under normal circumstances, I wouldn't be thirty-four weeks pregnant with his kid either.

ON SUNDAY AFTERNOON, we leave the apartment for the first time all weekend to attend Gemma's barbeque, which I now regret agreeing to. He's flying out of LAX tonight, and it's a flight he will need to make.

"One hour, right?" he asks when we pull onto their street.

I tug him toward me for a kiss. "One hour. I'll pretend I'm going into labor if I have to."

"I'm honestly surprised you haven't already played that card."

I laugh to myself without mentioning where, exactly, I considered playing it.

The men are gathered near the grill and the women are standing by a long table spread with food, the exact kind of thing I never wanted to be a part of. Is this who I'm about to become? In a year or five, will I be saying things like, "*it's wine o'clock!*" while spending summer afternoons talking about travel soccer?

Maybe.

The kids run across the yard, barefoot little idiots, yelping and laughing, and I know I'm going to want my daughter to be part of this. I've already changed so much about my life for this baby and standing here I realize...those were just the first steps of many.

I find Drew and Tali sitting off in a shaded corner with their slumbering babies.

"Look at you," says Drew with a laugh. "Who'd have thought you'd wind up *here* last January? I'm so relieved."

I assume she's talking about how I wound up with Graham rather than Six, but I don't recall her ever suggesting I *shouldn't* be with Six last winter.

"Relieved?"

"I heard an earful about that weekend from my husband, believe me," she says. "But all's well that ends well, right?"

They start talking about something called "Ferberizing", which apparently involves letting your baby cry herself to sleep and which I already know I won't be able to do, and then Tali weighs the benefits of a preschool where they teach Chinese versus one where they hang out in the woods and only play with *"toys found in nature"*. A year ago, I would not have been able to imagine a more boring conversation, but a year ago, I couldn't imagine loving anyone so much more than I love myself.

I look across the lawn to Graham, who's at the grill doctoring a burger for me. I'm pretty sure I now love two people way more than I love myself. He looks at his watch twice, which makes me laugh, and I cross the yard to him.

"You've got to stop checking the time," I say near his ear.

He hands me a plate. "I have to leave for the airport in four hours, Keeley. And I don't want to spend those hours talking about draft picks."

Actually, neither do I. I can think of way better ways to spend it.

The two of us take our plates to the table and eat while we watch the kids running around on the lawn and parents dealing with babies. I'm starting to realize how demanding even one child can be. Any time Tali and Hayes's baby needs something, there's shuffling and a discussion and one of them rummaging through a diaper bag while the other holds the kid. Drew's husband now has their son over his shoulder, because she needed a break.

"It helps," I say quietly, "having a father around. It's a lot to do on your own."

It's more subtle than saying, "*I think you should stay with me for good, person I've only been coupled with for forty-eight hours.*"

"That's part of why I need to be in New York this week. I put my condo on the market a while ago. It goes to settlement on Tuesday."

My jaw falls open. "A *while* ago? How long is a while ago?"

He laughs to himself. "From the day of the ultrasound."

I stare at him. "That was *months* ago. How could you have kept it a secret that long?"

He holds my eye. "It made you feel safe, for a while, thinking I was leaving. Right?"

I nod. "Yeah."

He's right. If he'd told me he planned to stay, I'd have freaked out. I'd have geared up for a daily custody battle. I just can't believe he sold his condo without anywhere else to go.

"But where would you have gone if all this hadn't happened?"

He hitches a shoulder. "I've been looking for houses," he says. He nods to the yard. "I know you love your apartment, but I want this for our kid. So, at the risk of freaking you out, I was kind of hoping I might convince you to come with me when I moved."

I picture our daughter chasing after the ice cream man in bare feet. Biking home from a local pool with popsicle-stained lips. Walking to school every day. I love my apartment, and I love living in the city, but I think I might like *this* even more.

"I can't tell if you're okay or about to catch the first flight to Cabo because I've pushed you too far," he says quietly.

"That depends." I rest my head on his shoulder. "Are we talking about a house like Ben's, or some kind of Warren Buffett-style 'look how frugal I am despite all my money' thing?"

He laughs. "Yes, Keeley, you'll get your Mariah Carey closet."

"You have no idea how horny that just made me."

He laughs again, and his fingers twine with mine. "I know it's a lot, but while I'm piling on here, I wish you'd at least consider quitting your job. You could have the baby, take some time to get settled into it, and find something that suits you better."

"I'd feel like I was being kept by a Saudi prince."

He smiles. "I thought you *wanted* to be kept by a Saudi prince."

"I do. It's a good thing. We might need to do some roleplay."

"Saudi prince roleplay and anniversary anal. I like it. Just out of curiosity, are we going with January eighth for our anniversary? Because I want to make sure I mark it on my calendar."

I place my mouth against his ear. "Graham, once I get this kid out, you aren't going to have to wait for once a year *anything*."

"Jesus," he says under his breath. "Are you ready to get out of here? I'm tired."

"How can you be tired? This was the laziest day I've ever seen you have."

He gives me a sidelong look, one that starts at my eyes and lands on my mouth for a long moment. "I'm not actually tired, Keeley."

Ohhh.

"I hate to eat and run," I announce to the table, as I rise.

"You just got here," Gemma argues.

"Don't push this or she'll just pretend she's going into labor, Gemma," Graham warns.

I'm beginning to think marrying him was the smartest thing I ever did.

41

KEELEY

He leaves for New York, but it all feels different now, in a good way. I don't hand in my notice because I intend to get as much paid maternity leave out of Kathleen Fox as possible before I quit, and the rest of my life is so good that a little aggravation at work hardly seems to matter.

We're staying together. We're going to have a baby, and a house, and I'm going to have my Mariah Carey closet, and once we've waited the required length of time after the delivery, I'm going to reacquaint myself with the *not* careful, *not* gentle side of Graham Tate in bed.

The only person more excited about this whole thing than me is Gemma.

"I found you a house," she says, calling me for the sixth time in two days. "When we were walking Lola last week, we met this couple who said they were getting ready to move, so I stalked them, and she said it goes on the market next month. It's perfect for you."

I laugh. "Gemma, I don't even know our budget."

"Please. Graham could afford ten houses in my neighborhood if he wanted. How soon can you get out of your lease?"

I ignore the fear that this is all too much good fortune at once, that I'm building up to a life it will hurt too much to leave. I remind myself that having a life you don't want to leave is a *good* thing.

"Graham has a copy," I tell her. "I'll check when I get home."

I leave work at a reasonable hour—I now have loads of made-up doctor's appointments going forward to prevent a week full of ten-hour days—and go into his room. His desk is neat as a pin, his bed is made, every folder in his file drawer labeled.

I flip through a lot of things that look financial, seeking something labeled with the word *apartment*, and land on *Contracts, Keeley*. Gemma calls just as I'm grabbing the file. "I think I've got it," I tell her, flipping it open on his desk.

Gemma's saying something about getting out of my contract but I don't really hear it. Because it isn't a rental agreement in this file. It's a different kind of contract entirely.

"What the fuck?" I whisper.

Gemma asks if I'm okay and I can't even answer her. I stare at the paper in front of me as my stomach slides to my feet. "Oh my God."

"Keeley, answer me! Are you okay?"

"No," I tell her, my voice breaking. "Gemma, he's thinks I'm going to let him buy my kid."

"What? That can't be true. What does it say?"

"I, Keeley Maureen Connolly—" I begin and then I start to cry.

I, Keeley Maureen Connolly, do hereby voluntarily and irrevocably relinquish all legal and physical custody of (name) to Graham David Tate.

"Oh God, Gemma, this is bad. It's really bad." There's a paragraph about compensation and a paragraph about visitation—at his discretion but *generally discouraged for the welfare of the child*.

"I'm on my way." She's using her stern lawyer voice, but behind it, I hear a hint of worry. "Stay there and don't jump to conclusions. I'll read it over. It can't be the way it appears. I know him, Keeley. *You* know him. It can't be as bad as it looks."

I desperately *want* her to be right. I'm just not sure how she could be.

Twenty minutes later, she's sitting at Graham's desk, her mouth moving as she skims the contract, her brow furrowed. And then she picks up his pen jar and slams it against the wall.

"I'm going to *kill* him," she says.

I sink onto his bed and bury my face in my hands. He's on his way home right now. He thinks he's going to waltz in here and pretend everything's good. The way I guess he's been pretending all along.

It feels as if I should have a response, but instead I'm just... empty. There's nothing inside me right now but shocked, echoing silence.

"Are you going to call him?" she asks. "He needs to explain this."

"He's flying home right now," I whisper. I truly can't even grasp what's happened, can't make sense of it. And I'm not sure there's an excuse or explanation in the world that's going to make this okay. He thought he could give me a million dollars to have no contact with my child, ever again. He really thought I'd sign this. Even Shannon, with her sickeningly low opinion of me, wouldn't believe that.

So what has this been, these past few months? Was he was stringing me along all this time, simply to gain my trust? Did he really want us to stay married and get a house? Or were all these things just little insurance policies for him? A homeless, unemployed mother could be made to look unfit pretty fucking easily.

It seems impossible, but it would be naïve, at this point, to think anything else.

No wonder he wasn't worried about sharing custody. He never fucking planned to.

~

HE CALLS WHEN HE LANDS, and I let it go to voice mail. He texts, with more of that worry of his, the worry I thought was legitimately about me as a person and not about me as the vessel for his seed.

God, I was such an idiot.

I go put on makeup and the cutest dress that still fits and then sit on the couch.

He opens the door and the sight of his face breaks my heart a little. He looks so convincingly...besotted. I thought he couldn't lie to me. It never occurred to me he might just be really, really good at it.

His smile fades. "Hey," he says slowly. "Is everything okay? I texted you."

I climb to my feet and set the folder on the counter closest to him. "I went to your file cabinet because Gemma wanted me to check the lease on the apartment. This is what I found instead."

He flips the file open, and the moment he realizes what it is, I know there won't be a good explanation. I'd held out the ridiculous hope that *someone else* had placed the contract there, but he isn't surprised by what it says. He's just surprised he got caught.

"It's not how it looks," he says quietly. He turns, reaching out a hand.

I take a step away from him. "Really? Because it looks like you thought I was the kind of person who'd *sell you* my child."

His eyes fall closed. "Keeley, when I first came here you weren't even sure you wanted to have a kid. You were talking about drinking at *Coachella*."

He isn't wrong, but doesn't he know me better than that by now? Doesn't he realize I didn't mean it? "I was fucking with you, and you've had months and months and you never got rid of this. Which suggests that you were just holding onto it, waiting to see if I'd fuck up."

"That's not what it—"

"Out," I say quietly. "I want you out."

"Keeley—"

"I'm not interested in a goddamn thing you have to say. Gemma's taking care of the annulment and I'll be in touch when the baby is born."

"Keeley—"

"Look, I've got a date. Be out by the time I get home."

He stares at me. "You've got a date," he repeats flatly, his voice hoarse. "You've got to be fucking kidding me."

"You were going to take my *baby*," I reply, and I have to swallow hard so the words don't turn into a sob. "Don't think for a minute you get to judge me now."

I turn away from the pain in his face. *Good. I hope it hurts.* He can't be nearly as hurt as I am.

I walk out the door and he doesn't try to stop me. I wait until I reach the elevator before I burst into tears—it went exactly as I planned...I just can't believe it's all over with that quickly.

I pull it together and drive out to Silver Lake, to see the friends I haven't laid eyes on since Graham first showed up at my apartment. They're going to dinner and a club. I already know I won't be joining them for the second part of the night, but I've got to pass the time until Paul calls to say Graham's out of the apartment. If he's not gone when dinner's done, I'll crash on someone's couch—which is exactly the sort of thing Graham would expect of me, isn't it?

My friends are all assembled by the time I reach the restaurant, and I'm welcomed back with open arms, though that might have to do with how drunk they already are.

They all saw my video. More than one of them comments on how gross it must have been. Then they talk about how their tents blew away at some festival and they wound up with sunstroke. They tell me about another wild weekend in which they got a guy we know really drunk and dropped him off over the border with no identification. As a joke.

I want to be the old Keeley, who laughed at everything, but maybe that ship has sailed. Or maybe I just need to become a different version of me once I give birth: *Less Fun Keeley* who drinks but does so responsibly and excuses herself when her friends decide to strand someone in a foreign country.

They start chanting "*blue meanie*" for some reason, annoying most of the diners surrounding us. Aaron pushes away from the table and knocks into a waitress with a whole tray full of drinks, which go flying. There's glass everywhere, the people at the table beside us are covered in red wine, and my friends are laughing like it was a victimless crime.

"Erik," Aaron shouts, "tell Keeley what you did!"

Erik laughs. "Nah, bro, you tell it better."

I already suspect I won't like it.

"So Erik and I have all this LSD, right, and we're on this playground," Aaron begins. *Yep, I won't like it.* "Right in the middle of the fucking day. And Erik's talking to this little kid and then he's like, 'we're already dead. I'm dead and you're dead' and this kid starts crying and runs for his mom."

Everyone roars with laughter. And I don't want to think about Graham now, but I do. I wonder what he'd say if he was listening. I wonder what he'd have done if this guy came up to *our* daughter and told her she was *"already dead"*. I guarantee fists would have been involved, and I don't want to approve of anything Graham says or does right now, but I'd approve of that.

I'd probably help.

"You can't say that to a kid, Erik."

Erik laughs. "Well, obviously. That's why it's so funny."

"It's not funny. It's fucked up." I throw some cash down on the table. "I'm out, guys. Good seeing you."

They boo. "Pregnancy turned you into an old lady, Keeley!" Leila shouts.

No, it turned me into a fucking adult. I just wish I was a happy one.

I'M ABOUT to get a hotel room for the night when Paul calls to say Graham is gone. I wait for him to add something that will give me a little hope, somehow, but he doesn't.

"Did he say anything?" I finally prod. It's pathetic, me needing this reassurance.

"Nah," Paul says. "Just thanked me for letting him borrow the hand truck. Sounds like he had a lot of files to pack or something?"

Jesus. He did this to me and all he was worried about were his fucking files.

I go to my apartment and look around me, staring at the kitchen where he cooked and the couch where he'd cover my feet and it hits me that we really must have been *nothing*.

All the times he seemed to look at me a moment too long, all the times he laughed and let me hope I'd made him happy —perhaps not a single one of them was even real.

I search the counter but there's no note, no apology.

I guess I thought he'd at least say, *"I know you better now. I know you would never have gone along with it."* But he just walked out of here more concerned with his fucking files than me, so he probably doesn't know it at all.

42

GRAHAM

I refuse to tell Ben where I'm staying until he threatens to stop giving me updates on Keeley.

He shows up at the executive apartment I'm renting twenty minutes later. A week in, it's a little worse for wear: the trash is overflowing, the desk is covered in files, boxes are stacked up to the walls.

"So this is how you're living, huh?"

When Gemma broke up with him and he couldn't get on the next flight to DC to see her, he chartered a private plane, so I'm not going to be lectured by *him*.

"How quickly you've forgotten what it's like to be dumped."

"What *I* remember about being dumped is how quickly I tried to fix it," he replies, sitting on the couch. "From what I've heard, you've made no such effort."

I go to my desk and turn on my computer. "You can save the speech, Ben. It is what it is and I don't need your help."

"Fuck you, Graham. If nothing else, you owe me a goddamn explanation. My wife has been smashing things for a week because she's so furious with you, and she's spending more nights at Keeley's place than our own. I mean...what the hell were you thinking?"

I run a hand over my face. I knew Keeley would tell Gemma, and Gemma would tell Ben...I just never really considered how bad it would sound. Every single person who hears about it, even my own mother, will tell me I'm a fucking asshole.

And I am. I'm a fucking asshole, and there's no way to even apologize for it sufficiently.

"I messed up," I tell him. "It was her worst fear, having someone fight her for custody, so she's never going to forgive me. Just stay out of it."

"Graham," Ben says, leaning forward, his elbows pressed to his knees, "you need to tell Keeley why you did it."

"She already knows why I did it," I spit out. "She came across as someone who couldn't raise a child and I made assumptions I shouldn't have."

He swallows, clasping his hands between his knees. "That's not what I meant. You've got to tell her about all the shit that happened with Mom."

I freeze. We do not speak about the months after my dad died. Colin and Simon don't remember them, and it's too hard for my mom to discuss. If I'm being honest...it's too hard for me too. "I have no idea what you're talking about."

"Bullshit," he says, not unkindly. "I know you remember it, and it's why you've looked so goddamned haunted any time someone mentions the baby to you. We've both tried to keep it in the past for Mom's sake, but you can't tell me that it's not what made you panic and get that agreement drawn up."

"That was more than two decades ago," I reply stiffly. "I'd have to be insane to let something that happened two decades ago still influence me."

He shrugs. "Maybe you are a little insane. Maybe we both are. You think that whole thing hasn't fucked me up a little too?

What set Gemma apart for me is that the girl is made of steel. I've never, not once, worried she'd crumble under pressure." He smiles for a moment. "I have, obviously, worried that she'd *kill* someone under pressure, but that's a different sort of fear."

If the whole fucking city fell into the San Andreas fault, Gemma would be the first person you'd find clawing herself out of the rubble. She'd step on your shoulders to get there too. But she'd make sure Keeley and my daughter got out, so I don't mind.

"Keeley isn't Gemma, though," I tell him quietly. "She's not Mom, but she's fragile in her own way."

"*Everyone* is fragile in their own way. But when you find the right person, you don't want to run from it. You want to take care of her and throw yourself on every grenade the world launches just to make sure she's safe."

I sink my head in my hands. That *is* how I feel, about Keeley, about the baby. It's what's made all this so hard—I did this to protect our child, and I've wound up hurting her and her mother in ways that might last forever.

"She isn't going to forgive me," I tell him. "I wasn't what she wanted in the first place and she's never going to forgive me."

I'll never forgive myself either, but I guess that's nothing new.

43

KEELEY

I am staggering through my days.

I want to curl into a ball under a blanket and eat ice cream until it all feels bearable, but I can't. I have a horrible job to get through, day after day, and a baby to prepare for.

Gemma, Mark, Paul, and Jacobson are godsends. Gemma checks on me multiple times a day and convinces Jean to cancel the surprise baby shower she'd planned. Mark helps me set up a 529 plan and a savings account and shows me how much to set aside next year for a nanny.

Paul and Jacobson push Graham's mattress against the wall when the rest of the baby furniture is delivered and politely suggest I let them know if I need help "moving anything out."

When they leave, I stand in my daughter's room. I thought I'd feel better, seeing everything in its place, but with the mattress against the wall and no splashes of color anywhere, it's all a little grim.

I don't want to be like my mom—trying to buy us a better life with money I don't have—but looking at this room simply makes me feel like I've failed.

I guess I'd probably feel like that anyway, though.

"You look like shit," Mark tells me when I bring him his breakfast.

I laugh. It's kind of nice to have someone refusing to skirt around the obvious truth. *Just like Graham did*, I think, and then I'm sad all over again.

"I'm thirty-six weeks pregnant. I'm supposed to look like shit."

"Tammy says—" he begins and I tune out the rest. Mark has found himself a lady friend who is slightly less homeless than him. She lives in one of the tents over on Venice Beach and was, once upon a time, a dispatcher until her child overdosed and her husband left and she found herself in bad shape financially. A series of hard blows at the wrong time...I can see now how that would make you just walk away.

"You know...Graham really cared about you," he says. "I mean, the guy was head over heels."

"He had a contract written up," I reply, assuming he's forgotten. "He was going to try to *buy* my baby."

Mark shakes his head. "Nah. He'd come down here, ostensibly to talk about the markets but really because he wanted to talk about you. You were his favorite topic and the one thing that made him smile. A guy doing that isn't trying to buy your baby."

I feel my temper ratcheting higher. "Mark, I saw it with my own eyes."

"I don't care what you saw. That guy was never, ever going to do anything to hurt you, and I think somewhere inside, you know that."

I brace myself to stand—it's nearly impossible at this point. "I need to get going."

"Keeley, you know what people see when they look at me now? They see a guy they assume is on drugs, or crazy, or just lazy as shit. And maybe all that is true, but you knew I could be homeless, and might also have gone through some stuff, so you listened. *You* got so drunk that you married a stranger in Vegas, but you'd gone through some stuff too. My point is that everyone has a story. And if you ever cared about Graham...you at least ought to ask. Because maybe he has a story too."

I want to believe that. I can feel the way hope is already blooming in my chest, and I squash it flat immediately. If anything Mark's saying was true, Graham would have tried to explain, or defend himself.

He didn't care enough to do either.

"I'd better get going."

"Did you sell the stuff from the storage unit?" he asks.

Last week, at his suggestion, I pulled some of the unworn or barely worn designer things from the storage unit and put them up for sale—three pairs of Louboutins that hurt too much, the Tom Ford dress I never wore once, a few Hermes bags, including the Birkin. I need a safety net for the not unlikely possibility that Fox fires me. I'm not asking Graham for shit.

"The Birkin already sold. I sent it out yesterday."

"That had to hurt a little."

I shake my head. "It wasn't bad."

All that matters going forward is this baby, and nothing else.

Unless Graham finally comes to his senses and tells me why he fucking did it. And then maybe I'll allow him to matter too.

I guess I haven't squashed all the hope after all.

"SORRY WE KEPT YOU WAITING," I tell the woman sitting on the exam table the next afternoon. I'm fifteen minutes late, which is what happens when you've got double the number of patients any doctor could squeeze into a three-hour period. "I'm Dr. Connolly. What can I help you with today?"

She smiles. "I'm Ally. We've actually met before. Last winter. You were outside Native Planet with Drew Bailey. I guess you don't remember. It was pretty early in the night, like nine."

I gulp. She's referring to the night I married Graham which is, obviously, quite a blur. And she's claiming we were still in LA at nine. So how the hell did we get to Vegas before *midnight*? "Oh, sorry. It was kind of a crazy night."

She nods. "It was. Anyway, right before the fight with your boyfriend—Graham, I think?—you told me I should get this mole looked at, so here I am." She stretches out her forearm, and I know immediately that Drunk Keeley was right.

"Do you see how the borders are irregular?" I ask. "We need to do a biopsy."

She shrugs. "Sure, whatever."

I turn to the nurse assisting me and ask her to get the lidocaine.

"So are you still with that guy?" Ally asks, glancing at my stomach.

My throat tightens. I wait for the sadness to pass, knowing it won't, entirely. "Um, no. But given that you saw me fighting with him even last January, it's probably for the best."

"Oh...I meant the fight *he* got in, when that guy tried to kiss you? Man, I thought he was going to kill him."

I've just inserted a needle into the lidocaine but stop to stare at her. "I don't remember that."

She tilts her head, dumbfounded that I could have forgotten. My ability to appear sober when I'm not strikes again. "Remember that guy just grabbing you? He, like, threw you against the wall, and Graham had him on the ground in seconds. It was crazy."

I smile weakly as I return to what I was doing. I'm a little embarrassed both my nurse and my patient are aware of this story, especially when I'm *not*. I must look extremely classy right now. "Yet somehow, I managed to notice a mole on your arm. One-track mind, I guess."

"I wanted to talk to you about it but you guys went around the corner, and then like two seconds later, Drew grabbed you both and pushed you into a limo."

I stare at her. I *should* play this off and act like I remember, but I'm too stunned. "She did?"

Even as I ask the question, though, I'm starting to put some things together. Like Drew telling me how *"relieved"* she was. Like how she'd *"heard an earful"* from her husband, but *"all's well that ends well"*.

Like the fact that we were still in California at nine but somehow got to Vegas well before midnight...which we could only have managed by private plane.

Something Drew would have on speed dial.

~

DREW CALLS me back within the hour.

"I heard about you and Graham. I'm so sorry. You guys were so cute together the other week, at Ben's house. I really thought it was all going to work out."

Maybe it's my imagination, but she sounds guilty.

"Actually, this is related: that night, the night we went to Vegas? I don't really remember how we got there."

She is very quiet, for a long moment. "I'm so sorry," she finally says. "You seemed okay. I mean we were all drinking, but according to Josh, *I* was the drunk one. You don't remember *anything*?"

I run a hand over my face. I can no longer claim I regret getting that drunk because I wouldn't have this baby coming if I didn't. But it's probably going to remain embarrassing for a good long time. "Very little. Did you...get us a plane?"

She sighs. "Yes. *Fuck*. I took care of the plane; I took care of getting you to the airport before you'd even *agreed*. I even had my assistant arrange everything in Vegas. I was drunk and felt like I was playing fairy godmother, and it wasn't until I woke up that I realized it might have all been a really bad idea. I'm so, so sorry."

"It wasn't your fault. I mean, clearly, *I* was the one pushing to marry a stranger."

"Oh," she says. "Not really. I mean, you were on board, but the whole thing started with Graham."

"*Graham*?" I repeat. That can't be right. Graham Tate was coerced into this nonsense by me and me alone, possibly with Drew's assistance.

"Wow," she says. "You really don't remember anything, do you? It was so cute. He said he knew he was going to marry you the first time you ever spoke on the phone."

If things hadn't ended the way they did, I'd think that was the most romantic story ever. But they did end, so now it's just really sad.

And really confusing.

44

GRAHAM

"Graham," barks a sharp voice. I'm sweating profusely and a little disoriented from the run I just finished—excessive exercise is the only thing keeping me going these days.

I wipe my face with my t-shirt and pull my earbuds out as I turn to find my sister-in-law stepping out of her car in a suit and sky-high heels. Her sunglasses are on, and her cheekbones look like they could cut glass. I'm far taller than Gemma, but if I weren't...I'd probably be a little terrified. Given how much she must hate me, I probably should be a little terrified anyway.

"Is Keeley okay?" I ask immediately.

Even behind her sunglasses I can tell she's rolling her eyes. "No thanks to you."

I pinch the bridge of my nose. "You can yell at me all you want, Gemma. You can't make me feel any worse than I already do."

"Do you honestly think I don't know what you're doing?" she demands. "My husband and I have been together nearly two years, and he has never asked me once about Keeley. Now he's asking me multiple times a *day*, detailed questions he wouldn't even know to ask, about her blood pressure and the baby and her job and if all the furniture's arrived and if the car seat was installed. You two are idiots!" she says, throwing her hands in the air. "Why the hell aren't you just asking me directly? Why aren't you just asking *her*?"

I push my hands in my pockets. "She's not speaking to me. I assumed you weren't either."

"I shouldn't be, but my friend is devastated and it's your goddamn fault, so you need to pull your shit together and fix it."

"Do you think I wouldn't fix it if I could?" I demand. "She kicked me out and told me not to contact her! She's seeing someone else anyway."

She groans loudly. "Did you honestly believe that? Who exactly do you think she suddenly started dating?"

Ethan. He'd take her back at any point, I'm certain. It was written all over his face. "I figured it was someone from before."

"You smitten asshole, even if she was *willing* to date someone at this point in her pregnancy she wouldn't, and you're the only person *whipped* enough to think one of her exes is going to date her when she's eight months pregnant."

Maybe she's right. It's one of the things I found too painful to even contemplate fully...and thus all the working out.

"I still don't know how to fix it."

"By telling her why you did it, Graham. Why you *really* did it. And by telling her you know her better than that." Gemma pushes her sunglasses on top of her head and brushes at her eyes. I've never seen Gemma tear up before. I sort of thought she wasn't capable of it.

What I've done to Keeley is *that* bad.

"You know why this is so hard for her?" she whispers. "Because you took everything she hates about herself and everything Shannon told her she was and you put it on paper. That's what she saw when she looked at that contract: that the guy she fell in love with only saw the side of herself she *hates* and nothing more."

"Gemma, I'm—"

"Don't," she barks, pulling the sunglasses back on and opening her door. "Do not fucking *apologize* to me. *Fix it.*"

She climbs into her car and drives off, leaving me sick to my stomach.

I've been so focused on how Keeley must feel about me that it never occurred to me how this must have made her feel about herself.

And I can stand a lot of things, but not that.

45

KEELEY

I lumber out of my desk chair, forcing myself to go get lunch, though I haven't had much of an appetite since the whole thing went down with Graham.

"You don't look so good," Trinny says as I walk out.

I blink. She's right. I feel...not *ill*, but off. As if something has disrupted the balance inside me in a way even growing a human in my stomach has not. "I've had better days," I tell her.

"Maybe you should go to the hospital?"

I shake my head. "It's not...I just don't feel good. Maybe I should go home."

She grins. "Of course you should. You're thirty-six weeks pregnant, and *Dr. Fox* has a very light schedule today. I'm sure she won't mind being double-booked."

I laugh wearily. "Yeah, she kind of has it coming, doesn't she?"

I've just reached my apartment when Graham texts, and even the sight of his name hurts.

Graham: Can we talk when you get home?

I figured this was coming. At some point he was going to

want to discuss custody. I'd like to put it off, but I guess I need to know what I'll be fighting him over in a few weeks.

Me: I'm already home.

My phone rings immediately. The picture I took of him pops up. In it, he's on my couch, reading and trying to appear irritated with me, but fighting a smile. I swallow hard. He didn't hate me. I'm still sure of it. So how could he have done what he did?

"Why are you home?" he demands as soon as I pick up, his voice sharp. "Is everything okay?"

I put my feet up on the coffee table. "Why? Are you going to run to a judge to tell on me if I just wanted to go home early for once?"

"Jesus Christ, Keeley," he says. "Of course not. I'm just worried."

I've heard that before. How many times have my father and Shannon said the same?

"I'm fine," I reply. "Why are you calling?"

"I...was just following up on the email I sent."

I sigh. *Here we go.* I assume it's a contract of some kind, or an email a lawyer wrote on his behalf, suggesting a custody arrangement that works best for *him*. "I don't know what you're talking about."

"I sent you an email last night. I knew I should have texted you. You never check your email."

"Yes, because I'm not a hundred years old."

"Can you check it, please?"

I'm in no mood for this. "If it's about your contract, I think you know where you can shove it. If this is about custody, just send it straight to Gemma." I'd worried once that she might be on his side, since he's a relative. Instead, I think she's angrier at him than I am. It was a little too much like the bullshit her dad pulled on her mom, and she can't deal with seeing me sad.

"I tore that contract up the second you walked out for your *date*. And it's not about custody. Please, Keeley."

Sighing, I reach across the table for my laptop and click on the message he's sent.

"It's a letter?" I ask quietly. "Should I just read it and call you back?"

"It's not a lot," he says. "I can wait."

I set the phone down and pull the laptop closer.

SEPT 9, 2022

I don't know how to begin, so I'm just going to say it: I fucked up.

I can't fix anything at this point. I'm putting it all on paper simply because I hate that I hurt you. It's the worst thing I've ever done, which is really saying something.

I was thoughtless and I was irresponsible, but that's nothing you don't already know. So just let me tell you the rest:

After my father died, my mother started refusing to come out of her room. I tried to feed Colin myself and spilled boiling formula on us both. Colin wouldn't stop crying, so I called 911, which led to Colin and Simon being placed in emergency foster care. It took three months for my mom to get them back. She still can't look at baby pictures of any us...that's how raw it is for her even now, decades later.

I have never wanted the responsibility that came with having a child, and when I found out you were pregnant, I panicked. I can't defend my actions. I made assumptions I shouldn't have after one night in your apartment, and that's when I had the contract drawn up. As soon as you said you wanted to be a parent, I set it aside and never considered it again.

I doubt you'll believe any of this. I know it won't change anything. I just wanted you to know I love you, and there's no one alive I'd rather have raise our daughter than you. She'll know more about The Jonas Brothers and the cast of Dawson's Creek than any child should, but she'll also be loved in a way only you love the people you care about. Being one of them, briefly, was the happiest time of my life.

Graham

I'M CRYING by the time I'm done reading. Poor Graham, holding all this in and blaming himself. He's such a worrier. I can picture it: a crying baby, a burned arm, the chaos of it all. How it must have made him panic. When he was *eight*. Barely past being a baby himself.

I get it now. I just wish I could stop crying long enough to tell him this.

"Shit," I whisper then jump up from the couch. "Oh, shit."

"Look," he says, and I vaguely process how disappointed he sounds. "I don't expect anything. I know I dropped a lot on you at once, and if you've moved on with someone else, I'm not going to—"

"Graham, it's not that," I say, barely audible as I stare in shock at the large stain where I was just sitting. "I think my water just broke."

46

GRAHAM

I wanted to be with her for this, but I also accepted weeks ago that I might not be, so I already had a contingency plan in place.

I call Paul's cell. He will drop everything to get her safely to the hospital, and I don't trust this to some Uber with two other passengers and a driver who can't follow directions.

He has her in his car within three minutes. Mark comes along, too, just in case they need help.

They make it to the hospital in record time, but it takes me far longer. Traffic is snarled, and I've now got texts from Mark, Paul, and Jacobson—keeping tabs from his post at the building until his replacement gets in at nine—asking me where the hell I am.

I arrive at Labor and Delivery, frazzled and worried sick. Yes, I want to be there when our daughter is born, but mostly...I just want to see my wife again. The past two weeks have felt like a lifetime. Mark and Paul both leap from their seats and join me at the front desk. An Indian doctor standing there turns when he hears me ask for her. "You're the father?" he asks with a small, quizzical smile. "That's good. That's very good. I'm Dr. Patel. I was just up here checking on her."

"Do you know where she is?"

"This isn't my area, but I'm sure one of the nurses can take you back and get you some scrubs. Rachel?"

A nurse pops up from a chair, and I nod to Paul and Mark. They nod back, worried and hopeful at once.

She waits while I change into scrubs, then walks me down the hall to Keeley. "She's not quite thirty-seven weeks," I tell the nurse just before we enter. "How big a deal is that?"

She shakes her head and gestures to the room, which is full of laughing hospital staff. "As you can see from these idiots, who are *violating the rules* and should not be here, it's not a big deal at all."

I shove my way through, expecting to find Keeley cracking jokes and holding court, but her gaze is strained when it meets mine...and relieved, deeply relieved.

She needed me here, and she needed me while we were apart. God, I hate the way this has all unfolded. I hate that the past two weeks ever happened at all.

"Hey," she says, her voice quieter than I expected, her face less joyful. Keeley, who loves drama and celebration more than anyone I know, is pale and tense.

"Are you okay?" I ask.

Her eyes close and she shakes her head. "I'm about to have another contraction, and they're really bad. I thought women were kind of overdramatizing things, but...they weren't."

Only Keeley would think *centuries* of women were exaggerating the pain of childbirth.

She squeezes my hand, her eyes fall shut, and her mouth moves as if she's silently counting.

"You've got this, bestie!" shouts a woman in scrubs. Someone else cheers. I think I'm going to fucking kill all of them.

Her breath explodes when the contraction finally ends and her grip eases. She looks exhausted as her gaze meets mine.

"Do you actually want all these people in here?"

"Well," she says, "no, but they just want to celebrate and—"

I stand. "Everyone? I'm this kid's father. Nice to meet you. Now get the fuck out unless you're assigned to this room."

People glare at me and glance at each other, undoubtedly thinking *"what did Keeley ever see in this asshole?"* I don't blame them. It's a question I've asked myself many times.

But they leave, and once the room is empty, aside from a lone nurse currently taking Keeley's vitals, her sigh is pure relief.

"They're all going to hate you," she says. Her eyes fall closed. It seems early in the process for her to be this tired.

"Like I give a shit," I begin.

"You *need* to give a shit," she says with a too-small smile. "We can't piss them off in case we ever decide to have another one."

My heart stops. I didn't write that letter hoping to change her mind about us, but that she wants me here and is talking about a future *us* has me hoping for it anyway. "You mean... together? We'd stay together?"

"God, Graham, you haven't already changed your mind, right? I mean, you only sent that email *last* night."

I can't speak for a moment. I lift her hand and press my face to its back. "No, I haven't changed my mind," I say. "I just thought..."

I don't finish the sentence. I can't.

"People aren't quite as unforgiving as you seem to think," she says. "And besides, we both know I can't afford a Mariah Carey closet on my own."

I squeeze her hand. "I'm so sorry, Keeley. I'm so fucking sorry."

"I know," she whispers.

Her eyes close, and I wait for them to open so she can tell me about all the things she wants in her new closet, or describe the outlandish *Real Housewives* mural she'd like to paint on our daughter's wall.

It takes me a few seconds to realize she's fallen asleep.

Keeley, in one of the most exciting moments of her life, has fallen asleep. It's wrong. It's wrong for her in particular, but aren't women in labor, at the very least, supposed to be red-faced and hyper-alert, screaming obscenities at the guy who did this to them?

I look at the nurse on the other side of Keeley, who's writing something in a chart. "Is this normal?"

She glances at me with a frown. "Her blood pressure is really high. We gave her something but it's not helping. Dr. Seever is on the way."

Keeley wakes with the next contraction, squeezing my hand through it, watching the second hand of the clock like it's her only lifeline. She exhales in relief as it ends and her gaze turns to mine, followed by another weak smile.

"I'm glad," she says.

"Glad?"

"I'm glad you had a story. Mark said you would. I had stories, too, but I think they were my mom's stories." Her eyes close. "I'd rather have my own."

I look up at the nurse, on the cusp of demanding she find someone who's available now, but I don't need to.

She hits a button on the machine next to Keeley. "Get the attending," she announces. "Her pressure's up and I need more hands *now*."

Within seconds, a woman I've never seen before walks in, with several others behind her. She looks at the monitor and after a hushed conversation with the nurse, she looks over her shoulder to a tech behind her.

"We've got to get this kid out," she says. "Open an OR."

Keeley's eyes open slowly, as if by force, and she swallows.

"Keeley, I'm Dr. Asif," the woman says. "The mag isn't controlling your blood pressure, and the baby's in danger. We need to do a section right away."

The old Keeley would make a joke here, something about bikini season or her vagina. But she just nods. Everyone is moving, someone's on the phone issuing urgent demands and things are being unclipped. The only person in the entire room who is still and settled...is Keeley.

No, not settled. *Resigned*. She reaches for my hand. "Graham," she says quietly, "you're going to be such a good dad, and she's so lucky to have you—"

"Stop," I demand. "You're fine."

"I'm sorry," says the nurse. "We need to leave now."

They push the bed from the room and Keeley grips my hand as I walk alongside her down the hall. "Listen to me, okay? I love you. I love this baby, and I don't regret any of it. Convincing you to marry me is smartest thing I ever did."

I open my mouth to tell her to stop talking like this. To tell her she's going to be fine, and that the truth is that *I* was the one who wanted all of this, that I was the one who convinced her to go to Vegas. But we've reached a set of double doors and a nurse moves in front of me.

"I'm sorry," she says. "They have to put her under, so you can't come back with her."

I look from her to Keeley. There is so much I need to say and there's just no time. "I love you," I whisper.

Tear well in her eyes, but her smile is quiet, and peaceful. "I know."

The doors open and she's gone. Someone leads me to the waiting room, and I go blindly, struck by the way we just said goodbye. It felt...*final*.

I call my mom, and Ben, and Keeley's father, and within thirty minutes, they're all here.

"I didn't even know she was pregnant," her father says, taking the seat across from mine.

"You're lucky I called you at all, after the way you let your wife treat her," I reply.

Harsh, perhaps, but true. And he fucking knows it. He simply nods, and then buries his face in his hands.

Gemma barks at Paul to move and takes the seat beside me. Her hand slips through mine.

"It all happened so fast," I whisper. "There was so much I should have told her."

She squeezes my hand. "I'm sure she knew."

Staff from other parts of the hospital are trickling in now, huddled around the nurses' desk, whispering, and I don't know what it all means, but it doesn't seem good.

Julie enters Labor and Delivery at a jog and nods to me as she heads to the nurses' station. She converses with someone and then takes a phone call, her face increasingly grim before she walks in my direction. I jump to my feet and Gemma is right behind me, followed by Ben, Keeley's dad, and the guys from the building. "They're still in there," she says, wiping her arm across her forehead. "The baby's in the NICU. Nothing to worry about but she was breathing a little fast so they're keeping an eye on her. But Keeley..." She swallows. "Graham, her blood pressure went too high during the delivery. She had a seizure."

Ben's hand lands on my shoulder, keeping me in place.

"A seizure," I repeat.

She nods. "I'd like to tell you that she's going to be okay, but..."

"But?" I ask weakly.

Her gaze meets mine. "I'm sorry. There's no way to tell."

I want to ask how bad things might be, but I already know. I already *knew*, simply from the worry on the staff's faces.

"Can I see her?"

She isn't meeting my eye. "Not yet," she says. "They're still finishing up. They'll want to make sure she's stable first."

Julie returns to the nurses' station, and Keeley's father begins to cry, as if he already knows what's going to happen. I just sit, feeling numb. All these responsibilities I once thought I didn't want...now I'm not sure how I'll continue to exist without them.

It feels like hours have passed by the time Dr. Asif appears, quietly conferring with Julie before turning to me. Her face is strained as I propel out of my seat and toward them.

"Congratulations," she says. "You have a beautiful five-pound, nine-ounce baby girl."

She pulls off her surgical cap and uses it to wipe her brow, her shoulders sagging.

"Keeley?" I can barely get the question out. "Is Keeley okay?"

"It was a close one," she says, "but you still have a beautiful wife as well."

Everyone cheers. All I can do is grip the counter as my knees threaten to buckle. For a minute there, I really saw the world the way Keeley has, for most of her life. It was terrifying.

47

KEELEY

When my eyes open, I'm in a recovery room, and Graham is beside me, his face planted on the mattress next to our linked fingers.

"Hey," I whisper. My throat feels raw which I assume means I was on a vent. So I didn't die, but I was perhaps not all that far from it.

He raises his head, pale and stone-faced, and my stomach drops. I was knocked out from the second I got into the OR and I have no idea what happened.

"The baby?" I whisper.

"She was in the NICU," he says. His smile is wooden and forced. "But she's fine."

Our baby is fine, but he is not. He picks up the phone and calls the nurse, but even inches away I know he's retreated somewhere I can't reach him again. I don't understand.

The nurse comes in and places our daughter in my arms. She has a head full of dark hair like Graham's, and a sweet, pursed mouth that begins moving in her sleep. I've waited forever for this little girl. I didn't even know I was waiting, but I know it now. I blink back tears as I press my lips to the top of her head. She is half of me and half of Graham and more perfect than I ever dreamed she could be.

"You've got friends waiting outside to see you when you're ready," the nurse says.

I glance at Graham. "Not just yet, okay?"

She nods and walks out. I pull my gown down and our little girl latches on like a champ. It's all so perfect. All of it but Graham. I thought he'd be *happy*.

I trace the pad of my index finger over her soft cheek. "It can't even taste that good," I coo to her. "Just wait until I get ahold of some Hot Tamales."

Graham's head falls into his hands, his shoulders shaking, and for a moment I think he's laughing until I realize he's not.

"Hey." I reach over and run my hand over his head. "*Hey*. Everything's fine. What's wrong?"

It takes him a second to answer. "You really scared me, Keeley," he says, his voice rough. "You really fucking scared me."

I find his hand. I worried I was too weak to do this. To be with someone, to be a mother. But he'll keep me on course, and every once in a while, I'll keep him on course too.

"It's all okay now, Graham."

He nods. "I know. I just...you weren't waking up, and I...I'm just having a hard time shaking it off."

He likes to be the practical one, the one who sees the world as it really is, and I like to be the dreamer, seeing the world as it could be. But today got a little too real for him, and I know exactly how to get us back to normal. "I want a wedding," I tell him. "A big one. With a carriage. And doves."

He scrubs his face and looks up at me, astonished for a moment, but then his mouth softens. "Yeah?"

"Yeah. And a parade. Like they have in New Orleans."

His smile grows. "I'm not sure they could do that in LA."

"I thought we could do it in Santorini. And then we'll do our honeymoon on a murder mystery train."

He laughs. "You're just throwing in as much crazy shit as possible right now because you know I'll agree. I guess that means you're going to name her Kalamity too?"

"I was thinking about Delilah—"

"You realize that's in the Bible—"

"Please don't ruin this for me. Anyway, we'll name her Delilah but we'll call her Daisy."

He winces. "Or we could, you know, just call her by her actual name."

"I nearly died, Graham."

"Daisy it is, then," he replies.

Her tiny moving mouth slows, then stops.

"She's sound asleep already," I whisper. "She got that from you."

He lowers the side of the bed and sits beside me. I place her in his arms and he swallows hard as he takes her in, his eyes bright once more.

"Hello, Daisy," he whispers. Her tiny hand wraps tight around his pinky and I rest my head against his arm. There's no one alive I trust more. I'm so glad she'll have him to lean on.

I'm so glad we both will.

OUR DAUGHTER REMAINS in the hospital for four days, and after pulling some strings, we're allowed to stay with her. Just before she's released, Graham goes to install the car seat in the back of the Volvo. Daisy's asleep in the nursery, so I roam the halls, catching up with people.

Dr. Patel is *not* supposed to be one of them.

"Do you have a minute?" he asks.

"Do you have another case of *Mycobacterium marinum* you want me to diagnose?" I ask with a small laugh.

He smiles. "Still resentful over that, I see. Come along. I need coffee."

I guess I can hear him out. I've been realizing this week how much I missed a lot of things about working in the hospital.

"I saw your segment on *Mindy and Mills*," he says as he pours coffee into his cup.

"I don't suppose you're going to tell me I was amazing."

He raises a brow. "You *did* actually attend medical school. It would be sad if you *couldn't* do those things."

Which is exactly what I said, but he could have humored me.

"You did, however, remain commendably composed," he continues. "I assume you asked the surfer if he had a tetanus shot?"

I roll my eyes. "Of course I did."

"And the newborn—you felt for the cord as you pulled him out? And you cleared his nose right away?"

He's really pissing me off now. "*Yes.*"

"Do you know why I'm asking you these questions, Keeley?"

"I assume it's because you think I'm incompetent."

"No." He takes a sip of his coffee. "It's because every doctor misses things at some point, and it's learning from those misses that turns you into a better doctor. You didn't ask a patient with fish handlers' disease what he did for a living, but I bet you never do it again."

I frown. I *suppose* he's right. "It still felt like you singled me out. You gave me a patient with a rare disorder and then described in detail how I messed up."

"I absolutely did single you out," he agrees, setting his coffee down. "Has it ever occurred to you, though, that I perhaps did that because I knew *you* could figure it out, and suspected the others wouldn't?"

I grin. "So you're saying I'm actually the greatest resident you ever had?"

He laughs. "No, far from it. But you could become a very good doctor. And if you ever tire of telling rich women which retinol to use, I'd be happy to find a place for you here."

He's a pain in the ass, but I'll probably become a better doctor because of him, and the idea of working here excites me in a way Beverly Hills Skin never could.

"I want to stay home with my daughter for a while first," I warn. "She hasn't seen the first two seasons of *Bridgerton* yet."

He sighs and shakes his head. "Yes, yes, of course. But for your daughter's sake, I hope her father is good at telling you *no*."

I smile. Our daughter is named Delilah Kalamity Tate.

He's not that good at it.

48

KEELEY

JANUARY

I'm unpacking, waiting for Graham to get home, when I come across the onesies Daisy wore as a newborn. As small as she still is, the tiny garments in this box look like doll clothes to me now. That's how it is though—you don't register most change as it happens. It just hits you like an anvil when it's well behind you.

And on this particular date, a year from the afternoon I met Graham, several anvils are hitting me at once.

Exactly a year ago, no matter what he says now, Graham had just arrived at the Langham and was probably trying to figure out how fast he could get back to New York so he could return to the office—the same guy who now cuts out of work just because he thinks I look tired, and who recently cancelled a shareholder meeting because Daisy had an ear infection.

A year ago today, I was being as rude as possible to him while planning to seduce another guy. It's a little shocking in retrospect, and it's taken me most of this year to understand that I was driven entirely by fear. I set my sights on the one guy I knew I'd never want to make permanent, and fought the real-ization that there was something about Graham—his irritating reliance on logic, his refusal to take any shit from me, and later, of course, that *mouth*—that I knew I'd want to keep.

I *did* keep it, obviously, and now I'm a wife and the mother of a four-month-old and a *homeowner* of all things, and it was only when I heard Coachella had sold out that I remembered I'd ever considered going.

I hear Graham's key in the door and throw the onesies down. He was in New York for three days—his longest trip since Daisy was born—and I'm just uncool enough to run down the hall to see him faster. He's just uncool enough to drop his bag and pull me against him tight as if he's been gone for a month.

"How was it?" I ask.

He tugs me closer, and I listen to the steady, constant beat of his heart beneath my ear. *Steady* and *constant* are things I didn't even know I wanted last January. Now I can't imagine life without them. "I'm glad to be home," he replies.

I bite down on my smile. "How *glad* are you, exactly?"

He pulls away just enough for me to see him raise a brow. "How glad are *you*?"

Ugh. So, I'm *not* getting laid. All because I jokingly suggested I might take a page from Gemma's book and not sleep with him until we left for tomorrow's anniversary trip, to which he'd replied, *"as if you have that much self-control."*

Why did I insist I'd prove it? Graham has way more willpower than me. I know this. Graham knows this. Hell, Daisy even knows it.

"Not as glad as you wish I was," I reply, pulling him by the hand.

He peers into our living room as we round the corner to the stairs. The room looks even worse than it did when he left town.

"If you say a word about my lack of progress, you'll be waiting a lot longer to get laid than you think," I warn.

He smirks. "As I said the last time you suggested this, you'll cave before I do."

I nearly remind him I've made it three days, but I'm not sure I can laud myself for days he wasn't even home.

He presses a kiss to my forehead and tells me he's going to peek in on Daisy. I only have to wait a minute before I see him in the moonlit nursery, settling into the rocking chair with his jacket off and her snug against his chest. For all Graham's concerns that I'd be too soft, he's nearly as bad.

And the sight of him like that leaves me doubly determined not to wait until tomorrow to get laid. I hustle to my closet when he rises to return Daisy to her crib and get out the sheer black lace nighty he hasn't seen yet. This thing is even risqué for me, and that's saying something. I own a *lot* of lingerie.

He's in the shower when I emerge. "Did you look at her ear?" he calls over the sound of the running water.

I laugh to myself. Thank God I'm a doctor because as it turns out, Graham is the world's most paranoid father. He's now read more *JAMA* articles on ear infections than most pediatricians I know. We'd be at the hospital every other day if it wasn't for me.

"It's not Ebola, hon," I reply, reaching for the toothpaste. "Ear infections are really common."

"But you looked?" The water shuts off. "They did this study on—"

His words trail away as he steps out of the shower. I spit toothpaste in the sink, leaning over more than necessary. I *know* he's looking at my ass.

He steps up beside me with a towel around his waist. I wipe my mouth and smile at the sight of those two butterfly tattoos on his chest—one for me and a smaller one for Daisy— because he finally loved two things enough to mark himself on their behalf.

"I think you forgot to dry off," I tell him.

He ignores me, his eyes grazing over the black lace as he reaches for his toothbrush.

"Is that new?" he asks, his voice rougher than it was.

"Uh huh."

"It's...very sheer."

I look at my reflection. "Oh, look at that. It really is. You can see *everything*, can't you? I'll have to remember not to wear it around the house while they're here painting next time."

He stares at me in the mirror as he starts brushing his teeth. His Adam's apple bobs. "I know what you're doing."

I hop onto the counter, and the slip rides up to my hip bone. He'd be able to see my panties...if I was wearing any.

"Remember the night your mom and Walter kept Daisy and we had the apartment to ourselves?"

A muscle in his cheek flickers. "Yeah."

If I even *reference* either of two things—that night in the apartment or my vibrator—Graham loses it. I once waved the vibrator from across the room when he was in a Zoom meeting and he told them our power had gone out to end the call.

"That was so hot," I purr. "I'm not sure if I ever told you this, but when you left the next morning, I started thinking about it and had to get out my vibrator."

He flinches as he spits out the toothpaste and rinses his mouth.

"We can end all this very easily," he says, voice lower than it was, rasping with desire. "Just admit you want it."

My fingers move between my legs and his eyes jerk toward the motion. "I want to try what we did in the apartment again, but I want you to do it harder."

"Fuck," he groans, pushing my thighs apart and stepping between them. "You win."

His hand slides around the back of my neck as he pulls my mouth to his. The towel appears to fall on its own, having realized it was no longer necessary, and then he's pressed against me, hard as steel. I have to silence my groan, but *it's about fucking time*.

"*Who* is it that has no self-control?" I ask as he lifts me up and turns us toward the bed.

The sound he makes is half laughter/half grunt. "It might not be me but it's not you either." He dumps me on the bed. "I guarantee you bought that lace thing in multiple colors and it cost a fortune."

I laugh. Well, yeah, obviously. I haven't changed *that* much.

I get on my hands and knees and he growls at the sight. His hands grip my hips, squeezing for a moment as he considers how he's going to do this, and then he flips me on my back like a rag doll and a large palm circles the base of my throat.

"I thought you'd want me on my hands and knees, like last time," I say, sucking in a breath, arching toward him.

"I'm saving it," he says against my ear. His hand skims down my chest and stomach in a smooth stroke, barely pausing before pushing two fingers inside me, inhaling when he feels how ready I am. "Because when we do *that,* I want it to last for a good *long* time."

"Oh God," I beg. "Please fuck me."

He shoves inside me hard, without warning, just the way I knew he would, and holds my gaze under heavy-lidded eyes, watching me shiver with pleasure through the first thrust.

Instead of continuing, though, he pulls one strap of the slip down to expose a breast. His palm is gentle as he cups it, and then he pinches my nipple simply to hear me gasp.

"More," I plead.

His jaw is tight as he pulls my legs over his shoulders and grips my hips the way I like.

He pulls back slowly, but slams forward with enough force to jolt me up the bed, hitting every nerve on the way. He does it again and again, his eyes locked on mine through the punishing pace.

This is Graham, unrestrained, holding nothing back, not being careful, and taking everything he wants because he knows, beyond a shadow of a doubt, that it's his to take.

"God, I love you so much," he hisses as he gets close.

Someone telling me they loved me would once have sent me running. Tonight, it simply pushes me right over the edge and I'm whispering all my *"I love yous"* back when he follows with a low groan.

He collapses beside me and pulls me close. Within a minute, his voice is slurred with fatigue because he was up thirty-six hours straight getting ready for today's presentation. By the time I press my lips to those butterflies on his chest, the way I do every night, he is sound asleep.

So very boring. And I wouldn't trade him for the world.

49

GRAHAM

Ben and Gemma arrive at our house the next afternoon, politely saying nothing about what a disaster it is at present—that's what happens when you've only lived somewhere for two weeks and you have a four-month-old, but it certainly doesn't help to have your wife simultaneously discover that some designer once made tiny baby shoes and they can still be bought new in the box on eBay if she enters auctions rather than helping you unpack.

Gemma sighs as her phone buzzes. "Your mother is already asking if we're sure we don't want her to come over," she tells Ben, showing him the message. "If I can take care of a puppy, I can take care of a baby."

Keeley's smile fades and Ben laughs. "Gemma, save those jokes for after they leave or he's going to have to drug Keeley to get her out of here."

He isn't wrong—Keeley's love for our daughter is a staggering thing, and I suspected it would be. It's a big part of the reason she's only going back to work half-time when she starts at the hospital in a week. The other part is that she just realized there are eight seasons of *Love Island UK* and she and Daisy have only watched two of them.

She told me and Daisy last week that Jonny from season two is a douche and if Daisy brings home a guy like that, she'll make sure he's dead by morning. Our daughter gave me a big toothless grin when she said it—Daisy looks like me, but she's an O'Keefe through and through. I'm in so much trouble.

"I typed up some instructions," Keeley says, handing Gemma the packet.

"You're only going to be gone for one night, right?" Gemma asks. "Because this has me worried you're actually taking off for Europe."

"Just one night." Keeley pulls Daisy close. "We'll be back first thing in the morning."

"We'll be back late tomorrow *afternoon*," I correct, pressing my lips to the top of Daisy's head. "And we're not going to get any surfing in at all if we don't get out of here."

Keeley concedes, placing Daisy into Gemma's outstretched arms. "Just make sure you put her on her back when she's asleep, okay? And you can't put breast milk in the microwave. Use the bottle warmer. Are you sure you remember how to—"

"I've used your bottle warmer at *least* ten times," says Gemma. "Stop worrying. We'll put her on a leash and take her for loads of walks and she'll be fine."

"Just so we're clear, you know she can barely support her own—"

"Keeley," I groan, "she *knows*. And I'd really, really like to get on the road."

We exchange a glance, and her lashes lower in the way they do when she's thinking about sex. Which is surprisingly often, even for Keeley. I'm a lucky man.

We say our goodbyes and head out. Keeley doesn't notice there are no surfboards on the roof, and she's so busy telling me about some couple she likes on *Love is Blind* that we are well into town before she even notices we've gone the wrong way.

"Hey," she says, "you realize we're not on the PCH, right?"

"Yeah, we're making a pitstop." I pull into a parking lot. "We're here, by the way."

She frowns at the building's shiplapped façade. "I'm hoping it's a sex club, but I doubt it because it's too early for that. Why are we here?"

I take a quick breath. "This is where I proposed. I figured this was a good place to tell you how it all happened."

50

GRAHAM

THE PREVIOUS JANUARY

I wake to find two fingers on my neck, checking my pulse, as a woman's voice, husky with sleep, says, "God, not again."

And even though I've got a headache beginning and I'm not quite awake, I laugh.

Keeley.

Obnoxious, over-confident, logic-impaired...and the only voice I've wanted to hear on the phone for the last six weeks.

I dream, for a half-second, that I've taken those two fingers of hers and pulled them into my mouth, wetting them to push inside her. *I make her get herself off until she begs me to fuck her and then...*

The hand leaves my neck and I wake again, then roll over to look at her. She is all lush lips and wild hair, looking like exactly what she is: a woman who was up most of the night getting fucked within an inch of her life; a woman who made me wild and unhinged in ways no one else ever has. There was actually a point, in the early hours of morning, when I caught myself thinking *"I need to marry this girl."* Me—a guy who has spent his entire life swearing that's the one thing he'll never do.

I'm sure it was just the dangerous combination of alcohol and Keeley naked, but it wasn't an entirely new thought. It's been in the background, barely repressed, for a while now, as if my world had been in black and white and I didn't know it until I first heard her voice.

Who'd have thought my life would be transformed by a woman who'd called me both *"boring"* and *"cheap"* during the first five minutes of a phone call? I'd laughed over that conversation for days afterward.

"Did you just check my pulse?" I ask.

She stares at me. And then she scrambles out of bed.

"This didn't happen," she says, and I'm regrettably slow to understand. When I finally get it, it hits me like a hammer.

Everything I assumed was wrong and even the words she said *aloud* were completely meaningless. The whole fucking night meant nothing to her.

"Because you're still on your mission to fuck the rock star," I say. It's an effort not to sound bitter. But how can she possibly want that *moron* after the night we just had?

"If mankind let every simple mistake get in the way of its goals, we'd still be communicating via cave drawings," she replies, shimmying into her dress.

She's hunting the floor for something while my shock morphs to disappointment. Never in my life have I so misread another person's feelings, but I certainly had some help...a few hours ago, she was saying she wanted to marry me and have a million babies. I knew even at the time it was standard Keeley hyperbole—it's something I've heard her say of ice cream as well—but it turns out it's what she says to someone she doesn't even *want*.

Thank God I never told her what I was thinking. I'll get through today and process my misery back home...the sooner the better. It's an afternoon party—I can definitely make a late flight. I can't believe I ever suggested I might stay the full week.

I reach for my phone to text my assistant.

Me: Jana, please get me on the redeye back to JFK tonight.

But just as I send it, Keeley turns to say goodbye, and there's something in the way her eyes drift over me for a moment, as if she isn't entirely sure she wants to leave. As if there's some small piece of her that wishes this was different.

I wait until she's gone before I send Jana a second text.

Me: Scratch that. I think I'll stay.

I gamble at work, I take risks. But I've never taken one with my personal life until now. It's not likely to pan out, but my God...if it did.

I guess I'm willing to find out.

TEN HOURS LATER, the party is over, and Keeley's still by the rock star's side.

This gamble of mine does not appear to have been worth taking, and yet I can't look away from her. She's in a white dress with a v cut so low she can't possibly be wearing a bra, and all I can think of is sliding my hand inside to feel her nipple harden against my palm. I want to hear that small gasp of hers again, the way her eyes will fall shut and her head will roll backward when I do it. The fact that Six is looking at her like he wants to hear her gasp, too, has me on edge...and hearing him refer to her as *his* girl, earlier, nearly put me right over it.

She'd just asked what I remembered from last night when Six interrupted, and she had that glint in her eye, as if she already wanted to repeat it, no matter what she'd said this morning. I wish I'd gotten the chance to tell her. To step close enough for my breath to brush her ear as I described watching her on her knees in front of me, how my hand wound tight in her hair as I tried not to come. How it felt to slowly push inside her for the first time, how it took all my self-restraint to be careful with her, and when she whispered, *"more"* and dug her nails into my back, I gave in, and it was wilder and rougher than I'd ever been.

I'd have told her how fucking alive I felt during those hours, and that the desire to take care of her—unexpected, and something I've never felt for anyone else—still hasn't left.

But he did interrupt, and he hasn't left her side since, and the longer it goes on, the more I find myself drinking, and assuming I won't get that lucky twice. She's across from me now, at some club Drew's brought us all to, and Six—again—is trying to look down her dress.

I've got to walk away.

I go to the bar and order another whiskey—God knows how many I've had at this point. My stepsister appears by my side a moment later and politely waits until I've slammed my drink before she speaks.

"You might want to slow down," Noah says. "This isn't like you."

"Did you see how drunk Drew is? And Colin and Simon are over there lighting shots on fire. *I'm* not who you need to be concerned about."

Her gaze goes back to the table. "The difference," she replies, looking at my brothers, "is that they're having the time of their lives while you look like you're at a wake."

I should have gotten on a flight to New York tonight. Hell, I should have left this morning, the minute she walked out my door. This situation is *that* fucking unbearable.

Except just as I think it, Keeley's eyes meet mine. She's been looking at me, on and off, the whole goddamn day, but this is the first moment where I know I didn't imagine that look on her face this morning...the indecision there, as if she'd suddenly remembered what she saw in me.

She rises, holding my gaze as she walks to the dance floor.

"You know what to do," that gaze says. *"Exactly what you did last night."* There's a petulant voice inside my head saying, *"she should be coming to me"*, and I ignore it. This is the moment I've waited all day for and I'm not letting it slip past.

"Sorry, Noah," I announce as I rise. "I need to take care of something."

I push my way through the crowd on the dance floor. When I find her, she grins at me, and I want to stay mad about this morning but, somehow, I can't. I grab her hand, tugging her deeper into the crowd—if Six sees us together he'll be here in a moment's time trying to stop me. I'd be thrilled to set him straight, but turning the situation violent can wait until she's agreed to leave with me.

"State dependent memory," she says as if answering a question I'd just asked. "You're more likely to recall things when in a similar state of consciousness to the original incident. If you're inebriated when an event takes place, then you're more apt to remember it when you're inebriated again. That's why this is happening."

My mouth softens. The funny thing about Keeley is that the more she drinks, the smarter she sounds. Right now, she sounds like she's getting ready to lecture doctoral students at MIT. Six hours ago, sober, she was asking everyone who the "hottest" Spiderman was.

"Why *what* is happening?" I ask, fighting a smile. Once again, the world is in color.

"Why I'm remembering last night," she says, reaching up to run a hand over my shirt. "I like this shirt. Where did you get it?"

"You don't give a shit where I bought this shirt," I say with a grin, stepping closer. I suddenly need to feel a lot more than her hand on my chest. "I didn't realize you'd forgotten last night. You didn't even seem drunk."

"It's my superpower," she says. Before I can ask what the

hell that means, she's sliding her hand into my shirt and pulling my mouth down to hers.

It feels like falling, as if I have no sense of where we are, of where she ends and I begin. But it's also like being found, and it's a feeling I don't want to lose.

"How am I going to keep you from forgetting again?" I ask against her mouth.

"I won't."

"Prove it," I say, pulling her snug against me, my erection throbbing painfully now, and she groans when she feels it for herself.

She grabs my hand and turns for the exit. "Let's go back to your room. I'll prove anything you want me to prove."

Yes.

No.

Yes, I'd very much like to see Keeley attempt to prove something, *anything* in my room.

No, because I don't want to go through another day like today. I don't want to wake up tomorrow to have her rushing out of my bed, acting like I was a regrettable mistake.

I want more. I want more than one night. I want more than anything she's planning to offer.

I take her in, her hair falling out of its careful updo, looking angelic but fragile in that goddamn dress...which is *way* too low cut. I rest my hands on her bare arms and they're cold to the touch, so I pull off my jacket and drape it around her.

I've never wanted to be responsible for anyone. I've never wanted to *belong* to anyone. But I want both those things with her, and I don't want the job of keeping her safe and happy to belong to anyone but me for the rest of our lives.

"Marry me," I say, and when the words emerge, I *expect* to regret them. I expect to want to pull them back...but I don't. I'm simply stunned by how perfect a solution it is. "That's how I want you to prove it. Marry me."

She laughs. "Sure, I'll marry you...like, eventually. But right now, we really need to go back to your room."

Yes.

No.

"Tonight. Before you forget and decide you'd rather be with Six Bailey."

She stops in place, blinking up at me. Maybe it's because she's the only one of us sober enough to see this whole thing clearly, but I feel clearer than I ever have in my life.

"You don't think you'll regret it in the morning?" she asks. "You seemed pretty unhappy with me a few hours ago."

"You were letting Six fucking *molest* you all afternoon. Of course I was unhappy."

Her mouth opens to argue, which is when Drew pushes between us, drunkenly throwing an arm around Keeley's shoulders. Poorly timed interruptions are apparently the primary character trait of the Bailey family.

"What's up, kids?" she asks. "We're taking this party back to my house because my pool is way better than the one at the hotel. I just called for the limo."

My gaze locks with Keeley's. *Don't go with them*, I silently plead.

Drew looks between us. "Umm...what's going on right now?"

Six is Drew's brother-in-law, so this is definitely a conversation she shouldn't be privy to. "Just party stuff. Some issues with the—"

"Graham thinks we ought to get married," Keeley says. "Like, tonight. In Vegas."

Drew's eyes widen, and I wait for her to say, "*that's insane*" or "*you guys hate each other.*"

Instead, she looks at Keeley. "Wow. What are you going to do?"

"I still don't even know why he asked," Keeley says, but she's smiling, and it gives me hope that I can still sell her on this.

My fingers twine with hers. "Maybe I just wanted someone who'd force me to go to Santorini."

She grins wider. "We both know that's not true."

I was joking, of course. But maybe I wasn't. Maybe I do want someone to force me to go Santorini. Maybe I've been locked up for a long time and I'm starting to think she's the key to the outside.

"I want to marry you because you don't wear enough clothing when you go out, and I want it to be my jacket you wear home at night. And because a part of me has wanted to marry you since the first time we spoke. You bring my entire world into color, and I don't want to go back to the way it was."

Tears spring to Keeley's eyes. "I wasn't planning to ever get married," she whispers.

"I wasn't either," I tell her. "But I want to marry you."

"Oh boy," says Drew, pulling Keeley away. "We're going to have a chat outside. Meet us out there in five."

Keeley allows herself to be led, but at the last moment she turns and smiles at me.

I'm pretty sure it was a *yes*. And for the first time in decades, the future is technicolor and open wide, and I can't wait for it to start.

51

KEELEY

I listen breathlessly as he describes the night we wound up in Vegas. He's told me bits of this, of course, but never in such detail. I feel like I can almost remember it now too. And then he stops.

"Come on," he says, climbing out of the car.

"You can't just end it there!" I protest.

In my head, he's still inside the building a year ago, and I've gone outside with Drew. Even though I know things worked out okay, I want to scream at story-Graham and say, *"go outside and get her, idiot, before Drew convinces her not to marry you!"*

"We're getting to the rest," he says, reaching into the trunk and hoisting my bag over his shoulder before he grabs his own. It's only now I realize he never put the surfboards on the roof, or packed our wetsuits. I'm shockingly unobservant at times.

He slams the trunk shut and comes over to where I stand, twining his fingers with mine as he leads me to the building's entrance.

"What happened next is that Six stormed outside and grabbed you," Graham says. "So I clocked him, which I'd been dying to do all day."

I put a palm over my face. "Oh my God," I groan. "You punched *Six*? Look, I know he's kind of a douche, but he isn't a bad person—"

Graham's nostrils flare. "If you remembered the way he grabbed you, you might feel otherwise."

I hide a smile. He's still irritated over the attention I paid to another man a *year* ago. Then again, Anna Fucking Tattelbaum will never be my favorite person either. "Please continue."

"And then I brought you over here," he says, pulling me around the corner, to an empty patio on the building's west side. In the distance, the sun is already beginning its descent in a glorious haze of pink and salmon.

He drops to one knee, and I don't entirely understand why until he fishes a small blue box out of his bag. "I asked you to marry me again, and you said yes. But I figured it was time I did it the right way."

I blink back tears. Yes, there was a part of me that always wished I'd gotten a big romantic proposal, or had at least been asked when he was thinking clearly. I told myself it didn't matter as long as I wound up happy, and...I did. But I love that he's asking now anyway.

He climbs to his feet. "Aren't you going to open it?"

I pluck the box from his hand. "I'm just worried it's, like, a tiny stock portfolio instead of a ring."

His eyes crinkle at the corners. "Even *I'm* not that bad."

He's *nearly* that bad—I mean, we still don't have a Silver Cross stroller. I fully expect a diamond chip so small I need a magnifying glass to see it, but it doesn't matter what the ring is like. I love him and I love that he's done this.

I open the box and my jaw drops. Not out of horror.

It's a *massive* rose-cut diamond, just like the one Lily Collins has. "Oh my God," I whisper. "How did you know this is what I wanted?"

He laughs as he slides it on my finger. "You've shown me

that ring every day since you got out of the hospital, Keeley. You made a TikTok about your love for that ring."

Okay, yes, I did do those things. I laugh but it comes out a little like a sob.

He frowns. "Is it okay?"

I swallow hard and press my face to his chest. "It's better than okay. J Lo only wishes Ben Affleck loved her this much."

He holds me tight. "So that's a yes?"

I nod quickly. "Yes." I wipe my eyes and pull back to smile at him.

His gaze holds mine for a long moment. He already knew how I felt about him, and I knew how he felt about me. It's still nice to stand here and live in it all for a second. We're so lucky it worked out the way it did.

"So are you going to tell me the rest of the story?"

He pushes my hair out of my face. "After the limo ride to the airport, it's mostly a blur for me too." He nods toward the street, where a limo I hadn't even noticed awaits. "I know it's not a parade through Santorini, but I thought maybe we could redo the rest of it together. It's the most important decision I ever made. And the best one. I'd like to remember it."

I'm blinking back tears again. It was by far the best decision I ever made too. I'd be inclined to wonder if Drunk Keeley was some kind of all-knowing genius, except Drunk Keeley also once thought it would be "funny" to try to sneak over the border into Canada. So probably not.

I slide my hand into his. "We probably need a classy, elegant story to tell Daisy one day."

He grins. "So this is going to be classy and elegant? That's disappointing."

"We're 100 percent still having sex in that limo."

He laughs and pulls me against him again. "We're only ten minutes from the airport," he whispers. "It'll have to be fast."

I pull his mouth to mine. "That's okay."

I'm no longer certain the O'Keefe curse is going to get me, but the one thing I'm sure of is that it's not about how long things last.

It's about making sure you love the time you have, and the people you spend it with.

And I do. I really, really do.

ACKNOWLEDGMENTS

Thank you to:

My beloved developmental editor, Sali Benbow-Powers, for her brilliant suggestions and for being willing to Vox me at midnight to tell me I need to add a sex scene even though she knows I'll have a tantrum about it.

The wonderful Entirely Bonkerzz, whose tweaks and suggestions were invaluable.

My beta readers: Michelle Chen, Katie Foster Meyer, Tawanna Williams and Jen Wilson Owens. As always, you've made this book so much better than it would have been without you.

To my publicist, the wonderful Nina Grinstead and the entire team at Valentine PR—Christine, Kelley, Kim, Sarah and everyone I've forgotten.

To Kelly Golland, for understanding subordinating conjunctions so I don't have to and Julie Deaton for knowing that "seatbelt"and "goosebumps" need a space between them.

To Kathy Schofield and English Michaels, my labor and delivery experts, for their expertise, and to my amazing dermatologist and her residents (who shall remain nameless in case I messed something up) for letting me grill them.

To Deanna Heaven, for giving me just enough info about hedge fund managers that I could pretend to be one, and convincing me I'd never want to be.

To my PA, Christine Estevez, for keeping me on track.

To my besties—Deanna, Katie and Sallye. FKA The Capital

Grill Club, FKA The Bad Ass Middle Aged Assassins. Now dubbed The Cul-de-Sac Crew because I'm determined to make you all move to Florida with me in old age.

And finally, to my daughter Lily, for all the snide commentary during *Bridgerton* (credit for the comment about Daphne needing cardio goes to her). Lily, as you leave for college, please remember which male contestants I hated on *Love is Blind* and *Love Island* and know this: I was serious about killing them in their sleep if you ever bring them home.

The Summer We Fell

He was my boyfriend's best friend—and the
bane of my existence. I wanted to hate Luke Taylor.
I did hate him. I just never hated him enough.

Now, a decade later, tragedy has brought us
back to the place where it all happened—my
best times, and my worst.

Our lives have changed, but that pull
between us is just as strong as ever.

Only this time, it's more dangerous too.

**Keep reading now for a sneak peek of
Juliet and Luke's epic story . . .**

Available now

PIATKUS

1

NOW

I t wasn't that long ago that I could get through an airport without being recognized. I miss that.

Today my sunglasses will remain on. It's one of those obnoxious *"I'm a celebrity!"* moves I've always hated, but that's better than a bunch of commentary about my current appearance. I slept most of the way from Lisbon to San Francisco, thanks to my handy stash of Ambien, but I'm still fucked in the head from the call I received just before I got on the flight...and it shows.

Donna has always been a ball of energy, cheerful and indefatigable. I can't imagine her any other way. Of all the people in the world, why does it have to be *her*? Why is it that the people who most deserve to live seem to be taken too soon, and the ones who deserve it least, like me, seem to flourish?

I've been promising myself that I just need to hold it together a little longer, when the truth is that I've got three straight weeks ahead of holding it together with no end in sight. But if I think nothing of lying to everyone else, I'm certainly not going to quibble over lies to myself.

I duck into the bathroom to clean up before I head for my

luggage. My hazel eyes are bruised with fatigue, my skin is sallow. The sun-kissed streaks the colorist added to my brown hair won't fool anyone into thinking I've spent time in the sun lately, especially Donna. Every time she's visited me in LA, she has said the same thing: *"Oh, honey, you look so tired. I wish you'd come home"*, as if returning to Rhodes could ever improve anything.

I step back from the mirror just in time to catch a woman taking a picture of me from the side.

She shrugs, completely unashamed. "Sorry. You're not my taste," she says, "but my niece likes you."

I used to think fame would solve everything. What I didn't realize is that you're still every bit as sad. You just have the whole fucking world there to watch and remind you you've got no right to be.

I walk out before I say something I'll regret and head down the escalator to baggage claim. It wasn't until I started to date Cash that I understood the kind of chaos that can descend when the public thinks they know you—but today there's no crowd. Just Donna waiting near the base of the escalator, a little too thin but otherwise completely fine.

She pulls me into her arms, and the scent of her rose perfume reminds me of her home—a place where some of my best moments occurred. And some of my worst.

"You didn't need to pick me up. I was gonna Uber."

"That would cost a fortune," she says, forgetting or not caring that I'm no longer the broke kid she was once forced to take in. "And when my girl comes home, I'm going to be the one to greet her. Besides...I had company."

My gaze follows hers, past her shoulder.

I don't know how I didn't see him, when he stands a foot taller and a foot broader than anyone else in the room. Some big guys go out of their way to seem less so—they slouch, they smile, they joke around. Luke has never done any of those things. He is unapologetically his unsmiling self, size and all.

He looks older, but it's been seven years, so I guess he would. He's even bigger now, harder and less penetrable. His messy brown hair still glints gold from all those hours he spends on the water, but there's a full week's beard on a face that's normally clean-shaven. I wish I'd been prepared, at least. I wish someone had said, *"Luke will be there. And he'll still feel like the tide, sucking you out to sea."*

We don't hug. It would be too much. I can't imagine he'd be willing to do it anyway, under the circumstances.

He doesn't even smile, but simply tips his chin. "Juliet."

He's all grown up, even his voice is grown up—lower, more confident than it was. And it was always low, always confident. Always capable of bringing me to my knees.

It feels intentional, the fact that I'm only learning he's here *now*. Donna knows we never got along. But she's dying, which means I'm not allowed to resent her for this tiny manipulation.

"He offered to drive," Donna adds.

He raises a brow at the word *"offered"*, arms still folded across his broad chest, making it clear that's not *exactly* the way it happened. It's so like Donna to attribute far kinder qualities to us than actually exist.

"How many bags do you have?" He's already turning toward the carousel, manning up to do the right thing, no matter how much he hates me.

I move in front of him. "I can get it."

It irks me that he walks to the carousel anyway. I press a finger to my right temple. My head is splitting, finally coming off everything I took yesterday. And I just don't feel up to polite conversation, especially with him.

I swallow. "I didn't know you'd be here."

"Sorry to disappoint."

I see my bag coming and move forward. "That's not what I

meant." What I really meant was *"This is the worst possible situation, and I don't see how I'm going to weather three weeks of it."* I guess that's not much better.

I glance over my shoulder. "How is she?"

His eyes darken. "I just got in this morning, but...you saw her. A strong wind could knock her over."

And with that there's really nothing left to be said. Not easily or comfortably, anyway. The silence stretches on.

We both reach for my bag at the same time, our hands brushing for a moment.

I snatch mine back but it's too late. Luke is already in my bloodstream, already poisoning me. Making me want all the wrong things, just like he always did.

He might not be the devil, but working under him for six weeks is my idea of hell.

Meet the temp assistant and the British boss she loves to hate . . .

Available now.

PIATKUS